D0922393

Murder in a Small Town

Mary Francis Allen

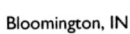 

Bloomington, IN   authorHOUSE®   Milton Keynes, UK

AuthorHouse™
1663 Liberty Drive, Suite 200
Bloomington, IN 47403
www.authorhouse.com
Phone: 1-800-839-8640

AuthorHouse™ UK Ltd.
500 Avebury Boulevard
Central Milton Keynes, MK9 2BE
www.authorhouse.co.uk
Phone: 08001974150

First published by AuthorHouse 9/12/2007

ISBN: 978-1-4259-6832-8 (sc)

Library of Congress Control Number: 2007902149

Printed in the United States of America
Bloomington, Indiana

This book is printed on acid-free paper.

This book is dedicated to my loving and generous parents Stanley Franklin Allen and Harriett McMorrough Allen.

Introduction

1976

The Big Four, as they were affectionately known, had been the best of friends since the first grade in the small town of Upton, Georgia, population fifteen thousand. They had been student leaders—good kids—and at thirty, they were still as close as when they were growing up. After college all but one had moved back to their hometown. However, the lives of these four and their families were about to change. Harbored secrets and a crime against one of the members would tear their idyllic existence apart. How would these friends survive amid death and suspicions of murder?

The group consisted of:

Kate Stroud, a petite blond with big blue eyes, made you want to smile. This person had been endeared with a wonderful personality which made her a natural at winning every honor in high school. She was still considered the town sweetheart. Kate had dropped out of college at the end of her sophomore year and married Ted Stroud after his graduation. Though he was from Savannah, they moved back to Upton and Ted went into business with Mr. Sanders, Kate's dad. Ted handled the financial end of the construction business and store. They were the parents of seven-year-old Todd and four-year-old Anna Kate.

Tom DePau, tall, with dark hair and blue eyes, had made all the girls swoon. He was from an old and moneyed Georgia family. No one could challenge their wealth. They were headed now by his grandmother, Maria Antoinette DePau. Even with all of his family's credentials that he enjoyed, Tom was very grounded and genuine. A good athlete and student, he had always been popular. Much to his family's delight, while in college he met and married Beth Anne White, an Atlanta debutante. After graduation they moved to Upton, where Tom went into one of the family businesses. This couple had a six-year-old boy, Thomas Jeffery, known as Jeff; and a three-year-old girl, Elizabeth Jane, known as Liza.

Smitty Jarvis grew up in Mill Town. Though this was not an incorporated place, it was on a tract of land outside of Upton, and was basically owned by the mill. Most of the people there were from generations who had made their living at the mill. They did not mix with others outside their community. The only exception was that the children attended Upton schools, but many dropped out before completing high school. Smitty had always been the exception. A natural athlete, leader, and scholar, he had led the school to many academic and athletic victories. Tall,with an easy-going manner, sandy blond hair, clear blue eyes, and a few freckles, Smitty was not handsome, but was nice-looking, very popular, and well-respected by all. Though able to mix with both those from Mill Town and Upton, he became thoroughly entrenched in The Big 4 when he was in the first grade.

In the summer before his second year in law school, Smitty began dating Karen Stokes. Karen, who was two years younger, was also from Mill Town. Her good grades and school activities had helped her get into the University of Georgia where she got her master's degree to become a school counselor. They had married at Christmastime during Smitty's last year in law school. After graduation, the couple moved back to Upton, where Smitty set up a law practice and Karen taught for a year and then became a counselor at Upton High. They had three children: Four-year-old James Copeland, or James; followed by Richard Stokes, or Dick; and three-month-old Margaret Karen, or Maggie.

Jen Saxton: Like Kate, she too was pretty, and had been popular. At five-foot-seven with shoulder-length, dark brown hair and distinct, large green eyes, Jen was outgoing and friendly. She also possessed a reserve that almost made her seem distant at times. Those who knew her understood this was her way of withdrawing into herself to get her thoughts straight. Jen tended to see the big picture and made decisions very methodically. Unlike the others, after graduation she had moved to Atlanta, gotten an apartment and begun her teaching career. Jen loved being on her own, but hoped to someday marry.

Part 1

Chapter 1

Though it was Labor Day weekend, a storm late the night before had pushed the temperatures down to about eighty-eight degrees, and for August in Georgia, that was cool weather. It had been a perfect day for a picnic. As the sun was slowly setting, Jen thought about the weekend. Labor Day had always been such a joyful experience. The holiday would start out with the town festival on Friday night. This event consisted of a dinner, entertainment, and a silent auction. The proceeds were used for a predetermined town need. This was always a big affair that people looked forward to. The day after the festival, the group—the Big Four—would go out to the Great Stone Palace for the night. This tradition began when they were in high school, and continued to the present. The Big Four reveled in their closeness and rituals.

The Great Stone Palace was a huge stone house that had been left to the town. It stood on the highest point in the county about five miles outside of Upton. On a fall day when the trees were bare, the place could be seen from miles around.

As twilight fell, Jen took a walk to sort some things out in her mind. As she returned to the house, Liza ran up and said, "Aunt Jen, let's get the jars ready." Jen gave the child a hug and then dutifully went into the kitchen. Kate, Karen and Beth Anne were already putting holes in the lids of jars so the little ones could catch fireflies and watch them before releasing them. The older kids played chase. Tom, Smitty and Ted were down at the lake fishing.

Jen observed the different activities. Being with the group and sharing their traditions brought her a sense of joy, for they were family to her. She had no way of knowing that within the year the closeness of the Big Four would be broken. The culprits would be secrets harbored by those she had long known, loved, and trusted. The disaster would bring Upton to its knees.

A breeze caused Jen to shiver. She looked up through the pine trees. Dark storm clouds were forming in the starlit sky.

⸙ *Chapter 2* ⸙

November

A white light flashed and then there was blackness. This recurring dream played itself out as Jen lay in a semi-comatose state. After two days of this, she opened her eyes. Her mouth was so dry her throat hurt. Getting out of bed to get water proved to be impossible. She was too weak to move. As if in a haze, Jen surveyed the room. Instead of the familiar surroundings of her bedroom, this place was white, and the bed had rails on it. Her mother and father were sitting beside her.

Barely able to speak, she said, "Where am I? Water."

Her mother moved quickly to get the glass with a straw and answered. "You were in a wreck, and this is the hospital."

To keep from breaking down, Mary Virginia concentrated on giving her only child the water.

Jen closed her eyes and slipped back into the blackness where she would remain for the next twenty-four hours.

For two days after she came out of her coma, Jen was extremely weak and asked no questions, but on the third day, when she and her father were alone, she spoke.

"What's wrong with me?"

"You had a wreck. The authorities believe that something happened to your brakes. You went off of one of the steep inclines in the county."

"Where was I going?"

"Back to Atlanta. You had spent Thanksgiving and the day after with us, but left on Saturday as you had a date that night. You must have decided to go the back way."

By all accounts, she should have been killed, but miraculously that did not happen. However, Jen was hurt badly: she suffered a broken leg, broken ribs, a head injury, and internal injuries. Because she needed help, she stayed in Upton with her parents until the middle of January.

One night when Mary Virginia, and Joseph were alone, she expressed her puzzlement. "I am surprised at the group."

"What do you mean?" Joseph said as he laid down his newspaper.

"Well, both Smitty and Kate have acted rather strangely. Smitty hardly ever comes, and when he does, he is not himself. He is stiff, rather distant. Kate stops by often, but she is preoccupied. I can't put my finger on it, but something seems odd. I hope Jen has not noticed."

"Maybe it's just the horror of one of their own being hurt so badly. These four kids have been insulated from trouble. I suspect they are pretty frightened by what has happened. Besides, with the holidays, they have probably been busy."

"I hope you are right." Mary Virginia replied in a dubious voice.

By the first of January Jen was able to return to Atlanta and to her job. For the first two weeks she only worked half days. After that, she easily slipped into her old routine. The wreck just seemed like a minor setback.

Chapter 3

February

The bell that ended the school day had rung about fifteen minutes before. Jen was straightening up her room when Janice Thompson, a fellow teacher and friend, came in.

"Hi. How was your trip to Upton this weekend?"

"Oh," Jen sighed, "different. You have time to get a cup of coffee? I surely could use a pair of listening ears."

"I could do you better. I made some great soup, so why don't you come over. The kids will not be home until about eight o'clock, and Mark is out of town. You can talk all you want." Janice answered.

"Thanks."

After the two women settled down to a bowl of soup and bread, Janice asked.

"So, why did you go to Upton this past weekend? Was there something special?"

"No, dad and mom were having some work done at the house on Saturday and they were going to be out of town. They wanted me there."

"So what happened?"

"It's Kate. She came over Saturday afternoon. From the beginning there was a coolness—a distance about her. When I asked if everything was okay, she jumped down my throat. But that was not the worst."

Let me digress here. The group always gets together sometime in January, after the holidays, to have its own dinner to celebrate the coming year and to exchange New Year's gifts. Everyone takes turns hosting the affair and it was Tom and Beth Anne's time. This year we all decided that January 25 would be a good time for the dinner. But when I had not heard anything by January 20, I called Kate. She said that they had decided not to have it this month; that everyone was too busy. Well, I was just getting back into the swing of things here and did not think too much about it. This past Saturday, however, Kate mentioned the new year celebration dinner that they had had. In her mind, Jen went back to that afternoon.

Jen looked surprised. "What dinner? You told me that we were not doing that this year."

In a halting and rather embarrassed voice, Kate answered, "Oh, uh, well, we did this on the spur of the moment. It was fun. I wish you had been there."

Angrily, Jen answered, "Well, I would have liked to have been there, but it's hard to attend something that you don't know anything about. You said spur of the moment. Does that mean an hour, a day, what?"

Sounding exasperated, Kate said, "Oh, Jen, I don't remember. We just assumed you could not come on such quick notice."

"That should have been my decision. This really stings, Kate."

"There you go again, blowing everything out of proportion. You need to learn the world does not revolve around you."

"Kate, Where is this coming from?"

Kate rolled her eyes. "Listen, people make plans—it's just that simple; I didn't mean to hurt you."

Feeling shocked by her friend's response, Jen answered, "Well, you did."

With a look of triumph and a voice devoid of anything but pleasure, Kate answered, "I'm really sorry; I should not have said anything. It's four o'clock and Todd is waiting for me at the gym."

Jen came back to the present in her mind and looked at Janice. "And she left."

Janice was astounded. "Jen, that does not sound like the Kate you've always talked about."

"Well, there is more. As if by divine appointment, as Kate reached her car in the back driveway, Beth Anne was ringing the front doorbell."

Again, Jen went back to that afternoon in her thoughts as she told the story.

"Oh hi Beth Anne, come on in."

In something of a curt voice, Beth Anne answered, "Well, just for a moment. I came to deliver your New Year's gift. Remember, Tom and I drew your name."

Jen was astounded. "I don't understand. You did not invite me to the party, and now you are bringing me a gift. What is going on?"

Beth Anne was obviously shocked. "What do you mean we did not invite you to the party? Didn't you get my invitation?"

"No. In fact, several weeks ago Kate said that all of you had decided not to have the dinner. Then about ten minutes ago she said that you had the get-together on the spur of the moment and didn't think that I could get there."

Beth Anne was staring in disbelief. "Jen, we would not do that to you. Remember, we set the date for the party for January 25. Tom and I were leaving for North Carolina January 10 for two weeks. The day before we left, Kate stopped by my house and offered to help with the dinner since Tom and I were not getting back until the twenty-fourth. I told her that I had everything taken care of, except I had not mailed the invitations. She said she would do that, and took them. I was upset because you did not acknowledge yours."

Coming back to the present again, Jen said to Janice, "It even gets weirder. Later that day, I saw a duffle bag sitting in the corner. Thinking it was Mom's, I decided to wash any clothes that were in there, so I dumped out the contents. It was then that I realized that it was Kate's. As I put everything back, there was the invitation."

9

Janice shook her head and said, "That is one odd individual."

Agreeing, Jen continued, "What I couldn't get over was the fact that Kate seemed to be taunting me about the party and enjoying every moment."

"She obviously is very angry. You don't have any idea what that's about?" Janice questioned.

Jen looked at Janice and said, "No, but I will tell you this. I have never seen Kate as mean as she was Saturday."

Chapter 4

March

The quietness was punctuated only by beautiful music. Jen closed her eyes; she was filled with disbelief and shock. Just as she was feeling as though she might faint, the minister began to speak words that brought comfort:

"The deaths of Dr. Joseph and Mary Virginia Saxton create a sadness and bewilderment in all of us. It is unfathomable to think one family should experience two such horrible wrecks in a period of five months.

"This popular couple moved to Upton thirty-eight years ago. Joseph, or Dr. Joe, as he was affectionately known, legendarily determined that everyone deserved the best of medical care and medicine regardless of ability to pay. Mary Virginia's many hours of volunteer work at the library and the church will be sorely missed. They served the community and church well. Of course, they would always tell you their most important accomplishment was their wonderful daughter, Jen. Dr. Joe and Mary Virginia touched the lives of all they met. They were good parents, good friends, and good Christians.

"The children of Army officers, these two decided early in their relationship that they wanted to settle down in a small town, have children, establish roots, and make a good place for their family. The sadness in all of our hearts mirrors the fact that Virginia and Joseph met their goal."

Of course, the sorrowful expressions on the faces of a few were only a mask that concealed a horrible secret. One member of the congregation found that sitting through this funeral had not been easy, though it had been necessary. Had he not shown up, people would wonder. Feeling restless, he turned and their eyes met briefly. When she saw him, her look of grief deepened, but it was a mockery of the joy and triumph they both felt. He almost laughed. Their acknowledgement was but momentary. They must be careful. Thankfully, the minister began the benediction.

With the amen, the service ended. As Jen walked down the isle, she did not know that two people were looking at her and thinking, *two down, and you are next.*

Chapter 5

"Thanks for coming," Jen said. It was the last of the guests who had come by after the funeral. As she closed the door, she leaned against it for a moment and closed her eyes. There was silence all around. For the first time in four days, the house was almost empty. Since the accident on Friday, people had jammed the rooms.

Jen slowly opened her eyes and just stood there looking around. When Joseph and Mary Virginia had moved to Upton, they had known they were planning to stay. They met with an architect who drew up plans that allowed the doctor and his wife to add to their home as they could afford to do so. The house, which had evolved over the years, was a large, sprawling, one-story traditional place. The entrance way was small, and led into a large living room. To the left were the bed rooms. Straight ahead of the living room was a large den where the family spent most of their time, and to the right were the kitchen and dining room. The white brick home with green shutters was a stately looking place. Just about two months ago Mary Virginia had laughed and said that after thirty years, they had finally finished building. This house had been a symbol of stability and a promise that the family would not be uprooted with still another move--a lifestyle Jen's parents had gladly left behind.

The door to the den was open enough for Jen to see one of the two recliners and a medical journal that lay open on the table. In the corner sat a TV which had never played a central part in their lives. The molding around the ceilings along with the antiques and near-antique furniture gave the house a stately but welcoming and homey look. It also displayed Mary Virginia Saxton's good decorating taste—sadly, this was a trait her daughter did not share. Jen walked into the kitchen to visit with Kate.

"Here, sit down and have some fresh coffee," Kate said as she put a cup on the table.

Kate almost seems back to her old self—not quite, but much better, Jen thought.

Jen took a deep breath and sat down. How many times had she, her mother, and Kate sat around this kitchen table just talking. How she loved this room. The green and white decor was charming, and the fireplace at the other end of the big room gave it a feeling of coziness. People always gathered here. A feeling of intimacy prevailed. A lump began to form in Jen's throat. There on the counter lay a recipe book with a pair of her father's glasses on top. It reminded her of how Joseph had become interested in cooking in the last few years, and how he had begun routinely helping Virginia prepare supper. This new arrangement still made Jen shake her head, as her dad had never shown any domestic tendencies while she was at home.

"Kate, what am I going to do? I am so alone. I have no family!" Jen's voice was getting emotional.

"You are not alone. We will always be here for you—you are like my sister."

Jen smiled. Since both women were only children, they often referred to themselves as siblings.

"Thank you, Kate. I needed to hear that. I don't know what I would have done without you—especially since the accident." Suddenly, Jen began to shake. It was that word—*accident*—except now it was accidents that always caused feelings she could not explain, as though something were terribly wrong.

"Are you okay?" Kate asked with concern in her voice.

"What?" Jen asked absently.

"Are you okay? Jen, you are shaking."

Jen watched Kate as she washed some coffee cups. At thirty, Kate looked much the same as she did in high school. Seemingly, Kate could do no wrong.

Jen waited a minute before answering. "Every time someone mentions the accident, a feeling comes over me. I can't explain it, but I know that something is terribly wrong."

"What do you mean *wrong*?" Kate asked in a rather careful tone of voice.

"Like maybe my wreck and now that of my parents was no accident."

"Jen, how could you say that? Now; now you just stop that. You know that Uncle Harry investigated your mom and dad's wreck, as well as yours. He said there was no foul play. He told you, and now I am telling you; but you just don't want to accept what has happened. Don't go looking for trouble where none exists. That won't help anything." Kate's voice was almost shrill.

At that moment Jen experienced an anger she had never felt. How dare Kate accuse Jen of not wanting to accept her parents' death. After all, Kate would leave here and go home to her spouse and two children. Her mom and dad lived within walking distance of her house.

In a very measured but low and even tone of voice, Jen said, "Kate, don't ever say that to me again. You don't even know what you are talking about."

"Now Jen, you are just getting worked up. Calm down. You are tired."

"Kate!" Jen said in a loud voice, "Yes I am tired but more that that I AM SCARED! Will I be next?" There, she had finally said it.

"What? That is crazy talk," Kate said in a flustered, almost angry voice.

Kate continued as if talking to a tired child. "Look, I think what you need is a good night's sleep. You will think clearer in the morning. Anyway, it's getting late and I have to get home."

Yeah, you go home to your family and I'll get a good night's sleep after losing mine, Jen thought bitterly.

"I'll call you in the morning Jen."

"Actually, I'm going back to Atlanta tonight," Jen replied in a rather icy tone. "My friends, Jack and Helen, who came for the funeral, are visiting with some friends. They are driving me home."

"Are you going back to work?"

"I have to. I was out so much with my wreck. Anyway, it is just a month and a half left in the school term. I need to be there. I want to be there. Work will help me survive."

Kate looked almost relieved. "I will be talking to you soon. Jen, I really am sorry."

They hugged rather stiffly, and Kate left.

Jen thought about her old friend. Somehow without her noticing it, Kate had changed. There was a time when Kate would have loved trying to figure out what the circumstances surrounding the wrecks were. It was now that Jen also let herself think about something she had kept below the surface—that when she had stayed in Upton after her own accident, Kate had not been her old self.

"Something is very wrong," Jen murmured.

As she was about to close the door, Jack and Helen arrived and interrupted her thoughts. Jen was grateful; she did not want to continue speculating.

~ *Chapter 6* ~

Kate did not go home immediately, but went where she always did when things got too much: to the Upton High School football stadium, home of the Screeching Owls. She sat high up in the tall bleachers. Somehow, watching the cheerleaders practice their jumps and yells helped Kate relax. It took her back to a time when everything was easy and life was happy.

As Kate watched the girls practice, she began to talk to herself. "Hold on to your youth. What happened? It was not supposed to work out like this." As she watched the girls practice, she pictured herself back in high school leading the cheers on Friday nights, going to dances: living life to the fullest. And then a night from just thirteen years ago came to life in her mind: The fall weather was perfect. One by one the convertibles, bearing members of the homecoming court, the girls dressed in their evening gowns, drove around the field. Waiting on the other side were the boys who would accompany them. When she got out of the car, Tom, the quarterback, was there to escort her across the field. They led Jen and Smitty and the rest of the court to the platform where Kate would be crowned the 1963 homecoming queen; Tom, the homecoming king. They were a beautiful couple. The crowd stood, cheered, and applauded for their royalty—Tom and Kate. Though she had never admitted it to anyone, the joy she felt that night had never been duplicated, not even by her wedding or the birth of Anna Kate and Todd.

"Where did it go wrong?" she said to herself. "Life was so perfect and easy, and now it's out of control. Worst of all, there is no turning back. What am I going to do?" Thinking about the deaths of Joseph and Mary Virginia made her shudder. The ex-homecoming queen put her face in her hands and cried softly.

Chapter 7

After the funeral, Smitty had put in his obligatory appearance at Jen's and gone back to his office. He believed that the last few days, especially the funeral, were the hardest of his life, and now he would have to live with his actions. Thankfully, Karen and the children were out of town for the week. Facing them now would be impossible.

"Smitty, can I get anything for you?"

"Oh, no thank you, Jane. In fact, why don't you go home early. I have some things to catch up on, but won't need any help."

"Thanks, I could use the time. Have a big test next week."

Smitty heard his secretary leave and was glad to be alone. The office was in the second story of an old building. The three large rooms were rather stark, with only the bare necessities: two desks, bookcases, and a place for clients to sit; but Smitty had always loved the place. He turned and looked out of his window. Not too far in the background, he could see the mill tower—the landmark of Mill Town. Until today, it had been a welcomed sight because it had represented the place where he had grown up: a "town" of good, hard-working people.

It was Jen's father who had saved Smitty's life. As a young doctor who had just moved to Upton from Atlanta, he heard someone talking about a child in Mill Town who was dying from thrush. The herb they usually used for this disease had not worked. When Joe Saxton, who had a child of the same age, found out that the only person who had seen the sick baby had no medical training, he went out to visit the parents. Doctors were just beginning to use penicillin, and though it was hard to get, Dr. Joe had some. He strongly believed that this wonder drug was the baby's best chance for survival.

Paul, Smitty's father, had been reluctant to listen; after all, Mill Town residents did not mix with outsiders. However, he was a fair man. He knew he had nothing to lose, and his child was dying. After a few days of the doctor administering the wonder drug, Smitty got well. Paul did not have the money to pay for this medicine, so Joe offered him a job at his drug store when the mill closed, as it did every spring for a month. Though Smitty's father worked his way up to the position of head foreman at the mill, he worked at the drug store every year until his death two years ago.

Joe had saved Smitty's life in more ways than one. As time passed, Paul introduced the doctor to some of the best fishing holes around, and each year Joe would take Paul to a football game at the University of Georgia. They would have dinner at Joe's fraternity house and then go to the game. Smitty could still see the thrill that had been in his father's eyes when he returned after the first time he had taken this trip.

It was late at night, and six-year-old Smitty had awakened from a bad dream. Margie, his mother, let him get up, and she made some hot chocolate and was reading to the child when Paul quickly walked into the house. In an excited voice, he began to tell the story of going to the game.

"I'll tell you Margie, I have never seen a place like that. We went to this two-story brick house—it sort of looked like the DePau home— anyway, they call it a fraternity house. That is an organization that a lot of college boys join," Paul explained in a very important-sounding tone of voice. "Anyway, we ate with lawyers, judges, doctors, even senators, and they talked to me and listened to what I had to say, just like I was one of them. After supper we went to the game. Oh, it was fun. The score was close, but the university won. I hope Joe invites me to go next year. It was great."

That was the beginning of Joe and Paul's annual trips to the University of Georgia football game. Paul never missed a year. Early on, Joe began urging Paul to encourage Smitty to go to college rather than drop out before high school graduation, as did many Mill Town children.

Smitty's mind went back to a morning when he was a junior in high school. Joe and Paul were slated to go to their yearly game. Early in the morning the phone rang. Smitty answered.

"Dad, it's for you. It's Dr. Saxton."

"Paul, Joe here. Say, I have to go to Atlanta. A friend of mine is going to have to perform emergency surgery later today and needs my help. It's an area where I have expertise. I have made the reservations at the frat house and the tickets to the game are there. Why don't you take Smitty; show him around the campus, and the two of you can eat at the house before attending the game. Who knows? Maybe Smitty will want to go to the university. That would be great."

"Are you sure there won't be problems with us eating at the house without you?" Paul asked in a dubious tone of voice.

"Positive. I have already talked with Jim Sherring. He is expecting you and says they look forward to seeing you again."

Jim Sherring was a high-powered lawyer from Gainesville. He took care of the alumni every first game. Paul liked him; he just seemed to be a regular type of guy. Paul also felt good that such an important person could look forward to seeing him.

That outing was something that Smitty and Paul talked about until Paul's death. Smitty recalled the pride on his father's face when they went to the frat house—a large antebellum brick home with columns— and when he introduced Smitty around. Paul had been proud of both Smitty and the important people he had come to know over the years. Smitty now suspected that Joe had planned not to attend because he felt it was important that Paul introduce him to college, not a friend. Next to his father, there was no other person Smitty respected more than Joe Saxton. The next year, Smitty was offered several scholarships, but chose the University of Georgia. When he got ready for law school, it was his grades and some of the men his father had met at the frat house who helped him get in.

"Joe Saxton saved me, and now he is dead. It's all my fault," Smitty said to himself. "How could I have done such a stupid thing?"

As he looked over at the mill tower, he said to himself, "The Mill Town star has fallen."

He got up, went over to the window, and closed the curtains.

Chapter 8

It was now May 26, two months after the funeral. School was out, and Jen was returning to Upton for the first time since her parents' deaths. There were many decisions to be made, such as what to do with the house. There was also the necessity of packing up everything. It was not a pleasant time, and she wondered what kind of support she would have. Even though Smitty was her dad's lawyer and was, Jen thought, one of her best friends, he had only called her one time since her parents were buried, and he had rushed that conversation. It was as if Smitty knew he should contact Jen, but did not want to. Kate had also been strangely quiet.

Jen glanced at her watch. It was almost twelve thirty and she was still twenty minutes from Upton. "I meant to start earlier so I could get home by noon," she admonished herself. Then reality set in. No one was there; it did not matter at what time she arrived. The truth hurt her so badly that she pulled over to the side of the interstate and cried.

"Stop it," Jen said to herself. "You have to make this trip. It is going to be hard, but necessary. Now pull yourself together and get going!" With a new resolve, Jen headed to Upton.

There was a sickening feeling in the pit of her stomach as she passed through downtown. The business section of Upton, a collection of old buildings constructed around the turn of the century, had been built on a square, and was dominated by a large, old courthouse. As she passed her dad's clinic, which was next door to his drugstore, Jen thought she would die. Just knowing that he was not there was like pouring salt on an open wound. But nothing could have prepared her for the despair she felt when she unlocked the door and walked into her childhood home. Virginia had always met her daughter at the door when she had arrived. Jen did not realize how much that had meant to her until this moment, when all she experienced was emptiness. Her mother's welcoming smile had made life seem so right, and the absence of it reminded Jen that she was now alone.

"Jen?" Jen had been so much into her thoughts that she did not hear anyone walk up.

"Kate. I didn't know you were here." Kate walked over and gave her old friend a hug.

"I couldn't let you be alone when you arrived. When your parents would go out of town, I watered their plants, and still have a house key. I decided to bring some sandwiches, if you haven't eaten. I even have some dessert and made some fresh coffee."

Jen had been a little upset with Kate for not bothering to visit with her in Atlanta, and for the fact that when she did call, she seemed preoccupied and rushed. However, Kate's presence today wiped out all of these sins.

"You will never know how much your being here means to me. Thanks!" Jen said as she gave her old friend a hug.

They spent time visiting. Kate had prepared a nice lunch, and Jen realized that she was very hungry. That afternoon the two young women looked at the scrapbook Virginia had started for Jen when she was a baby and had kept going until the present. It was simply called *Jen's Life.*

In the middle of the afternoon, Beth Anne stopped by with a casserole.

Jen thanked her for the food and invited her in.

Beth Anne joined Kate and Jen. "Hi Kate."

"Oh, hi," Kate said, trying to sound casual. Jen smiled to herself. Kate had never really seemed to accept Beth Anne. She insisted the Atlanta debutante was really just a snob. Jen believed that Kate had a hard time seeing someone else with Tom. Even though those two had never really dated, they had always received a lot of attention, which was something Kate craved.

At five-foot-seven with dark eyes, a complexion with just a tint of olive, and almost-black hair fixed in a pageboy, Beth Anne radiated a quiet, confident beauty. Even though she dressed simply, her appearance screamed old money. Many people thought that Beth Anne's reserved manner was one of snobbery. It didn't help that much of her social life revolved around the Atlanta society—a fact Miss Marie Antoinette had made sure everyone knew.

Virginia had known Beth Anne through volunteer work and had realized that what people thought was unfriendliness was really shyness. Virginia had also suspected that the spouses of the group found it hard to feel that they were a part of things. The Big Four had been together for so long that they had probably been exclusive in some of their actions without meaning to do so. It had been Beth Anne and Tom, though, who had been to Atlanta at least once a week to visit with Jen and take her out to dinner and to the movies. They had been a life saver.

"What is this certificate for graduating from Upton's School of Charm?" Beth Anne asked as she looked at some of the pictures from the scrapbook.

Kate and Jen fell down laughing.

"Come on, tell her how you almost got expelled and banished from polite society," Kate laughed.

"Oh *dahling*," Jen said with mock drama, "your grandmother-in-law almost single-handily decided that I was not worthy to be deemed a lady."

Coming back with her own mockery, in an English accent, Beth Anne commented, "Oh, what a pity, my dear, that you shan't walk in the company of Kate and me."

Laughter filled the room. Jen had never seen Beth Anne so animated.

"So, why did my sweet (this word was said with obvious sarcasm) grandmother-in-law almost decide that you were unredeemable?"

"Because she is a mean old bat," Jen answered with a smile.

"Jen! That is not nice," Kate said admonishingly, but laughing. "Come on. Tell the whole story."

"Well, if you insist. During class one day, the creep was saying something about how well-bred young girls were supposed to act and I told her that dogs and horses were bred, not people, and I did not want to be compared with horses. She pursed her lips. They got so thin I almost couldn't see them. Then she burst out, 'Young lady, you are impertinent. You do not deserve to get a certificate from the Upton School of Charm. Go call your mother. It is time for you to go.'"

"I did not know what impertinent meant, and I didn't care. I just wanted out of that place."

Beth Anne was a little confused. "You must have gone back—here is the coveted certificate."

"Tom's mother called mine and said I should return. Probably the only time in Jean's life she stood up to that old woman. Anyway, because she was so adamant, and because my mother decided I needed to temper what I had to say, Mom and I met with Jean and Miss Marie Antoinette. Anyway, I was allowed back in, and graduated, but the old girl has never really forgiven me. Not that I cared then nor now."

Kate and Beth Anne were laughing very hard.

"Jen, you have given social functions a new meaning for me. The next time Tom and I are at some party in Atlanta among the refined and well-bred, I will probably look out and see faces of dogs and horses rather than people."

Jen was enjoying herself. The laughter was a great respite from the burden at hand.

Beth Anne could not stay, but issued an invitation for Jen to join them for dinner. She declined, as the trip had tired her, but said she would take a rain check.

After seeing her friend off, Jen returned to the den to find Kate holding pictures of their prom. In a dreamy voice, Kate asked, "Do you ever wonder what would have happened if you had married Smitty and I had married Tom?"

"Have you lost your mind? That would have been like marrying my brother. Ugh." Jen screwed up her face in disgust.

"Aw, come on. Didn't it bother you just a little when he married Karen?"

"Well, I had to get used to the idea."

"I had already married and left college when Smitty and Karen became engaged. How did you find out they were marrying?"

Jen's thoughts went back to that cool October afternoon from her senior year in college at Agnes Scott.

"Jen, there is someone in the lobby to see you," The girl at the desk in the dorm lobby announced.

"Wait, I'll be right there."

In her gray slacks and pink sweater set, Jen looked very pretty. She was surprised to see Smitty. They had both been so busy that they had not really visited since June.

"Hi. What brings you over from the University?"

"Oh, thought maybe you would like to go get a hamburger."

After visiting and eating, Jen could stand it no longer. "Okay, what is going on?"

"What do you mean?"

"Smitty, I have known you all of my life. I know when you are up to something."

He smiled, and with a little sadness in his eyes, he said, "We have known each other for a long time. You have made my life special."

Beginning to feel a little concerned, Jen tried to keep everything casual. "Yeah, yeah, yeah; are you dying?"

Laughing, Smitty answered, "No, nothing like that. Do you remember Karen Stokes?"

"Sure, she was a couple of years behind us—student council, real smart—I always liked her."

"Yeah. You know she grew up in Mill Town and is at the University. Well, anyway, she has been riding back and forth to school with me, and we got to know each other better. This past spring we went out a few times. Nothing big. This summer, with both of us on work scholarships at school, we saw each other a lot."

Jen's heart was beating fast. She knew what was coming and, for some reason, did not want to hear it.

"I'm going to ask her to marry me." Smitty said hurriedly. Jen just sat there for a moment, and he rushed on. "I would have been fighting for you, but I know you don't want to return to Upton—you have always had your own dreams. Karen and I want the same things in life."

"Do you love her?"

"Yes, very much."

Jen went over to her old friend and hugged him. "I am so happy for you" she said genuinely.

"Were you upset?" Kate's voice brought her back to the present.

"A little. I didn't know why. I was not in love with Smitty. Mom explained that I was feeling displaced. It was a time of realizing that all of our decisions have consequences. I had always known that with little effort, Smitty and I could have gotten together, but he was right; I did not want to return here and live. But it was scary not to have Smitty in my corner. Say, how did we get on this subject? All of us made good choices. You have a great marriage, as do the others; and I love my life."

Kate didn't say anything. She left at about four o'clock.

Jen watched Kate go down the walk, and wished she knew what was wrong with her. "Kate has just not been her old self," she mumbled.

Jen continued looking at the scrapbook and remembering. Her parents were both children of high-ranking military officers. Though the families had known each other for years, it was only when Virginia had transferred to the University of Georgia that she and Joseph had begun dating.

Being a part of the town of Upton had been important to the Saxtons. They were very religious. Active in the Methodist church, their religion was an everyday thing. Joseph never turned anyone away who needed medicine or medical attention and could not pay. While he made a good living, he had made a choice to serve the people rather than make the big bucks. They had been a close couple who passed on their values to their only child.

Suddenly aware of her fatigue, Jen lay on the sofa for a moment. Before she knew it, she was fast asleep, clothes and all.

As Jen lay peacefully on the couch, she had no way of knowing that her findings the next day would make her life even more troubling.

～ *Chapter 9* ～

Jen opened her eyes. *What time is it*, she thought. *It's 5:30 a.m.; I slept here all night.* The familiar pain of loss began to saturate her. As always, Jen gave herself a little time before getting up. After a shower and breakfast, she felt better. Jen knew she was going to have to start sorting through things and making decisions as to what she wanted to do with the house. But for now she could not think about that. The uppermost thing on her mind was going through her father's papers.

Joseph Saxton had turned a small closet into an office. In it he made a drop-lid desk. When he was finished with his business each day, he would put the desk up and lock the closet. Jen was never permitted in there. Feeling strange, she turned the key and opened the door. She walked in, turned on the light, and looked around. The "office" was very neat and well organized. On one of the shelves, obviously displayed, was an envelope with her name on it. Jen knew it was her father's handwriting. Shaking a bit, she opened it, took the letter out, and began to read:

June 7, 1976

Dear Jen,

I hope that you never have to read this letter, because if you do, my worst fears will have come true.

Your mother and I have reason to believe that someone is trying to cause problems for us and that maybe your wreck was no accident. Do you remember that I lost the county supervisor's race? Well, I didn't think too much about that. Just figured that Andy White, who wanted the job, campaigned harder, and it was time for a change. However, in the back of my mind I began to realize that my business was falling off a bit. I just chalked it up to the economy. But when I saw the list of nominees for church officers and my name was not there, I knew there was a problem. I have served that congregation for thirty-eight years. In the meantime, George Cameron, the pharmacist in Georgetown, suggested we meet for lunch. When I arrived, he was sitting there with Rod Steal, who is head of the state drug division, and Jim White, our pastor. George had wanted us to meet so that he could tell me that there was a rumor going around that I was involved in selling illegal drugs.

It seems that a newly hired nurse, Barbara Sills, got to work early one morning, and found a sack full of illegal drugs and drug paraphernalia, sitting out on a cabinet. There was a note on it to me saying, in effect, that this was what I ordered and payment would be expected in full at the usual time and place. She immediately took the evidence to Atlanta. This is when Rod Steal got involved.

Later that day she called me and said she would not be in. Her mother had had a stroke. The next day I received a short note from Barbara saying that she was returning immediately to Athens to take care of her mom. Though I called several times to see if there was anything your mother and I could do for her, she never returned my calls, nor did she tell me about the sack of drugs. However, before leaving Upton, she must have told several people, and, unknown to your mother and me, rumors began to fly. Rod said that they started an investigation into my activities, but as soon as they did, it was evident that there was nothing to the allegations, and he suspected that someone was trying to set me up. We devised a campaign to restore my reputation. With a speech by Rod to the Town Board as well as the Rotary Club, the newspaper doing an article, and Jim supporting me from the pulpit, things cleared up, and business returned to normal. All of this came to light soon after your wreck. We were going to tell you about what had happened when you got better. Your mother and I have been dumbfounded as to why this has happened.

This past Tuesday Old Jim stopped by to see us. I realize many people don't think he is too bright, and they don't listen to him. I believe he is okay, just very quiet—maybe a little slow. Sometimes at night he walks for miles. When he came by on Tuesday, he was upset and wanted to tell me something. He said that the night before your wreck, he was walking by our house about 1:00 a.m. when he saw a man with a tool box run from our garage and get in a green car. He said that it was an odd-looking car—one like he had never seen before. He told the sheriff, who said he would check it out; but I suspect Harry just brushed him off.

In light of the drug rumors, what Jim said, and the fact that you had some questions about what really caused your wreck, your mom and I are concerned. Our trip to Atlanta later today is not only to visit with you, but also to see a private detective we are going to hire to find out what is going on. His name is Tony Antone.

Jen, just know that your mother and I love you very much and are very proud of you.

Love,

Dad

Jen looked at the date on the letter and realized that it was written the day before her parents' deaths. She suspected her dad had gotten up in the middle of the night and written it. Suddenly, she lost her composure and cried for a long time, both for herself and for her parents. When at last the tears stopped and composure came about, Jen knew she must see that detective as soon as possible. Though it was only six thirty, she called for fear she would miss him.

"Hello," a groggy voice answered. There was no doubt that this person had been awakened.

"Mr. Antone?"

"Speaking"

"This is Jen Saxton."

"Who?" he said in an annoyed tone.

"Jen Saxton. Actually you don't know me, but…"

"Say, it is only six thirty, can we have this conversation later?"

"No, we can't. I am sorry to awaken you, but my father and mother, Virginia and Joseph Saxton were to meet with you two months ago."

"Yeah, they didn't show." This was said in sort of a grumpy way.

"That is true. On the way to Atlanta they had a wreck and were killed."

"Oh! I am so sorry." His manner immediately changed from annoyance to sorrow. "How did it happen?" he asked with concern.

Jen told him about the wreck and the letter. "Mr. Antone, obviously my father was concerned for our safety. I know this is last-minute, but could you please see me today?"

"Yes. Where are you now?"

"I'm in Upton, but can come to Atlanta."

"No. Do you know where the Green Lantern is?"

Jen smiled. It was a nice restaurant halfway between Upton and Atlanta. When she was in high school, this was the place for a date to take you when he wanted to be impressive. How grown-up it felt going thirty-five miles away for a dinner. "Yes, I know the place."

"Let's meet there in say about two hours."

"Fine. By the way, how will I know you?" Jen asked.

"Well, I'm about six-foot-one with dark hair. I guess that you could say I'm tall, dark—and the handsome is your decision," he said with a laugh.

His attempt at humor put Jen at ease. "I'll see you there."

Who, thought Jen, *could be responsible for all of this horrible mess—the wrecks and rumors of illegal drugs? Were they related? Why? Will I be next?*

Her head swirling with questions, Jen dressed and left to meet the tall, dark, and possibly handsome detective.

Chapter 10

The Green Lantern was a rather pretty restaurant. It was in an old, large building just outside of the small town of Cameron, Georgia. The arched, white stucco walls, adorned with lush green plants and black lanterns, gave the place a Spanish look. Not only was the décor pleasing, but the food was equally as good. People came here from miles around for a fine dining experience. When Jen arrived at the restaurant, Tony was not there. After being seated, she scanned the place for any familiar faces, but saw none. This was a relief. Being seen with someone might prompt unwanted questions. Across the room were two high-school boys and two girls. Jen wondered if they were on their way to the University of Georgia for Senior Day. This took her back to the day she, Tom, Smitty and Kate had stopped here for breakfast on their way to Senior Day. They were so excited and felt so mature to be on their own.

"Penny for your thoughts."

Startled, Jen looked up. *It must be Tony—tall, dark, and yes, very handsome.* Extending her hand, Jen said, "Thank you for coming on such a short notice. Please sit down."

Tony smiled and sat down. "I'm starving. Have you ordered?"

"No. I just got here. I was watching those kids over there. They take me back."

Tony and Jen made small talk until the waitress took their orders. When the waitress left, Tony said, "I am truly sorry about your parents. Please tell me what happened."

"According to the sheriff, my father went off an incline—actually it's a drop of about twenty-five feet. There was a fire. Mom's and dad's bodies were burned beyond recognition." Jen almost broke down. She stopped talking to regain her composure.

"I am sorry to have to ask you about these events, but it is the only way I can possibly help."

Jen appreciated the young detective's obvious concern

"Tony, what did Dad tell you when he called and asked to meet with you?"

"Only that you had had a bad accident and there were some rumors of illegal drugs. I really didn't ask too many questions when he made the appointment."

"After my wreck, I told the sheriff and my parents that I saw a white light before leaving the road. They did not seem to think too much about it. Harry, the sheriff, believed my brakes went out. The car was so badly damaged there was no way to tell. It is just a miracle that I survived. Anyway, life got back to normal and I put the wreck behind me until my parents were killed. Then I began to believe there was more going on than we knew. This morning I found this letter."

She handed the letter her father had written over to Tony for him to read.

When he finished, he looked at Jen. "Your parents had reason to be concerned. What are your thoughts on all that has happened?"

"One of my first questions was what were they doing in that part of the county. The car was found along Old King's Highway, which is out in the country. Dad always took the freeway. The authorities said that the wreck happened around nine thirty, yet they were supposed to be meeting me at ten o'clock, which would have meant they would not have gotten to my place until at least eleven, and trust me, Virginia and Joe Saxton were never late."

"Was there someone who lived out there they might have been going to see before starting to Atlanta, or possibly an emergency at the hospital that had detained your parents?"

"I don't think so. No matter what, they would have called and told me they were going to be late."

"You said there were several reasons for your belief that these wrecks were not accidents. So far you have indicated that the facts of what happened do not add up to your parents' usual actions—which may or may not mean anything. What else?"

"This may sound dumb to you, but I have a strong feeling that more is going on than we know, and when I have these feelings, they are usually right."

"We should always be sensitive to a strong inner warning. Any ideas of who would want to harm your family?"

"I can't imagine anyone wanting to hurt us. Mom and Dad were very popular and gave a lot of themselves to the community. I will admit that dad made hospital administrators mad with his free treatment, but this was business, not personal. It just doesn't make sense."

"Who investigated both accidents?"

"Well, the sheriff was there. I doubt he did anything. I did talk to him about my misgivings, but he totally dismissed anything I had to say. He is my best friend's uncle and I have known him all of my life, but we have never liked each other. I don't trust him. And now with what has happened, I need to know there is someone on my side. Will you take the case?"

"Before I answer that, I want to get some preliminary things out of the way. First, we have to talk about the cost. This will not be cheap."

Jen held her hand up to stop Tony. "I know how much you charge. Dad had some information about your services in his papers. With the money my parents inherited, and now with what I have been left, the expense is the least of my worries. I will pay what it takes to find out what happened to my family. Besides, what good is the money if someone takes my life? Look, I need to know what is going on, and I'm willing and able to pay."

"The second thing is if I find out you are not being straight with me about things, I'm off the case immediately. You must be totally honest with me."

As Tony spoke, his soft brown eyes turned a steely cold. Jen knew that he meant business.

"Look, I have nothing to hide. Honesty is as important to me as it obviously is to you."

"Okay. Is there the possibility that your dad had been involved in drugs and these problems had something to do with a drug deal gone bad? It's not uncommon for doctors to get hooked—long hours, little sleep."

Tony was watching for Jen's reaction as much as her answer.

"Absolutely no possibility. Dad wanted to serve people, but always said that his best service came when he took care of himself. Besides, he would not have seen that as compatible with being a Christian."

Tony sensed that Jen was insulted by the questions.

"You need to realize that any time an investigation goes on, offensive questions probably arise. There is also something else you must consider: very often, investigations bring out painful information that you might rather not know about."

"I don't care what you uncover. I want to know why these wrecks happened and who was behind them."

Tony looked at Jen. She had a determined look that made him realize that she feared nothing but the secrets behind her parents' deaths and her accident.

"Okay. Back to your dad. How did he take care of himself?"

"Didn't keep late hours unless he had to go back to the hospital. He and mother also would go away for a weekend almost every other month."

"What about you, Jen?"

"What?"

"What about you? Do you do drugs, or have you?"

The look of disbelief almost made Tony laugh. Jen obviously had not hit the drug scene, but he had to play this out just in case she was a good actress.

"Heavens no, Tony. What do you take me for?"

"Come on, Jen. Did you go to college?"

"Yes, Agnes Scott."

"I'm sure drugs were there. I know they were because I suspect we graduated from college about the same time. I got my degree from the University."

"Well, did you do drugs?"

"No."

"Okay. Neither did I."

"Any of your friends involved?"

"Not that I know of. I really don't think so."

"You indicated that your parents had inherited money. Was there a family member who maybe felt he should have gotten money your mom or dad got?"

"There is no family."

"No family?" The thought of no brothers and sisters was hard for this Italian from a large Catholic family to understand, let alone the absence of an extended family. After all, his mom and dad were still living, as well as his six brothers and sisters; and his extended family consisted of many aunts, uncles, and cousins.

"My mother's parents were only children, as were mom and dad. My dad had two aunts on his mother's side. One died when in her thirties. She had no children, and the other never married. Dad never really knew his biological parents. When he was a baby, his mother left him at a hospital in Houston. It just so happened that my grandparents were in Houston on business. Grandmother got sick and ended up in the hospital at the same time my father was left there. Because they could not have children, my grandparents asked to adopt my dad when the news broke that he had been abandoned."

"Did he ever search for his roots?"

"Oh, no. He loved his parents. The other didn't matter to him."

"What about friends. Any feuds?"

"No. Look, I know that these accidents were staged, but the reason has to be a secret in the mind of a very sick person."

"Or persons?"

"Yeah."

"If you think something might happen to you, why are you staying in Upton? Seems to me you would be safer in your own place in Atlanta."

"I need to be in Upton. For some reason, I have more peace there than anywhere and fear will not run me off. Besides, I have to make many decisions, like what to do with my dad's businesses, the house—lots of things."

They both sat and drank their coffee, neither saying a word. Tony was lost in thought. Finally, Jen could stand the silence no longer.

"Tony, what's wrong? Don't you believe me?"

"Oh—oh yeah," He said, squinting his eyes a little. "I have a lot of thoughts going on. But how do you do it?"

"Do what?"

"Deal with all of this alone. My wife, Susan, died two years ago and I don't know what I would have done without my family."

"That's horrible about your wife. What happened?"

"We didn't know she was diabetic. About three months into her pregnancy, she went into a coma and never came out of it."

"Oh, I am so sorry."

"As I said, my family saved me. Who helps you?"

"My friends." Jen told him about the Big Four and how she relied on them. But even as she spoke she realized that, except for Tom and Beth Anne, they really had not been there for her. *Surely things will change this summer*, she assured herself.

After talking and socializing a bit, Tony and Jen stood to leave.

"Go back and look in all of your parents' things. Study papers and anything else that might be a clue as to what is going on. Even if you don't know what it is, if something doesn't feel or seem right, let me know. You have my number. Call me anytime. I will start my investigation and call you—probably in a week, but sooner if I can find anything."

"Thank you, Tony."

As Tony drove back to Atlanta, he thought about Jen. She seemed to be a very nice person, but truly alone. He liked her, but he was worried. If these were no accidents, whoever was behind them would come back for her, and very possibly succeed.

The questions that lingered were who, and why?

Chapter 10

It had been a week since Jen met with Tony, and he had not called. She had never worked with a detective before and did not really know what to expect, but she had hoped to hear from him by now.

Her days were filled with people coming by, visiting, bringing food, and presenting generous and sincere offers of help. Tom and Beth Anne were very attentive. Kate came over every day, but her visits were generally short, and Jen felt that they were too often obligatory in nature. Smitty never called or came to see her.

Tonight she was having an early diner with Toady and Charles Jordan.

Toady's real name was Tory, but her brothers nicknamed her Toady, and the name stuck. Jen's parents met Toady and Charles while they were all in college. Both couples married about the same time. Though they were very different, Jen knew that her father and Charles were as close as brothers. About one year after Virginia and Joseph moved to Upton, Toady and Charles also decided to move there so that he could open his own CPA firm. At sixty, they were a striking-looking couple. He was a tall, very erect man with a stern face and dark hair that was heavily peppered with gray. She was tall and large-boned with laughing eyes and a great tan from weekly tennis games. The couples shared many interests. Toady and John were like family to Jen.

She arrived at six thirty. Their magnificent home was a large, two-story brick house. Toady and John liked everything about their home to be perfect. She had hired an interior decorator to help her put the place together. The furniture consisted mostly of fine antiques, and was accented with oriental rugs. Never did anyone see anything out of place or a speck of dust. Both of them were the most organized and neat people Jen had ever seen. Virginia always said it was a good thing Toady and John never had children, as they would not have been able to accept anything less than perfect. Also, John would have resented the cost of a child because there was never enough money to please him. Even with their differences, the two couples loved each other very much.

At the dinner table Jen noticed that John looked awful. "Oh, Jen, Tony Antone came to my office today." Jen almost jumped. Her surprise, and maybe a look of fear, registered on her face. She was not sure why this comment scared her. Maybe it was because Tony told her not to tell anyone she wanted to hire him, or maybe it was because she feared John had bad news.

"It's okay. I was the one who sent your dad to Tony."

"Oh, how did you know him?" Jen seemed surprised.

"Last year I had to deal with an embezzlement situation. This happened in an Atlanta firm that is one of my clients. Tony was the detective who cracked the case. I was very impressed with his work and with him as a person. Nice man—good man." Jen knew that for John to say that about anyone was a real compliment. Unlike her father, John did not have a lot of friends. He was a very strong, demanding, and proper individual who seemed to look down his nose at people.

Virginia always felt that John's background caused him to have a false feeling of superiority. John's parents had met when his dad, Austin Jordan, was stationed in Montgomery, Alabama. They married, but John's mother, Margaret, was never accepted by her wealthy, "old east" in-laws. Not only was she not one of them in a social sense, she was also poor, and they believed she just wanted to get her hands on the family fortune. John's early life was that of a privileged, upper-class child: boarding schools, horseback riding, country clubs, and large homes. They understood their place in society and John relished in his position. Unfortunately, Austin died when John was ten. He and his mother were then cheated out of any inheritance that was rightfully theirs and the only nice things John ever had were from cousins and uncles who felt sorry for him, or had grown tired of what they had.

Eventually, Margaret took her son and returned to Alabama. They moved into a small house, and John was reared in poverty, but he never forgot his earlier lifestyle.

John had been a good student and received a scholarship from the University of Georgia. After college he hired a lawyer and recovered the money that had been due his mother and him. His portion of the settlement made him a wealthy man, and he got even more when his mother died; but growing up poor and pitied caused a pain and fear that never left him. John covered the fears and insecurities he felt with his frothy personality.

"Why was Tony here?"

"He was looking at your dad's financial records."

"What did he say?"

"He didn't say anything. Just called and asked if he could ask me about people in Upton. There is really nothing more to tell."

Toady stopped eating and put her hand over her face for a minute and then very softly said, "Jen, I can't imagine what you are going through. We shouldn't be having this conversation."

There was silence, and then John spoke up. "We would like to have you stay here with us until Tony can find out what's going on."

"You are so nice, but you have to understand; just being in Mom's and Dad's house makes me feel close to them; it gives me some sort of peace."

"But Jen—John and I are scared for you. You don't know if you are safe."

"I understand, and I am very careful. Besides, Kate is coming by to visit with me later tonight. After supper, Ted is taking the kids to his parents' home for a couple of days. I think he is going up to fish with his brother."

"Speaking of Ted, do you know him very well?" Toady asked.

"Of course. Well, to be honest I have not seen too much of him the last few years, but according to Kate he has been working hard."

"I don't know. She is so sweet, but I don't like him."

Toady was a plain-spoken person, but this bluntness surprised Jen. "Why?"

"Well, he seems to be surly and rude. I had some work done here in my kitchen, and he came out to check on the workers. He was ugly and rude to them, and not too nice to me. I told him not to come back until he could act in a respectful way to everyone. He called later and apologized. Claimed he was taking some medicine and had a bad reaction to it. I accepted his apology, but decided I didn't believe him. I don't know. Something is wrong with that man."

After dinner Jen helped Toady clear the table and put the dishes in the dishwasher.

When Toady was sure John could not hear them talking, she turned to Jen and said, "Please be careful. We worry about you, and I worry about John. Your parents' deaths were such a blow to him. If anything happened to you, I don't think…" her voice trailed off.

Jen put her arms around Toady and said, "Please understand, I must be at the house, but I promise—I will be careful."

Toady regained her composure and said, "Call us if you need help."

As Jen drove home, she thought about how much she appreciated the Jordans' concern. But just as she parked the car in the driveway, a horrible feeling settled over her. "Could they be trying to isolate me from my friends?" She said to herself. *No! After all, it was John who got her father to hire Tony.*

Jen shook her head slightly as if to ward off such horrible and invasive thoughts—or were they really warnings?

Chapter 11

Tony was the first to arrive. The old Atlanta restaurant, The Forest, was frequented by people from Atlanta, but seldom used by outsiders. It had three large, airy rooms, two of which were screened-in porches, with many ceiling fans and plants all over the place. Tony always chose the back room, as he felt a sense of privacy there.

He arrived early today so that he could have a cup of coffee and think. Tony was always careful about the things he said to his clients. He did not ever want to give them wrong information or false hope, but he did not like delivering unpleasant news. What he had to tell Jen was not good. Obviously, she was a strong individual, but how much could one person stand before breaking? He closed his eyes, put his head back, and, for the first time, wished he were not a detective.

A noise caused him to look up. It was then that he saw Jen walking toward him. *That is one fine-looking woman*, he thought to himself. Tall, with navy linen slacks and a white linen blouse, she looked almost regal. Her dark brown hair and large green eyes would capture almost anyone's attention.

Tony automatically stood. Jen noticed that he was smiling, but he seemed nervous, and this worried her.

After they exchanged pleasantries and ordered, Jen looked directly at Tony and, with a no-nonsense tone of voice, said, "Something is wrong, isn't it?"

Tony was startled. She reminded him of Susan. They were both very gentle women, but they both had a tenacious directness that could catch the best off-guard. He smiled as he thought, *Lady, I would not want you for my enemy!*

He shook himself back to the present. "Well, my news is not good."

"Let's have it. Waiting will not change anything." Jen knew she sounded tough, but inside she was wilting. There was no doubt that the limit as to what she could handle was fast approaching.

"I told you a week ago I would look into your situation. I worked long hours, and couldn't find anything obvious that would make me feel that someone murdered your parents."

Feeling total despair, Jen said, "So you are dropping the case?"

"I didn't say that."

She felt better, but that was to be short lived.

"My instincts kept telling me that there was something there, and I came up with some information that could be helpful." This was the part that Tony had been dreading.

He continued. "There is a possibility that someone went after you and your family for money."

"Who, and what money!?"

"It had something to do with the Super Drug Store deal. What do you know about this chain that wanted to buy your dad out? Also, why did he own the drugstore? He wasn't a pharmacist, was he?"

"When dad moved to Upton, he bought out the medical practice of a doctor who was retiring. Part of the buy-out was the drug store. There was a pharmacist there at the time who retired eight years later. Dad realized that many poor people went without the medicine they needed. He brought in Doug Treavor who was just graduating from pharmacy school. Mr. Treavor's philosophy about medical care was the same as my father's: people should not be turned away because of lack of money. Their decision was to give credit. Doug was to buy the drug store when he could afford it, but three years after moving to Upton he learned he had MS. Fortunately, the disease has stayed in remission, but it tires him, and his strength does not allow for what is needed for a full-time pharmacist. He and dad worked out a deal with Georgia State and The University of Georgia where they would take in an intern each year. The program has worked great. The student becomes Doug's strength when necessary, and gets excellent supervision and experience. This internship is highly regarded, and there is a lot of competition to get it. Because of the health situation, Doug decided not to buy the drug store, but he is paid well nonetheless. Dad always said that Doug was one of the best pharmacists in the state.

"A year ago, the Super Drug Store chain started visiting with different people in Upton about buying out my dad. The chain's supervisors didn't feel that Upton was big enough to warrant two strong drug stores. They claimed that their prices were better and assured Dad that they would keep the policy of credit lines and let Doug stay as long as he liked.

"The problem is that many people in Upton, especially those from Mill Town, will use extended time to pay a bill but never get a credit card. I suspect some of them can't get any credit. Anyway, Dad researched the chain and found that they made all kinds of promises which they kept for a year, and then they would gradually phase out the local policies and institute their own. They even have their own pharmacists. Doug would have been out of a job by the time he reached fifty nine. Mr. Treavor, Doug, is not ready to retire. With his medical bills, he needs the money; and it also keeps his mind off his disease. Also, Super Drug Store historically accepts cash only. Dad knew this would mean that too many people would go back to doing without medicine. So, he wouldn't sell. But what does that have to do with the wrecks?"

"One of the ways this particular chain has found to get accepted, especially when they are buying out an established business, is to use a few of the local businesses to get them started. Ultimately, only a few people and the chain profit. What do you know about Tom's, Smitty's and Kate's finances?"

The question shocked Jen, but she answered. "I assume they are doing fine. Of course, Tom's family has always had money and he has done well. Tom and Beth Anne built a new home two years ago, and Ted and Kate bought a new home several years ago. Smitty, I suspect, does not make as much as he could if he didn't do so much legal work for the residents of Mill Town. But he grew up poor, and with what he makes, and Karen's salary, he has more than he ever has."

"Okay, time for a reality check. Since the opening of the Peach Tree Bank three years ago, the Upton Bank has lost many of its customers. Since this bank is owned, for the most part, by the DePaus, this has hurt them financially. Seems that Miss Marie Antoinette and Thomas, Tom's dad, are the major stockholders. The DePaus have a reputation for being very cool and unfriendly to customers unless the individual is someone of importance. Also, Mr. DePau's, Thomas's, car dealership, which is also partially owned by his mother, is in danger of closing. With skyrocketing gas prices, people are turning to smaller and more economical foreign cars. The senior DePaus are having to transfer money from Tom's business to keep them going.

"I can't find out why, but Smitty's finances are in shambles.

"For some reason, Kate's father's business is losing customers. A lot of these small-town stores are having to compete with the city superstores. I don't know why the construction end is falling off. Anyway, they are not in good shape.

"John Preston has also lost money because of bad investments, but he has enough that he should not worry."

"My dad always said there was never such a thing as enough money for John."

Jen had said that in a joking way, but Tony made a mental note of that comment nonetheless.

"What does all this have to do with my parents' deaths?" A knot of fear was beginning to build up in Jen's stomach as she asked the question.

"The Super Drug Store promised to do business with the Upton Bank. This would have been a generous amount of money. Tom would have handled all of the real estate sales, which would have added up. They wanted Smitty as their lawyer, which would have amounted to about $15,000, and Kate's father's business would have handled all of the building and remodeling. There were some big bucks involved."

"You don't seriously believe they would have committed murder for some money do you?" Jen asked, holding back a flood of emotions. "No, no, I have known these people all of my life. They are not murderers."

Tony's concern for Jen's safety overrode the sympathy he felt for her, and his answer was rather forceful. "Unfortunately, I have seen these jobs done for much less. Desperate people can be dangerous."

"Are you telling me that you think my best friends tried to kill me, and killed my parents?"

Looking her straight in the eye, but with a softness in his voice, Tony said, "At this time, they are the prime suspects. Again, let me remind you that if you decide to continue with this investigation, you might have to deal with some unpleasant facts."

For a moment Jen thought she was going to throw up. How much more could she take? First she suffered a lot of pain from her accident, then her parents were killed, and now she was being told that her best friends were probably behind these tragedies. She looked at Tony and wanted to scream at him over this news. Yet, she knew the young detective was only giving her the information he had.

In a slightly lower voice, but with very even tones, she looked Tony squarely in the face and said, "I have loved these people all of my life. They were my brothers and sisters. They were like an extended family. However, if any one of them had anything to do with the deaths of my parents, I want to see them put away. Do everything you have to do to find out the truth."

The pain and determination in Jen's face almost made Tony flinch, but he was comforted to realize that even in sorrow, she was reacting out of logic and not emotion. "I will find the killer or killers," he promised.

"Jen, is there any chance that I can talk you into getting out of Upton while the investigation is going on?"

"No. When I am in my parents' house, I experience a comfort that means more to me than anything else right now. Besides, these are the people I am around, and if they are guilty, I believe they will eventually give themselves away or say something that will help us to find the truth."

"If they are after you, you may not be around to learn the truth."

"Right now, death seems like a blessed alternative, and I'm not that lucky. Believe me, I know these people. The truth will come out!"

"I figured you wouldn't budge on this one, so I want you to call a friend of mine, Buddy Jamison, who is the new sheriff of Clayton County."

"You mean the Clayton County that is next to Carrolton County?"

"The same. Buddy and I served on the Atlanta Police Force together. About the time I started my own business, he was shot by some street punk. He came out of it okay, but for a few days, things looked bad. He and his wife decided they wanted to get into a smaller and hopefully more peaceful environment. Buddy went to Clayton County and worked with Julius Treemont, a sheriff who had been on the force for twenty-five years. After he retired last year, Buddy was elected sheriff. I talked with him the other day about the investigation—wanted to find out what he knew about your sheriff, Harry Crenshaw. He and I talked a long time with Mr. Treemont, who basically told us that he and Harry started out together with high ideals. After several years, Sheriff Crenshaw seemed to be living a high lifestyle. The other sheriffs are suspicious that he is being paid off for different things. He is slick and doesn't have to be as careful about what he does. Getting reelected is easy, because he is kin to almost everyone in the county, and he is very good to his family."

Tony handed Jen a piece of paper. "This is Buddy's number. He knows what is going on. If anything happens, do not—and I repeat, do not—speak to anyone but him; and then call me. Buddy can get to you faster, and even though it is out of his jurisdiction, he can protect you."

As Tony and Jen left, they elected to walk through a hall which was an archway covered with vines and plants. Suddenly, Jen stopped and held up her finger to her lips for Tony to be quiet. They stood and listened for a minute.

"What is it?" He whispered to her.

She whispered back. "It's Smitty and Kate. I'll tell you more. She sounds upset."

"Look, Kate, I have to go. Karen is expecting me home in an hour. I know this is hard, but what's done is done. We can't turn back. Just hang in there a little longer. Be careful, and watch what you say. I'll talk to you later."

"Thanks Smitty. I needed some reassurance."

They both stood and left.

Jen was in shock as she watched the couple leave. She and Tony waited about five minutes before going outside. As they approached the front door, Jen saw Smitty and Kate drive off in separate cars.

Jen then turned and explained to Tony, "Kate has told me three times since yesterday that she was going to LaGrange to see her Aunt. She even called this morning and said she was leaving."

"I would say Kate doesn't know her directions very well," Tony answered, with an attempt at a little humor. He continued with a very serious tone. "Look, I don't have to tell you that you are in danger. Don't turn your back on these people, or that might be the last time you turn your back on anyone."

Tony's parting words made Jen shudder.

∽ *Chapter 12* ∽

For the next few days, Jen made no attempt to see any of her friends. She found the effort to keep a calm exterior too troubling. Kate seemed more preoccupied than usual, but out of obligation—or to dispel any guilt—she called daily. The conversations were very short and stilted. After about a week the two women ran into each other at the post office. As they visited, Jen realized she was enjoying talking with her old friend, and she was close to letting down her guard, but that stopped with the appearance of Sheriff Crenshaw. Looking directly at Jen, he said:

"Well, little lady, I checked out any references you made to the fact that your parents' accident might have been staged. It was, as I reported, a wreck."

His deliberately patronizing tone of voice made Jen seethe. Gritting her teeth, she looked directly at this despicable character and, in a not-so-low voice that rose as she spoke, said, "Sheriff Crenshaw, the name on my birth certificate is Mary Virginia Saxton. You may call me Mary Virginia, Mary, Virgnia, Ms. Saxton, or Jen, but Little Lady never has been nor will ever be one of your options!"

With that, she turned her back and walked away, but not before noting a look of total shock on his face, and one of fear on Kate's.

As Jen closed the door, she heard him yell, "You city folks, just too big for your breeches!"

Kate talked with her uncle briefly, and then noticed Tom across the street.

"Excuse me." She walked swiftly over to where Tom was standing. "We've got trouble. Can we talk? I must tell you what happened today."

"Sure," he said.

Earlier in the day, Miss Marie Antoinette had been admitted to the hospital. Jean DePau, Tom's mother, tried calling Thomas to let them know of the medical situation, as Miss Marie Antoinette had been demanding to see her son, but Jean had not been able to reach him by phone, so she drove downtown to see if she could find her husband. When she reached the post office, Jean saw Tom talking with Kate, so she parked the car to go over and see if he knew where his father was. However, Jean did not get out immediately. As she watched the two of them, she wondered if he and Kate would have married had the family not always reminded Tom of the importance of marrying into Atlanta's social set.

Jean knew that if Tom were not happy, she bore as much guilt as anyone else. She put her head back on the seat for a moment and thought. It had been a hard morning; her mother-in-law had become sick, and now it was Jean upon whom the old woman was depending to find her beloved son. Jean found some pleasure in this new role. After all, it was the first power she had felt in many a year.

Looking back, Jean relived the ways in which her life had been altered when she was ten. It was her mother's death that triggered the changes. Jean's father had become a raging alcoholic who gambled away what little money he made. The people in the churches, her teachers, and her friends had seen to it that she had food and clothes. Secretarial courses had enabled her to make a living after high school. The day after graduation she had left Waycross for Atlanta. Jean could still see her father, in a drunken stupor, yelling as she walked out of the door, "If you don't come back now, I will never speak to you again. No daughter of mine walks away." It was the last time she saw him alive. He always hung up when she called. Sometimes his brother and sisters would call and berate her for leaving. Jean suspected they were tired of taking care of him and wanted her to be the caretaker, but she couldn't go back. Her dad had never shown anything but hate, and had done all he possibly could to make her life miserable. Jean never forgot the time he sold the prom dress she had worked so hard to buy. Even when a friend had offered to lend her one, he had not let her out of the house to go to the dance. He was extremely mean and hateful.

After a while, she had been able to turn her back on her past. It didn't even hurt her anymore. Her job at the bank was good, and for the first time, there was some money to spend. Jean's plan at this time was to start attending college and get a degree. Because she had always been a good student, she knew she would have no trouble doing the work. Her plan changed when one day, a young man, Thomas DePau, had walked in to see her boss. They talked while he waited for his appointment, and a few days later Thomas had called and asked her out.

For several months they would talk and see each other some, but at this time Thomas was still in love with an Atlanta society girl who had called off their wedding just two weeks before it was to take place. He was devastated when this happened. Jean found herself falling in love with Thomas soon after they met. He seemed to offer stability, and though she knew he was only somewhat fond of her, she believed that in time, Thomas would come to love her. Too late Jean found that the real strength lay in the hands of Miss Marie Antoinette, who handled all of the money and ran the family. Marie did not like Jean and never let a day pass that she did not remind her of her poor upbringing and that she was Thomas's second choice. Thomas did not have the backbone to stand up to his mother. Over the years, Jean had lost the fierce determination and independence she had learned as a girl. Today, seeing the old woman beg to see her son was almost fun.

"Stop it," Jean said to herself. "Miss Marie Antoinette is very sick; you must get help." With that she got out of the car and went over to Tom.

Chapter 13

After Susan died, living in their house became too painful for Tony, so he had sold it and moved into a one-bedroom apartment. It was obviously a place he used only for sleeping and changing clothes. Except for several pictures of Susan, the interior consisted of only the necessities of making the apartment livable.

When he was home, Tony thought a lot about his cases. This kept his mind occupied and helped him forget his loneliness. He more than thought about Jen's situation; he was obsessed with it. She was a wonderful person and he did not want anything to happen to her. He believed with each passing day her life was in danger.

While lying on the couch, Tony went over in his mind the disturbing phone call he had received from Buddy earlier:

Hi, thought you might be interested in this. Today we had the County Sheriff's monthly meeting. Several people asked Sheriff Crenshaw about the Saxton accident. He said that he had run into Jen earlier in the week and thought she might be losing her mind. [Buddy explained about the situation in which Jen had blown up at the sheriff.] Even though Sheriff Crenshaw was trying to pass it off, I believe that he was worried about her attitude, and that he wanted everyone to believe that Jen is crazy.

"She probably is going off the deep end, and who wouldn't in her situation?" Tony said to himself. Laying all the papers about the case on the desk, he was about to study them when the phone rang.

"Tony, it's José."

José, A San Antonio detective, and Tony had met at special police classes that were held in Florida. They had spent a total of four weeks rooming together on two different occasions. When Susan and José's wife, Carmen, had joined their husbands in Florida, the four had become good friends. After Susan's death, the Texas couple had come to Georgia to visit and had also had Tony come to San Antonio to see them.

"Hey, what's going on?" Tony asked hopefully.

"I got some leads when I was in Houston that might interest you. You asked me to try and get some information about a baby being left at a hospital sixty years ago. As luck would have it, I found a small write-up in an area newspaper. Didn't give any details. But later I was talking with one of the police officers about it. His grandmother, Mrs. Johnston, had been a nurse at that hospital then. We went out and talked with her. She not only remembered that abandoned baby, but it was her friend who took the baby in. Her friend's name is Bessie Trotter. She is old and sick now."

"Man, I can't believe all of this. Do you think she would meet with Jen?"

"Mrs. Johnston talked with Mrs. Trotter and said that Jen was trying to find out something about her father's family. The suspicious death of Dr. Saxton was never mentioned, just said he had died. Miss Bessie, that's what she is called, said she would like to meet Jen. Seems she has always wanted to know what happened to the baby. Interestingly, Miss Bessie and Mrs. Johnston deny that Miss Bessie was the child's mother."

"This is great news! If Jen comes out tomorrow, you think you could set up a meeting for Tuesday?"

"I have Miss Bessie's phone number. Let me call her and call you right back."

"Good deal. Thanks, José; you don't know how much I appreciate this. Tell Carmen hi."

José called Tony back in about five minutes to say that the meeting was set up for Tuesday.

After the phone calls, Tony sat down in his chair, put his head back, and whispered, "thank you." Maybe Jen could finally find out some information about her dad's background. Though he really wasn't sure that this would help to solve the murders, it would get her out of Upton, give her a chance to possibly find family, and buy some safety time. Tony had a gut feeling that the murderers were closing in on his client.

"Jen, hi, it's Tony."

"Good to hear your voice. What's going on?" Just talking with Tony made Jen feel better.

"How does the idea of a trip appeal to you?"

"Traveling? Where?"

"I don't want to talk about it over the phone. Is there a possibility you could come by my office in the morning and be ready to fly out of Atlanta tomorrow afternoon?"

"I don't see why not. Nothing is going on here."

"Make up a story and tell Kate. Don't just leave without an explanation. That may arouse suspicion and concern."

Jen and Tony made arrangements to meet the next day. Jen started to pack, and thought of what she would tell Kate. She had an idea. Lil, her older friend from Atlanta, was visiting her son in Kansas, so Jen put through a call.

"Lil, hi, it's Jen."

"How are you doing?"

"Pretty well. Listen, I don't have time to talk, but I need your help. As you know, I'm trying to find some answers about my parents' deaths, and I need to go someplace. To be safe, I am telling my friends here that I am flying out to Kansas to meet you and your son's family. Is that okay?"

"That is perfectly fine, but please let me know where you really are."

"I will. I promise."

The two stayed on the phone a while longer.

"Lil, it's getting late, and I have one more call to make. I will phone you tomorrow."

Jen was afraid that she might not be able to tell Kate a convincing lie, and dreaded the conversation. However, she dialed the number.

"Hi. I don't have long to talk, but wanted to let you know that Lil, my friend from Atlanta, called just a few minutes ago. She is visiting in Kansas with her son, and invited me to come out and see them. I am leaving for Atlanta now to catch an early flight. I don't know how long I will be gone, but will call when I return."

"That's great, but isn't this kind of sudden?" Kate sounded strange.

The question concerned Jen and she knew she had to be careful.

"Actually, yes it is, but I was talking with her and saying how lucky she was to have a son to visit. It was then that she had the idea I should come out. I really need to get out of town for a while and a visit with a close family. It just feels right."

"You will be back for the Upton Celebration a week from Friday, won't you?" Kate asked in an almost child-like voice.

"Oh, sure, that's a week away. I'll be back." Actually, Jen had forgotten the big event, but she knew she could not miss it.

"Can I do anything for you while you are out of town? Water the flowers? I still have a key your mom gave me for when they were out of town."

Not wanting to tell Kate she had long ago changed the locks, Jen just said, "No, but thank you anyway. Kate, I really have to hang up if I am going to get out of here. I'll call when I get back."

"Okay. Have a good trip."

It worried Jen that she had so easily been able to lie to her friend.

As she pulled out onto the Interstate to go to Atlanta, Jen did not notice the blue car that was following her.

While listening to the radio, she wondered if this trip would help to uncover the mystery behind her parents' deaths.

Chapter 14

Work was impossible. It was late at night, and he was feeling impatient. This whole thing had gone on long enough. *Where is…*—his thoughts were suddenly interrupted by the ringing of the phone.

"It's probably my wife," the man groaned to himself.

"Hello," he said in a tense and curt tone of voice.

"Hi."

"Where have you been? I have been looking for you all day!" he screamed into the phone.

"Houston, Texas."

"Houston, Texas! Why? Why didn't you tell me you were leaving? I needed you here. A lot has happened!" He was now yelling almost uncontrollably into the telephone.

"Look, Jen got on a plane to Houston early this morning. I barely had time to get a ticket and board."

"Did she see you?"

"It doesn't matter. I am well-disguised. Works every time."

"Wait a minute. She went to Houston? She told Kate she was going to Kansas. She's on to something."

"Yeah. She was with Tony Antone at the airport."

"Who is Tony Antone?"

"Atlanta's up-and-coming private detective, and he's good."

He hit his hand on the desk. "She suspects something. We have to get her, and the sooner the better. Wait, get her there. No one will ever suspect us if she dies in Houston. Try to make it look like a suicide. Has she seen anyone there?"

"Not yet. She went shopping, ate, and went to a movie. I thought about finishing the job as she walked back to the hotel. Got my gun out. Was going to make it look like a common mugging."

"So what happened? Sounds like a good plan."

"Cop drove up, parked and got out of his car."

"Well, be careful. We don't want any trouble, and I think we have a pretty tight plan for the Great Stone House if you miss her out there. Whichever place, it has to be no later than this weekend. Time is running out!"

With that, he slammed the phone down.

∽ *Chapter 15* ∽

The Visit

Jen was thankful that Tony had offered to take her to the airport. Something about going there by herself made her feel totally alone. He promised to pick her up when she returned.

It was about 10:00 a.m. when the plane landed in Houston. This was the first time she had visited the city.

At the airport Jen asked a skycap where to find the hotel limo.

"Where are you staying?"

"At the Westin Galleria." Jen usually traveled on a strict budget, but she knew that she needed to have a nice vacation and could well afford one, so Tony asked José and Carmen about a good and safe place for her to stay. They said that this hotel was in the Galleria—the "in" place of Houston—and that it would be easy for her to get around in this location.

"The limo will stop over there." The man pointed to a sign.

"Thank you," Jen said as she took her bags and tipped the man generously.

The skycap liked her. He appreciated not only the tip, but also the fact that she was nice and polite.

This is a lovely hotel, Jen thought as she unpacked her clothes. Jen spent the afternoon at the pool swimming and reading. For supper, she settled on the Garden Room, which was on the third floor. It was a cheery-looking restaurant. This place was fascinating. Jen didn't know if she had ever been to a place where so many different languages were being spoken.

When she finished eating, Jen walked across the street to shop at a store named Sakowitz. After browsing and buying a few things, she returned to the Galleria to take in a movie. That night, for the first time since her parents' deaths, Jen felt relaxed and fell asleep almost immediately. However, had she noticed the man who was constantly shadowing her, she would never have rested.

The next morning the taxis were lined up at the hotel. "Could you take me to the Heights?" Jen asked a driver.

"Sure." She gave him the address.

"Is the Heights another town?"

"Used to be years ago, but been a part of Houston for a long time."

It was as though they had just driven into a small community. Jen marveled at how this could exist so close to the downtown skyline. The homes were, for the most part, old. It was a charming place. The taxi came to a stop.

"Is this it?" Jen asked, her heart skipping a few beats.

"It sure is."

"Thanks," she said while paying the driver.

Jen looked around. The house was a rather modest, nice brick bungalow. As she stood on the small concrete porch and rang the doorbell, a woman in a nurse's uniform came to the door. She was a very attractive and soft-spoken woman—probably about fifty-two.

"Miss Saxton?"

"Yes, I'm Jen Saxton."

"We've been expecting you. Come on in. I'm Guadalupé Cantu."

"Lupé? Was that someone at the door?"

"Yes, Miss Bessie."

A small and very frail woman appeared. Jen had been told by Tony that Mrs. Trotter was in very poor health. She had had heart problems for a long time, and was hardly able to get around.

Miss Bessie extended her hand. "You must be Miss Saxton?"

"Yes, but please call me Jen. Thank you for seeing me, Mrs. Trotter. I hope this is not a bother for you."

"Call me Miss Bessie. That's what everyone calls me. And it's a joy to see you. Come over here and sit down. Can we get you something to drink?"

"No thank you. I had a Texas breakfast this morning. I tell you what, if I lived here, I think I would be big as a barn. This food is great. They serve steaks and tacos with everything!"

Miss Bessie and Lupé laughed, and the three made a little more small talk.

Miss Bessie turned and said, "I have wondered about your father for sixty years. Please tell me all about him. Did he have a good life?" Her voice was full of anticipation and hope.

Jen told the woman all about her parents, but did not mention the murders. She only said that they had both died within the year in a wreck. When she finished, Miss Bessie wiped her eyes, but the smile on her face said that the story made her happy. For the first time, she was sure she had made the right decision so long ago. There was a pause, and then it was Jen's turn to ask for information.

"Miss Bessie, please tell me about my dad. If you were not his mother, how did you end up with him? Why was he left at the hospital?"

There was a long silence, and then Miss Bessie began. "It all started one night sixty years ago. First let me explain about my background. My husband and I were from west Texas—a little place called Wesley Community which no longer exists. It mostly consisted of a few farm families, a store, a gin, a one-room schoolhouse, and a church. None of us had any money, but we didn't feel poor. There was a lot of community spirit and support. We were just hard-working, plain people who didn't expect much. As my generation came along, we started moving to the city. Herb, who became my husband, came here and found a job as a carpenter. Was a good one. Built this house himself. Anyway, he moved here, made some money, and then came back and married me, and we left Wesley for the big city.

"I had two older sisters who have both died, and a younger one; Lee Anna. We called her Laddie. Jen, to this day when I think of that child, it takes my breath away. She had dark, almost black, curly hair, porcelain skin, and huge, dark blue, almond-shaped eyes. There was no one around who could match her looks. Needless to say, she was spoiled, and knew from a very young age exactly what she wanted in life. She used to say,'One day I'm going to be an important person. I may have been born in rags, but I will live and I will die wearing satin and lace.' She was very dramatic." Miss Bessie was laughing as vivid pictures of her strong-willed sister danced in her head.

"With Laddie's looks and intelligence, I believe she could have done anything she wanted. However, she was lazy. She knew how to charm her way out of chores—her work habits were sloppy. Laddie was the queen, and no one ever crossed her. That is, until she met a nice young man from another little town. It was the summer, and Laddie had just finished high school. He was a twenty-year-old college boy. Jeb—that was his name—was working on the roads. He would get together with all of the young people in the community, but I noticed that Laddie always made sure she was with him. She fell hard. Jeb was nice-looking and had lovely manners. Together they made a handsome couple, but he was not spoiled nor lazy, even though he was from a wealthy family. When Jeb went back to college, the letters were few. He finally wrote that he had met someone else, and wished Laddie happiness. In the spring she heard that he had married. A cousin from San Antonio told her the girl was from a wealthy family. Laddie decided that it was only because we were poor that Jeb turned elsewhere. I always thought that the time they spent together was of her doing, and that he saw through my little sister. Anyway, I don't think that girl ever got over him; the light went out in her eyes, and she hated Mother and Daddy for not having money. Sadly, I found out many years later that the girl Jeb married was not from a rich family. Someone had confused her with her wealthy cousin.

"About six months after Laddie received the letter from Jeb, a man, Jack Griggs, about twenty-eight, moved to Wesley. He was good–looking, in a gangster, swarthy sort of way, with dark, curly hair, eyes that constantly darted about, and secretive ways. Personally, I did not like him. He bragged about having money, but said he was working now because all of his wealth was tied up. Claimed to be from wealth. Laddie believed all of this. My father, though poor, was very smart. He begged her not to marry this fellow. Told her he was trouble, but she would have none of that conversation. They ran off to San Antonio and married. By this time I was married and living in Houston. Mama would write and say she hardly ever heard from Laddie.

"A year after the marriage, mama died. We had not seen Laddie nor heard from her, but she came to the funeral alone. She told me then she thought she was pregnant. When I asked about her husband, she gave some story about his being in South America for some land deal. I doubted that, but said nothing.

"About two years after she married, she showed up at my house one night with a baby—it was your father. Claimed her husband beat her, and the first baby had died at birth because of his cruelty. It seemed that Laddie had met a couple from Tampa, Florida who had promised to let her live with them and work in their store. She believed this would be a safe environment for her child. I had never seen her care about anyone but herself. Herb said at the time that he believed there was more to this story. He never trusted Laddie. I wanted to believe that maybe she was turning her life around, but I noticed she seemed frightened. When I asked her about it, she said she was afraid that her husband was going to come after her and harm her and the baby. Well, she stayed that night and the next day. She asked all about papa in sort of a wistful tone. I asked why she did not write. She said she didn't want to worry him. I believe that she was trying to break all ties to the past. Anyway, the next morning, the baby awakened me crying. I went in and took care of him, thinking Laddie had stepped outside. It was then that I discovered that sometime during the night she had packed all of her belongings and left. I went to the train station hoping to find her. The man behind the ticket counter looked as if he had been crying. When I showed him a picture of Laddie and asked if she had been there, he remembered her. She had bought a ticket to California, and had left about three hours before. The saddest look came over his face as he told me that about an hour out of Houston, the train derailed, and there had been no survivors."

Miss Bessie stopped talking for a few minutes. The room became very quiet as she took her glasses off, wiped tears from her face, and gazed into the unknown. Though clouded and sunken, it was obvious that her eyes had been the same beautiful almond shape as her sister's. Softly, the woman continued. "I was so sorrowful about my younger sister's death, but at the same time, I was angry. She had lied about Florida, and no telling what else. As usual, she was giving up her responsibilities by leaving the baby for me to raise. Oh, I had such mixed emotions.

"Jen, you must believe that I didn't give your father up because of a lack of caring. But Herb had hurt his back on a job. In those days we didn't have workman's compensation. To try and make ends meet, I took in washing and ironing and occasionally, when possible, babysat. We could just put food on the table for the family. I could not handle another responsibility, and my sisters had all they could take care of. Oh, I cried and cried. Didn't know what to do. Suddenly, I stopped bawling, held my head up, hatched a plan, and went to see a neighbor. Lula was a nurse at the hospital and she helped me to take care of the situation. We decided that I would leave your father at the hospital about three minutes before Lula went on duty. I would then hide and watch to make sure nothing happened to him. She would find the child, and turn him over to the administrator. The plan worked.

"The story of the found baby was in all the local papers. They didn't play it up much for fear that crackpots would come and claim the child. The authorities decided nothing would be done for three weeks. This would give relatives time to put in a disappearance claim—but no one came forth looking for a baby. About this time a young Lieutenant and his wife came to Houston on business. The wife got sick, and had to go to the hospital. She didn't know she was pregnant. She lost the baby, and doctors had to operate. They said she would never have children. Lula was her nurse at that time. When the couple heard of the abandoned child, they felt this was their chance to have a family, and were eventually allowed to adopt. I kept up with the child through Lula. Lula was very impressed with the couple. You can't imagine how relieved I felt that the baby had found a good home."

As she listened to Miss Bessie, Jen realized that this was a woman of compassion and sense. Jen then told her about her parents and their lives. It was only when Miss Bessie asked how he died that Jen told her the whole story of their death.

Very softly the older woman said, "Please, let me know if you ever find out what really happened."

"I will," Jen promised.

Miss Bessie had arranged for them to have lunch at the house. However, she seemed to be tired, so Jen left soon after eating. She had truly enjoyed herself, and knew that she had made a friend.

As she left, she turned and said, "One day, we will know what happened."

Miss Bessie watched as Jen left. She felt a sorrow for the young woman, but she was also relieved to know that the decision that was forced upon her so many years ago had been right.

Jen decided to stay in Houston for two more days. She spent her time reading, resting and walking around the Galleria. Once or twice she thought about renting a car and touring the city, but decided against it. In all of her time in Houston, Jen never noticed the tall man disguised with dark hair and dark glasses following her everywhere, just waiting to get her alone.

As the plane took off for Atlanta, Jen felt refreshed and more able to deal with what lay before her. She thought about how nice it was to meet a member of her family she never knew existed. Then she began to think about the visit, and knew that something felt strange. *What was it? Was it the house and something about Miss Bessie that seemed familiar? What was it?*

Chapter 16

It was late Thursday afternoon when Jen returned to Atlanta. As she left the plane, she was happy to see that Tony was waiting for her.

Tony broke into a wide smile when he saw Jen. "Hi, how was your trip?"

"Well, it was great to get away, but unfortunately, I didn't find out anything that would help us solve the case."

Though this news disappointed Tony, he was glad to see Jen looking more relaxed. "We have to pursue all of our avenues. Anyway, you look rested, so maybe the trip wasn't a total loss." The truth was that Tony had wanted Jen to get away. He felt that as long as she was out of Upton, she was safe. "What about an early supper?"

"Great."

"You going back to Upton tonight?"

"No, I need to go to my place. I'll leave in the morning."

As they approached the car, Jen saw Buddy.

Tony explained, "Buddy is joining us. His wife is out of town and he has the day off. Got bored, so came to see if he could help me in any way."

After the three arrived at the restaurant, settled at the table, and put in their order, Tony asked, "I want you to tell us everything Mrs. Trotter told you, and what your impressions were of her. Tell anything, even if it seems insignificant."

Buddy and Tony listened intently as Jen told them the story of how her father got to Miss Bessie's house.

Tony was the first to speak. "Okay, so we know that the mother is dead. What about the father? Did you get his name or any information about him?"

"All I know is his name was Jack Griggs, and he lived in the San Antonio area."

Something about Jen's demeanor caught Tony's attention. "Have you told me everything?"

"Well, I don't know how to put this in words, but there was something about Miss Bessie that seemed familiar. But I know, or feel rather certain, that I have never seen her before. I don't know what it was. I can't remember what it was, but she said something that set off a light in me. I've gone over the conversation in my head a hundred times and nothing catches me. I guess that it was just being in her home that an unconscious familiarity came out."

They went over the conversation again, but there was nothing.

Finally, Tony said, "If you think of what it was, let me know."

He continued, "What's on your agenda for the rest of the week?"

"Tomorrow night is the Upton Celebration."

"The what?" Tony asked somewhat amusedly.

"When I was in the first grade, Upton started having what they call the Upton Celebration at the Country Club, although anyone can go if they buy a ticket. The money raised is to be used for city projects.

"They have a dinner, and when we were juniors in high school, we talked them into having a silent auction. It was very successful. The four of us always did a lot of background work for this event, and Tom and Kate have headed it up now for four years. Kate loves it; she once again becomes the center of attention."

For reasons Jen could not understand, she did not want Tony to know that on Saturday she would go to the Great Stone House, so this was never mentioned.

"Anyway, I feel tired and need to go out to my townhouse."

Tony and Buddy dropped Jen off at her place. On the way to Tony's, he said to Buddy, "You have been very quiet all night; why?"

Buddy had known Tony for a long time. When Susan died, Buddy watched helplessly as his friend seemed to also die. Even though he had gone out with several people, some of whom Helen and Buddy had fixed him up with, no woman had interested him. That is until now. Buddy saw how Tony acted toward Jen. There was no doubt in his mind that his old partner had some strong feelings for his client. This worried Buddy.

"Look Tony, both of us know that very often, murder is done by someone close to the victims. Jen had money to gain, and you don't know what really went on between the three of them. Maybe this was not the lily-pure family it has been made out to be."

Tony gave Buddy an incredulous look. "Where are you going with this? Are you trying to put Jen in a bad light? Why?"

"All I'm saying is be careful. Don't let your feelings get in the way of good detective work."

"Yeah, I'll try." Tony said in a terse way.

With that, Buddy got into his own car and left. Tony was mystified by Buddy's reaction. Had he been taken in by personal feelings? He thought about this idea for a long time.

Chapter 17

Buddy's reaction to Jen made Tony do something he very rarely did—second guess himself. Was Jen the innocent victim? He had to admit that for the first time ever, his personal feelings about a client were strong, and that his objectivity had possibly been clouded. He went home, sat down, got his mind into a cold, objective state, and went over all of the facts. When he finished, Tony was certain that Jen was the victim, and his sixth sense was telling him that if he didn't act fast, she may not see another week.

Tony spread his notes out on the desk and read everything, trying to see if there was something he had missed. After reading them three times, it was evident that he had memorized all of the facts as he had them. Tony shut the folder, sat back, bowed his head, rubbed his temples, and asked himself, "What am I going to do? Jen's life depends on me." An idea that had always been in the back of his mind began to force itself to the front. What about Dr. Saxton's roots. Did he know more about them than Jen realized? Was that really the body of the doctor and his wife? They were burned beyond recognition. Were they trying to escape something?

It's my only hope, Tony thought.

Though it was already 10:00 p.m., he picked up the phone and began to dial.

"Hello," came a sleepy voice on the other end.

"Man, you go to bed this early? Fine cop you are."

"Tony! Hey, good to hear your voice. What's going on?"

"Jen didn't find out any information when she visited with Mrs. Trotter that can help me solve this case. I need to come out and see what I can discover. Could you help?"

"Sure. My shift is seven to four. What time are you getting in?"

"There is a plane that leaves here at eight thirty, and I should be there by ten."

"Carmen can pick you up and bring you to the station."

"No, I will get a car."

"Okay, just a minute."

There was silence on the other end, and then José came back. "Carmen says you will stay with us."

"Thanks. I look forward to seeing the both of you."

As Tony boarded the plane, he realized that he had failed to let Jen know about the trip. *Did I forget, or is it I don't want her to know? What I uncover may be bad news.*

Chapter 18

As Jen got dressed for the celebration, she knew this would be a difficult night. Her parents had always participated in this event. They always got a table with Toady, John, and another couple with whom they were good friends. Jen went alone. Several people had invited her, but she just didn't feel like being with someone who was not special to her.

Jen looked at herself in the mirror before leaving the house. The silk, emerald-green sheath with small straps was very becoming, and showed off her green eyes. The jewelry she chose was a diamond pendant her father had given her mother several years ago and a pair of small diamond earrings. "You can do this," she said to herself as she got in the car.

The Big Four and their families always sat together. Jen was the first to arrive. While waiting for the group, she visited with different people, and then walked over and talked with Toady.

Toady was glad to see Jen, but the older woman seemed somewhat upset. "We are leaving early. John is not feeling well. I think your parents not being here is too much for him. Anyway, we are going to eat and sneak out."

Finally Smitty and Karen, who were always early, came in. Smitty looked preoccupied, and Karen, uncharacteristically, somewhat angry.

Not too far behind them was Kate. Tom and Beth Anne soon entered. Dressed in a white, off-the-shoulder dress with a large emerald drop—a gift from Tom—Beth Anne looked elegant though somber. On the way, they had stopped by the hospital to see Tom's grandmother, who was in bad shape.

"Hey, where's Ted?" Tom asked.

Trying to sound light and nonchalant, Kate answered, "Oh, he's sick."

Jen saw her cast a sidelong glance at Smitty, but he didn't notice.

After a rather quiet meal, Kate excused herself so she could dress as she and Tom would soon start the entertainment. A little later, Tom went backstage.

First came a drum roll.

Tom came out from behind the curtains wearing his high school letter jacket. He held up his hands for the applause to stop. As the people stopped clapping, he said, "Thank you everyone. Judging from what I have on, you might have guessed that this year's theme is: Upton High School. Let me introduce Upton's sweetheart: Kate!"

As people clapped, he walked behind the curtains and escorted Kate to center stage. Jen gasped, almost out loud. *What is going on with her? She has her homecoming dress on. I can't believe this. Kate is actually recreating homecoming night when she was the queen.*

Tom and Kate showed slides of Upton High School from years past, and introduced some of the outstanding graduates. But most of the rhetoric centered on Tom's and Kate's experiences. Jen withstood as much as she could, but it soon became too much for her to bear.

"Please excuse me. I need to get some fresh air." As she picked up her purse, Smitty asked, "Are you okay?"

"Oh sure. Just need some air. Really."

Jen stepped out onto the porch. The club was a one-story brick building with a long porch across the front. The porch was lined with white rocking chairs. Jen sat down. Even though the weather was hot, there was a cool breeze blowing off the lake. The land between the lake and club was filled with tall pine trees and some magnolias. As she sat down, Jen noticed that the moon was almost full. The scene was pretty and restful.

She had been there about five minutes when someone said; "Mind if I join you?"

It was Beth Anne. "Oh, please sit down."

"How are you doing?" Beth Anne asked with sincere concern.

"Oh, I've been better . That show--I mean really; I could not believe that Kate showed up in her homecoming dress. She is losing it." Jen's voice held a touch of surprise and disdain.

"Well, I wasn't going to say anything. I know you are friends, but I agree. Frankly, I think she has sort of gone off her rocker. She calls Tom constantly. He was not happy about this show, but Kate insisted. Of course Tom hasn't been happy about too much lately. I guess with his grandmother sick. I don't know." Beth Anne's voice trailed off. Then she said, "I really miss your mother."

"So do I. She was an anchor for me."

"I think she was the first person in Upton who would believe that I am not a snob, but just quiet and reserved by nature."

Somewhat apologetically, Jen said, "We probably didn't make it easy for you to come into the group."

"It wasn't too hard. Kate has always had a problem with me. It's odd. She's okay about Karen, but I seem to trouble her. I try to be nice, but realized a long time ago if she were going to accept me, it would be on her timetable."

Jen thought to herself, *I know the problem. You are competition. In your own way, you are just as pretty as she, and I think secretly Kate wonders what it would be like to be married to Tom.*

Beth Anne broke into her thoughts. "Your mother was very proud of you."

"Really." For some reason this surprised Jen.

"I think she admired your gumption to do something other than marry when that's what everyone else was doing."

Jen smiled to herself.

Beth Anne continued. "Sometimes, Jen, I think you have the right idea."

"What are you talking about?"

"Oh, not following the norm. Don't get me wrong; I love my family and don't believe that people have to leave their loved ones to find themselves, but sometimes I wish Tom and I could just go somewhere else and start over."

"Why?"

"It's hard to explain, but too often I feel we are mini-parents and our parents are the real ones. The other day, for the second time in a week, I was leaving for a meeting in Atlanta. This was the first one for planning some event. Mom called and said it was crucial that I be there. Anyway, Liza started crying, and wanted to know why I had to leave again. I told her it was necesary that I go to these meetings. She answered with a very innocent 'I don't see why. Aren't you happy with us?' I looked at that child, and wondered at her wisdom. In a moment I made a decision that I knew would have a strong impact on my family. I changed my plans, and the two of us dressed and had a picnic. She still talks about the day I didn't go to Atlanta. My mother called later, and yelled at me for missing such an important event. When I told her what I had done and that I thought being with Liza was more important, Mother was just exasperated, and said that was what babysitters were for. I didn't care. What really bothered me was that I didn't seem to have the right to make the decisions I thought were best for my family. Of course, what I was doing was just the opposite of what mom had done and her mother before. I don't know. It just seems that our lives need to take a different direction. We have decided to cut way back in our Atlanta experiences. Both of our families, except for Jean, are upset with us."

"Well, what's wrong? Didn't you like Upton High School Night?" Tom asked in a rather sarcastic and dramatic voice.

Beth Anne looked up. "We didn't see you. Oh please, when do I get to get rid of that letter jacket?"

"What? Don't you know this is my life? Woman, where are your senses?"

They all laughed. "Seriously, are you going to stay out here all night?"

Beth Anne stood. "I guess it is time to go back in."

Jen observed them. They looked so happy. She just could not believe Tony's warning about the possibility of Tom being involved in her parents' deaths.

"If you will excuse me to the others, I'm going home."

"Are you okay? You want us to follow you?" Tom asked with concern.

"Oh, no thanks. I am fine."

As Jen drove away, she had no way of knowing what was facing her when she got to her house.

Chapter 19

Jen felt restless as she left the dinner. It had been hard to look at the place her parents used to sit and not see them. Her group had been quiet, almost sullen. She could hardly keep from screaming, "Who is responsible for the wrecks?"

It was only nine o'clock when she got home. Jen parked in the circular drive in front of the house. When she went in, she put her purse and keys on the table by the front door, and decided to change into some shorts and then go through her father's papers again.

After changing, Jen opened her dad's office. *Something's wrong,* she thought nervously. She stood and quietly observed the scene. Things were in place, but one of the file drawers had been left open just a little, and some of the files were out of order. *Someone's been in here,* she thought. When she turned around, she froze momentarily as she saw the curtains by the window move. Thinking to herself, *I never leave the windows open,* Jen realized that another person might be in the room watching her, and the last thing she wanted to do was to alert that individual of her suspicions. Going on the premise that someone was observing her, she quickly devised a plan.

Jen stretched, yawned, and said in a rather loud and dramatic voice, "Oh, I'm too tired to do this tonight. Think I'll go to bed."

She then started through the living room as though she were going back to her bedroom, but when she got close to the table with her purse and keys on it, she grabbed them, ran out the door, and jumped into her car. She was so nervous while trying to get her car started and deciding what to do next that she didn't notice the automobile that came around the corner from the back of her house.

"I know, I'll go to the all-night store up on I-75 and call Tony," she said to herself.

When Jen arrived at the store, she noticed that no one was using the pay phone. *Thank goodness the phone is free, but I wish it were inside,* she thought to herself.

When she could only get Tony's answering service, she remembered he had told her to call his friend Buddy, the sheriff in the next county over.

"Buddy, this is Jen Saxton. I met you in Atlanta when I returned from my trip to Houston. I was with Tony. He told me to call you if something happened because you could get here faster. Someone broke into my house while I was out tonight."

"Was anything taken?"

"No. Well, not that I could tell."

"Then how do you know that anyone else had been there?"

Jen did not like his attitude or tone of voice and started to tell him so, but thought better of it, as she did need his help.

"Things in dad's office had been moved around, and then I noticed the curtains swaying. Buddy, I know the window was closed when I left because I checked it. Someone came in through that window. It is on the back of the house, so they would not have been seen. I am positive someone was there."

"Where are you now?"

"At the Quick and Go up on I-75, south of Upton."

"Stay there. I'll come and get you. Stay inside the store, and don't tell anyone what happened."

"I won't leave or talk to anyone. Buddy, I do appreciate your help."

Jen browsed at the magazines and was surprised when she looked up and saw John. *I thought Toady told me they were going home early.*

He was the first to speak.

"What are you doing here?"

Trying to sound casual, "Oh, I am waiting to meet a friend."

"Meet a friend here? This time of night?"

Jen thought to herself, *I am thirty years old. If I want to meet someone at ten o'clock in the middle of the interstate, that is my business and I will do so.* She just looked at her father's friend. He must have read her thoughts.

"I'm sorry Jen. Toady and I just get concerned about you."

Jen smiled, but said nothing. She did not like people inviting themselves to get involved in her business.

John made a few purchases and left rather quickly. About five minutes later, Buddy showed up.

They decided to leave her car at the store and go to the house to check if anything was missing. When they were satisfied that nothing was gone, Buddy took Jen back to the store to get her car. Jen decided to go on to Atlanta for the night. She was a little afraid to go back to the house. The break-in had scared her.

As she drove to Atlanta, Jen realized that tonight had been proof that someone was getting too close. But a new thought arose: *Why were John and Toady at the Quick and Go? She told me at the celebration that they were going to go home early because John was not feeling well and wanted to go to bed. And besides, he didn't like places like the Quick and Go. Also, running out of Aspirin, which was what John had bought, was not the norm for this super-organized couple.*

"When will this end?" She said to herself.

Jen did not know that within twenty-four hours she would be fighting for her life.

Chapter 20

Tony arrived in San Antonio at about 10:00 a.m. After renting a car, he went straight to the police station. José did not see him walk in. By this time it was almost eleven thirty.

"José!"

"Tony!" José stood and both men shook hands. "Good to see you."

They talked for a minute and José introduced Tony around. Then they left to have lunch at a diner across the street. Once they had ordered, José said, "Tell me about this case. Oh, and by the way, I have arranged to take the afternoon off to help you—that is, if you want me to."

"Oh, that would be great."

"So what's going on?"

The Atlanta detective told his friend all about the case, and a number of things about Jen.

José observed the way Tony's manner changed when he talked about Jen. The San Antonio detective remembered all too well how his friend had been shattered when Susan died. This was the first time José had noticed any sign of interest in another woman, and it worried him.

When Tony finished, José said, "Something's wrong with this story."

"What do you mean?"

"Well, you have this wonderful family who would never do anything wrong, but there were drug stories circulating about the doctor."

"I told you he was cleared of that." Tony said rather defensively.

José looked down at his hands. He hated this. "Tony, what I mean is that it sounds like the good doctor might not have been so good. You don't really know that the bodies in the car were those of him and his wife. I also observe an almost reverence when you talk about Jen. Are you letting your feelings get in the way of good detective work?"

"What do you mean?" Tony said in an annoyed but interested voice.

"Have you avoided looking at the old man as a possible suspect because you don't want to have to upset her?"

"I'll admit I probably would have been here a little sooner. I don't know. This whole case doesn't add up. I'm here now."

"Does Jen know?"

"No."

"So what are you looking for?"

"Anything I can find out about Dr. Saxton, and I believe I need to go back to the beginning—when he was born. His mother, as I said, was killed, but I'm hoping that maybe his father can help us."

"Do you know who the dad was?"

"Mrs. Trotter told Jen that his name is Jack Griggs. Of course, there is a good chance he is not still alive, but if that is true, I am hoping that some of his relatives can give us some information." Tony knew as he talked that it was doubtful that the family could shed any light on this terrible crime, but he had to try every angle. Jen's life depended on him.

There were two listings under Jack Griggs in the phone book. Tony called the first one, but there was no one at home. The second phone call was a success.

"Hello."

"Jack Griggs?"

"This is Paul Griggs, his son. Who is this?"

"I'm sorry. My name is Tony Antone. I'm a detective from Atlanta, Georgia. May I speak to your father?"

In a rather puzzled voice, Paul said, "Mr. Antone, daddy died two weeks ago. Why do you want to speak to him?"

"Oh, I'm so sorry. Look, I know this must be a difficult time for your family, but I do need to talk with you and see if you can give me some information about some people from your father's past. I wouldn't bother you, but it could be a life-and-death situation." Tony sounded almost scared.

"Sure. I don't know what I can tell you. My sister and I are just going through dad's things. Come on out."

With the address in hand, Tony and José left for Jack Griggs's house.

Paul answered the door. After introductions were made, he invited the two men in. His sister, Lena Valdez, came in and joined the men.

While Tony was talking, José walked around the living room and the dining room. While he never got out of sight, the policeman was looking to see if there were signs that anyone else might be there.

"You said on the phone this has something to do with wanting information about some people from my dad's past? Why? Who?" Paul said.

"Mr. Griggs, as I mentioned earlier, this is a life-and-death situation. There is a young woman in Upton, Georgia whose life is in danger, and I need to find out some information about her father's roots."

"What does that have to do with dad?"

"Her father, we just found out, was your dad's son by his first wife."

Paul and Lena both looked astonished. "My dad was never married before he met my mother. In fact, he said she saved him; that he would have been a low life bachelor at the rate he was going. Mama was his inspiration. He wanted to please her so much. Settled down and made a very good living painting, papering houses, and doing almost anything else that needed to be done. Daddy's work is all over San Antonio. No. Mama was the first and only wife."

Tony was puzzled and discouraged. He must have found the wrong Jack Griggs. Then Paul spoke up.

"I'm curious. Why did you think daddy had another wife? "

Tony told him the story of the baby being taken to Houston, but he did not mention any names.

It was Lena who spoke up next. "Wait a minute. I remember several times hearing my mother saying something about a Laddie. When I was older, I asked her who Laddie was, and she said that Laddie had been a very beautiful young girl who had come to San Antonio with my father and they were going to marry, but as soon as they got here, she borrowed some money from him and he never saw her again. Heard years later she had been killed in a train wreck.

"They were not married? Did they have a child together?"

Paul spoke up. "Not that Dad knew of, but a saint he was not."

"Do you have any information about this Laddie?" Tony asked.

"I'm afraid not," Lena responded. "What I told you is all I ever knew."

"If you think of anything that might be informative, please let me know. Here is my card, and this is the number where I will be staying while I am here."

When they got in the car, José turned to Tony. "What now?"

"Well, there are several possibilities. First, Laddie could have been pregnant when she ran away from Jack; he could have known about the child and not admitted it to his family, or she could have kidnapped the baby."

"Kidnapped?" José said.

"I know it's a far-fetched theory, but I need to look at every possibility."

José spoke next, "Remind me—is there any family here who could possibly tell us anything about Laddie?"

"Not that I know of. According to Mrs. Trotter, all of the sisters are dead. No one who would have remembered her is alive."

Tony and José went to the city library and pored over old newspaper articles and cases. They were looking for anything that might give them a lead on a kidnapping sixty years earlier. The problem was that such old records and newspapers were scarce. By 9:00 p.m., both men were exhausted. They left, stopped, got a sandwich, and went to José's. When they got home, Tony went straight to bed. He was so exhausted that he forgot to call his answering service.

The rest did him some good; it cleared his mind. With a renewed determination, Tony believed that today he would find some information.

He smelled breakfast cooking, and walked out into the kitchen.

"Tony, it is so good to see you," Carmen said as she gave her friend a hug. She immediately recognized that their visitor was a million miles away in thought, so she did not try to get a conversation going. "Here, sit down and have some breakfast."

"What's the plan for today?" José asked.

"Thought I would go to the library and see what I can find."

"Good idea, I'll go with you."

The two men looked for about two hours, but none of the kidnappings seemed to be related to Jen's father. Tony was very discouraged. Sensing his friend's frustration, José decided to mention something that had been in the back of his mind. He excused himself and made a phone call. When he returned he said, "Come on, let's take a break."

"You mean get an early lunch?" Tony said.

"Yeah." As they ate, José explained, "There is a retired cop who would have been on the force during the time period we are looking at. He's in his eighties, mind sharp as a tack, and can remember cases no one else can. We use him sometimes when we are going back to the old days to try and solve something."

"Would he see us?"

"Yeah. I just called him and he said to be there in forty-five minutes. Just a ten minute ride from here."

"What can we lose? We're batting zero," Tony said, almost to himself.

Capt. Barlow, even in his eighties, was an imposing man. Tall and very erect, he commanded your attention and respect. Even Tony found him a little intimidating at first, but as they talked, he found that he liked the Captain.

"Tony—that is your name, isn't it?"

"Yes sir."

"Tell me about your case."

As the detective told his story, the older cop listened. It was obvious that he had heard thousands upon thousands of tales in his day, but that he treated each one as if it were the first one he had heard. José knew he would not miss a beat.

When Tony finished talking, Captain Barlow looked out of the window as he silently processed the story. Then with a piercing look he turned to his new friend. "You have searched all of the evidence?"

"All that I can find." Tony answered almost breathlessly.

The old man had detected a change of voice when Tony talked about Jen, so he watched his reaction very closely as he asked the next question.

"What about the daughter?"

"Clean as a whistle."

The retired cop just stared at Tony for a minute. *He's good and professional, but likes the daughter, although that obviously hasn't gotten in the way of a good investigation,* the Captain thought.

"I like you Tony. You are thorough."

Tony felt relieved. For a minute he had felt like a fifteen-year-old boy being scrutinized by his first date's father.

"Thank you, sir."

The old man drew quiet, and obviously withdrew into himself as he began to go over cases in his head.

Drawing a deep breath, he began. "I had just started working; it was a little over sixty years ago. I was on the front desk. One day a young father, Joseph Bradford, came in very upset. You see, San Antonio and the surrounding areas went through a flu epidemic that took many lives. It seems that both Mr. Bradford and his wife got sick, so their baby daughter was taken to one relative, and their two-month-old son to another relative. But the family with the boy all got sick, so they sent him to a home in San Antonio. Homes for children of sick parents had opened up. Joseph's wife lost her life to the disease, and he almost died. When Mr. Bradford got well, he went to get his son, but was told the child had died and had been buried at the local cemetery. This was not uncommon when there were outbreaks of a fever. The father was brokenhearted, but something in this man's mind would not accept this as being true, so he went back to the home. It had closed, but he found the head nurse, who had come by to pick up the last of some of her papers. When questioned about the specifics of his son's death, she admitted that she herself had gotten sick and had been off of work for a little over a week. Another nurse on duty had taken care of the child and his burial. When Mr. Bradford inquired as to who this nurse was, he was given her name, but could never find her. He later said it was as if she had fallen off of the world."

"What was her name?"

"Sara Cummings. I don't know why I remember it. I worked with the distraught man until we exhausted all means of locating her. Every once in a while he would stop by; we'd go to dinner and talk about the case. Very nice man. He was a rancher, and wealthy."

"Where was he from?"

"Little town about an hour and a half's drive from here called Juarez. I must warn you, he is dead. Died about five years ago."

"Maybe we can talk to someone who can help us," Tony decided.

The three men shook hands, and Tony and José left.

"Man, José, he is a walking encyclopedia of police information."

"Oh, he's the best. Still comes to the police station every once and a while. You can believe that everyone jumps to please him. But he is a great guy."

As Tony and José drove to Juarez, Jen was making preparations to leave for the Great Stone House and, unknowingly, step into a death trap.

Chapter 21

The morning after Jen arrived in Atlanta, she was tired. After breakfast and trying unsuccessfully to get in touch with Tony, Jen took a cup of coffee out onto her patio, sat down, and began to think about the night before. *Who was at my house? Why? If they broke in while I was gone, they must have been looking for something. But what? If they were there when I was, maybe they were after me.* This thought sent a feeling of terror through her and made Jen tremble. She put her cup down for a moment to steady herself.

Tonight the group was to meet at the Great Stone House, but the break-in the night before had scared Jen so much that she decided not to go. The fact that this landmark was isolated out in the country several miles from town and that Jen was increasingly suspicious that her friends might have been involved in the death's of her parents, made her even more frightened. Every member of the group had been late to the celebration, and had been anything but festive. Any one of them could easily have broken into her house, looked for whatever it was that was wanted, and come to the dinner. Additionally, if someone was after her, it would have been nothing for one of the Big Four to have gone to her house once Beth Anne or Tom had said she had left. They could have come in through the window while she had been dressing, or even before she had gotten home. After all, she had driven around trying to calm down for about twenty minutes after leaving the celebration.

After she finished her breakfast and started moving about, Jen changed her mind. *I am not going to be controlled by fear. Besides, as uncomfortable as it might be, there is also a strength in me that believes I need to be there. They won't try anything with their children present, and something may be said that will tell me for sure who is guilty, and then I can tell Tony,* She thought.

With the resolve that she was doing the right thing, Jen decided to meet her group at the Great Stone House. What she didn't know was that the plan for her to die that night, out in the country, would be carried out!

∽ Chapter 22 ∽

The last twenty-four hours had been hard for Kate. Miserably, she sat at her kitchen table. Even though it was 1:00 p.m., she was still in her bathrobe. She closed her eyes and thought. *I can't go on much longer. This whole mess is unbelievable. As if everything else is not enough, I made an idiot of myself last night. No one's called to tell me how great the celebration was. This is the first time that has ever happened. Always before, the phone would be ringing off the wall with congratulations. They were just laughing at me. What was I thinking? I'm a thirty-year-old woman, not a high school homecoming queen. Why can't I just accept that the time for happiness is gone? I can't go on much longer. I hope the next twenty-four hours are better.* She put her head down and cried.

Pulling herself together, Kate got up and got ready to go to the Great Stone House. This was the first time she had been to the group's Labor Day get-together since her marriage without Ted.

Chapter 23

About noon, just after Karen and the children had left to go to the mountains, Smitty went to the office. He and Karen had been fighting for two days. She was mad that he had suddenly left town earlier in the week and was gone on their daughter's birthday. They were both very angry when she had left earlier today. The office was the only place where he felt comfortable.

"Hi, Jane."

She turned around. "Smitty, I didn't expect to see you here today."

"Why?"

"I thought you and your group always went to the Great Stone House on the Saturday after the celebration."

Looking and sounding very somber, he answered, "Oh, we do, but I won't leave until three thirty. What are you doing here?"

"I needed to finish up some letters and filing. Things have been so hectic lately; I thought this would be a good time to catch up."

Jane noted that Smitty looked awfully tired, so she asked, "I'm going to make some coffee. Want some?"

"Thanks, that would be great."

Smitty then disappeared into his office. He was glad Jane was here; she made him feel less alone.

With work spread before him, Smitty soon realized that he could not concentrate. With all that had gone on, he began thinking. *What am I going to do? I have never seen Karen so angry.* He could still see her slamming the door in his face and driving off. He sat there, gazing off into space. *How could this happen? I am a nice person, and I've worked so hard. One mistake, and now I will lose everything I have worked for.*

Breaking into his thoughts, Jane appeared at the door. "Smitty, excuse me, but here is your coffee."

"Oh, thanks. I didn't even see you."

"I know. You look like you are in deep concentration."

"No, just thinking."

Jane left. She could tell that Smitty was upset and didn't want to talk.

About an hour later, she appeared at Smitty's door again.

"I'm going now. Do you need anything before I leave?"

"No. No, thanks. Have a nice weekend. Oh, Jane!"

She came back to the door. "Yes?"

"I really appreciate the great job you do."

After Jane got to her car, she sat for a few minutes and thought. *Since the Saxtons' death, Smitty has been very unhappy. He has changed, and he seems so upset and terribly nervous all the time. Such a change from the fun-loving Smitty I once knew.*

She also had a suspicion that all was not well in his marriage, but Smitty was strong and she trusted him to get everything straight. Yet, his compliment had the sound of finality to it. If she had not promised to take her mother to Atlanta for the afternoon, she would go back and work. *Please don't let Smitty do anything harmful,* she thought prayerfully.

Smitty could not concentrate, so he went over and lay on the couch. His thoughts began to drift to the Saxtons, how much they had meant to him, how he had worked hard all of his life to do well, and, of course, all of the trouble he was now in. Eventually fatigue took over and he fell asleep and did not wake up until it was almost time to leave for the Great Stone House. As he got ready, his thoughts were on what lay ahead.

Chapter 24

Probably because of fear, Jen did not leave Atlanta until three, and it was five before she turned onto the curvy and winding road that led to the great stone manor. She could see the place standing there with an imposing and, even more so than usual today, haunting look. Jen thought, *This house looks as though it belongs in a scary movie. It would be on a cliff overlooking the ocean, or possibly in an English setting with fog so thick that one could barely see the outline of the majestic creation.* Suddenly, Jen remembered a time when she was a five-year-old. The man who built this place, Mr. Harris, brought Jen and her parents out to see his home. It was then that he told Jen a secret about the house, but, try as she may, she could not remember what it was.

As Jen drove along, she could not help but think about the optimistic, happy feeling she had had just last year as she approached the house. Now the dread—or more truthfully, fear—made her realize that over the last twelve months her life had irrevocably changed, and the people she had always counted on now seemed to be her enemies.

Parking was crowded. The attendees usually left their keys on the table in the hall so that if someone needed to leave and he or she was blocked in, the other person's vehicle could be used or simply moved. Jen tried to park so that no one could block her in.

After turning off the motor, she just sat for a moment and thought. *I am positive they will not do anything as long as their children are around.* It was this belief that gave her courage and calmed her enough to get out of the car.

As Jen approached the house, she heard activity in the kitchen. Trying to sound casual and upbeat, she yelled. "Anybody here?"

"In the kitchen," Kate answered in a rather subdued voice.

Smitty and Kate were getting the food ready.

"Wow, where is everybody?" Jen asked as she entered the kitchen.

"What do you mean, everybody?" Smitty said without looking up.

"Like your wife, the children, and Ted."

Kate drew a deep breath as though answering these questions was laborious. "My two are with their father. They have gone to see Ted's brother. Karen and the boys are in the mountains."

Seemingly on cue, Beth Anne and Tom walked in. "Hi everybody. Sorry we're late, but we had to take the kids to Beth Anne's mom's house and then go by my parents'. They were leaving town, and we had to take care of some business."

Beth Anne spoke up. "Will all of you please excuse me? I am trying to get over a headache." With that she left and went upstairs to bed.

Jen felt as though she was frozen to the spot, and her mind began to race. *The children were my safety net. Why aren't they here? Something's wrong. I'm just going to pretend to go into the living room, but I'll quietly get in my car and, before they realize anything, leave.*

Jen walked into the living room and looked out the window. Tom's car was parked in such a way that she could not get hers out. Also, the sky was turning very dark and the wind was blowing hard.

"We're under tornado warnings," she heard Tom saying to the others in the kitchen.

Trying not to panic, and needing time to think, Jen announced that she was taking her things up to her room. For some unexplained reason, there had always been one room that Jen always insisted on having. She didn't have a reason except that it was comfortable to her, and the others always respected her wish. They affectionately nicknamed it "Queen Jen's Den."

For a few minutes, Jen just sat on the bed and thought. *I'm in a dangerous situation. If Tony is right and the killer is one, or all, of these "friends," this would be the perfect opportunity to get rid of me. Wait a minute. I knew of the danger when I decided to come, but after much thought and prayer, being here seemed like the right thing to do. I just have to believe I have made the right decision, and can't panic. I will go down, act as normal as possible, and keep my eyes and ears open to whatever I need to see and hear.*

Jen rejoined the others in the kitchen. She could not help but notice that the mood was extremely subdued. The others refused to talk, as though they were lost in their own world.

Supper was eaten in silence except for the pelting rain and harsh winds. Beth Anne was still upstairs. During the meal there was a knock at the front door.

"I'll get it." Tom said as he got up. "Yes?"

My name is Scot Reed. I'm an author and photographer for *Deep South Magazine*." He handed Tom a very important-looking business card. "I have been in this part of Georgia all day taking pictures for an article I need to write. My car started to act strange, so I drove into Upton and got some mechanic to fix the car, but with the bad weather moving in, he suggested I not try to leave for South Carolina until tomorrow. Since the motels are full, he suggested this place. He said there would be a group here and that there should be plenty of room for me. I won't be any bother."

"Sure. That will be fine. I had heard that there was a photographer for a magazine taking pictures. Can't keep a secret in a small town. Come on in and join us. We have plenty of food." Tom stood aside to let the man in.

"Thanks, but I have a sandwich with me. I've got a deadline and have some work to do, so if you will just show me to my room."

"Don't you want to meet the others?"

"Let's wait until tomorrow. That was a pretty harrowing ride out here. Just want to go up, relax, and work."

"Sure."

Jen could only see a profile of Mr. Reed as he and Tom talked.

When Tom rejoined them, he said, "He seems like a nice man."

Jen felt very uncomfortable, as though she was being set up.

After washing the dishes, they all went into the living room. Jen had decided to act as normal as possible, wait until the others had gone to bed, and sneak out.

Because of the storm, the TV reception was not good. They just turned it on to get the weather. They heard that tornadoes had touched down in different places. Phone lines were out all over the county and in parts of Atlanta. The group just sat and read. Finally, about nine o'clock, Jen got up, went and fixed a cup of coffee—her regular routine—and went up to bed. She took a couple of sips of coffee, and was asleep before she could finish the brew. About 2:00 a.m. Jen sat straight up in bed. Everything seemed fuzzy, but as her mind cleared some, she realized that the storm had stopped. But there was something else. She got up, splashed water on her face, and took an aspirin. Her head was hurting, and it felt strangely heavy. She sat back down on the bed and tried to clear her mind. As Jen began to focus, she thought, *That man Scot Reed looked familiar. Now I know. He is not a writer, he is an auto mechanic. He worked at a place where I took my car. Oh my gosh. I had my car in for a routine checkup just before my wreck. Buck—that was his name. He always kept his back to me, but once I saw his face and name tag.* Feeling scared, Jen began to try to stay calm and make plans to escape. A knock at the door broke into her thoughts.

"Jen." It was Beth Anne; she was whispering loudly, but obviously did not want anyone to hear her. "Jen, you have got to let me in." Of all of them, Beth Anne seemed the most trustworthy. Jen opened the door. Beth Anne had obviously been crying and was visibly upset.

"What's wrong?" Jen asked with sincere concern.

"When the storm stopped, Tom, Kate, and Smitty went to the lake to go check on the boat. I went back to sleep, but about thirty minutes ago I awakened, felt good, and went downstairs to get some food. Mr. Reed, as he calls himself, was talking to someone, but I couldn't see who it was. Mr. Reed was saying that your hour had come, and this time your death would not be botched. His plan was foolproof. In fact, he said he had already started the procedure. Jen, they plan to kill you!"

Jen put her hands up to her mouth and closed her eyes momentarily. "I knew it. Beth Anne, think—who was that man talking to?"

"I don't know. I could not see them."

"Them? Was there more than one?"

"I don't know. I just used that word. I really couldn't see anyone."

For a minute the two women stared at each other, fearing what they knew, and what they didn't know.

Chapter 25

Juarez turned out to be a town of twelve hundred people. The stores were old stone buildings.

"Wow, this place could be right out of some western movie," Tony said.

José pointed to the other side of the street. "Look over there."

It was the sheriff. They parked their car, and by the time the two men caught up with him, he was unlocking the door to a building with a sign on it that identified the place as the sheriff's office.

"Sheriff?" José said.

The sheriff, who immediately noticed José's gun, asked in a courteous tone of voice, "Can I help you boys?"

José pulled out his police badge. "José Perez from San Antonio Police Department."

Tony identified himself as a private investigator from Atlanta, Ga.

The sheriff had a pleasant look: not friendly, but not unfriendly. His expressions gave no clue as to what he was thinking.

With a pronounced twang, the sheriff said, "Wel'ome to Juarez, Boys. I'm Jeff Larson. C'me on in and sit down."

Tony guessed the man to be about thirty-four. At six-foot-five and dressed in jeans, a khaki western shirt with a badge over his left shirt pocket, cowboy boots, and a Stetson hat, Jeff Larson was the personification of the tall, detached, small-town, Texan sheriff.

"Want some coffee?" Sheriff Larson motioned for José and Tony to sit in two wooden chairs in front of his desk.

"No thanks."

After getting his coffee, the Sheriff turned back to the two visitors. "How can I help you?"

Tony spoke up. "I am investigating a case in Georgia and believe it possibly ties back to a kidnapping that happened sixty years ago—the Bradford child."

Though the sheriff retained his cool, almost passive expression, Tony saw a flicker. He knew he had his interest. So he told the story of what had happened to Dr. and Mrs. Saxton. While he spoke, the sheriff leaned forward, with his arms resting on his long legs, and his stare never left Tony. When the detective finished, Jeff looked at both Tony and José.

"I'd say ya'll been living right."

"Does that mean that you have information for us?" Tony asked with some hope in his voice.

"I don't, but Mrs. Rachel Bradford DeGeorge is visiting my aunt. She was the sister of this child."

The sheriff picked up the phone. "Aunt Carolyn, you busy? I have a couple of fellers from San Antonio and Atlanta, Georgia. They need to ask Mrs. DeGeorge some questions about her brother."

They talked a minute.

When Jeff hung up, he said, "sixty-five is not what it used to be. They were just about to dress to go jogging—needed the exercise—but said they would wait until later in the day when it is cooler, and for us to come on over."

The home of Carolyn Dixon, the Sheriff's aunt, was beautiful, and when they stepped into the foyer, Tony could see that it was also beautifully decorated. One thing Tony had learned during this case is that small towns were not synonymous with ignorance and want.

"Mrs. Dixon greeted her nephew with a hug. "Oh, Jeff, it's so good to see you."

"Aunt Carolyn, Mrs. DeGeorge, I want you to meet Lt. José Perez, with the San Antonio Police Department, and Mr. Tony Antone, a private detective from Atlanta."

"Please come in and have a seat. Would you like some iced tea?" Carolyn gestured for the men to sit down.

She served the men and then Rachel spoke up.

"Which one of you has some questions about my brother?"

"That would be me ma'am." Tony was captivated by this woman's looks. She had a beautiful olive complexion, white hair, and large, clear blue eyes. Her manner and dress announced that she reeked of money.

The sheriff cut in. "Tell them what you told me."

Tony noticed that Rachel glanced at the sheriff, and that he nodded. He wondered what was going on, but proceeded with what he knew about Dr. and Mrs. Saxton and how they had died.

When he finished, he saw that Rachel looked perplexed as did her lawyer who had slipped into the room as Tony had started his story.

When he finished, Rachel was the first to speak. "I don't understand, Mr. Antone. My brother has been here twice in the past five months. In fact, he was just out here three days ago." She looked over at the woman who had come in late.

"I'm sorry. I have not met you. I am Carla Armstrong. My father was the attorney on this case until he died. Of course, it all started long before I was born, but I grew up hearing of the missing child. My brother and I have a law practice together. He is out of town this weekend. The two of us have been working on this case since the death of our father. We were finally able to track Dr. Saxton down, and have been in touch with him many times over the last year."

"You were in touch with Dr. Saxton? He's been here?" Tony was flabbergasted.

"Yes."

"How did you find him?"

Carla spoke up. "A little over a year ago, my husband and I were in Houston at a convention of hospital administrators. My husband, Rick, is the county medical administrator. One night there were several couples sitting around the table talking about strange things that happen in hospitals. One of the women told a story that had happened about sixty years ago, when her grandfather was a hospital administrator. It seems a baby was left at a hospital and no one claimed him. I immediately spoke up and asked questions. I told her how my dad had a client who had been looking for his son whom he believed was kidnapped and it had happened sixty years before. We knew it was a long shot, but she made an appointment for me to talk with her aunt, her grandfather's daughter, who was a young adult when the incident happened.

"Mrs. Cromwell, the aunt, told me that when the baby was found he was in good condition. According to the police, there had been no reported kidnappings. When, after two weeks, no one came forward to claim the child, the authorities decided that the parents probably could not afford to keep the baby.

"About the time the child was found, the wife of a young army officer was admitted to the hospital after a complicated pregnancy in which she lost her child. The couple was told they could not have children, so they asked to adopt the found baby. Eventually, the courts granted them adoption rights.

"I contacted the army and got information that helped me get in touch with the baby who was now an adult. It took some doing, but I got an address and wrote Dr. Saxton. I told him that his father and family had been looking for him and would he please call. He did so immediately."

Tony was curious. "How did you know it was your client's son?"

"I asked Mrs. Cromwell if there had been anything to identify the child. She said that on the tag of the child's top he was wearing was the name Baby J. Bradford. Mrs. Cromwell's father contacted every Bradford in Houston, but no one knew anything about the child."

Tony spoke again. "You said it was about a year ago you contacted the doctor?"

"Yes."

"Are you sure?"

"Why, of course." Carla said confidently.

"That's strange. Jen, my client, knew nothing about this."

The detective was puzzled. Why would Joseph and Virginia Saxton stage their own deaths and then show up here? He decided there was more to this story.

It was Rachel who spoke next.

"Mr. Antone, let me be frank with you. My brother stands to inherit around fifty-five million dollars."

"You said, 'stands to.' He hasn't received any money yet?" Tony questioned.

"No. That is the reason I am here. I live in Colorado, but my brother is to meet me here tomorrow night. On Monday, the papers will be signed, and his part of the estate left by my parents will be turned over to him. You see, my father left everything so that there were only certain times of the year when the estate could be settled, and Monday is one of those days."

José spoke up next. "Tell us about your brother."

Rachel drew a deep breath, and in a careful but bothered voice, she began. "He wasn't at all what I expected. My father was a tall, well-built—a good-looking man with beautiful blue eyes—and though he was astute in business, and a person who worked the ranch, he had beautiful manners. People liked him; he was funny and fun to be with, and oh, so nice." Her voice was soft when she spoke of her dad. It was obvious that they had been very close and she had loved him very much.

"When I met Joseph, I was surprised. Oh, he was tall and erect. He wore sunglasses—claimed something was wrong with his eyes and he couldn't take them off—but he was arrogant and rather sullen when he found out he couldn't get the money immediately. He tried to hide his anger, but it was very apparent. There was something coarse about him."

"You said that you talked with him several days ago?" Tony asked in a confused voice.

"Yes. Claimed he needed to go to France on business and was hoping we could sign the papers just four days early. To be honest, we could have, but I told him it would be impossible. To make it legal, we would have to wait. He suggested we put the correct dates on the papers, but sign them early because he had to leave for Europe immediately. I stood my ground. Finally, he conceded and said that he would postpone his trip four more days. I don't really know why I put this off."

Tony spoke up. "You obviously have some doubts about him?"

"I do, but we've checked him out and he is who he says he is."

"How do you know?" Tony asked.

Carla broke in. "My twin brother, Carl, was in Atlanta about five months ago. He called and said he would like to come to Upton. Dr. Saxton met him at the airport and took him to his house. They talked and then Carl had to leave. He didn't have much time there, but wanted to get a feel for the man in his home."

"Did he meet his wife or daughter?"

"No. He said they were out of town."

"Why was Carl convinced that he was Dr. Saxton?"

"Well, a young man called after him as Dr. Saxton and my brother were walking to the car at the airport. Dr. Saxton had met the plane. Also we have checked his driver's license."

"Do you have a picture of him?"

Rachel spoke. "No. I wanted a picture of the two of us together, but he said that he wanted to wait until he could remove his dark glasses."

Carla intervened. "Yes, we do. Unknown to him, my secretary secretly took a picture with a small camera that was hidden." She looked in her briefcase and pulled out the copy of his picture and handed it to Tony.

A fear shot through him. "This is the man claiming to be Joseph Saxton?"

"Well, Yes." Carla answered.

"You have reason to be uncomfortable. This man is not Joseph Saxton. Do you have the original letter you sent him?

Looking shaken, Carla answered. "Yes I do. Here."

She handed Tony an envelope with the information.

"Do you mind if I keep this?"

"Of course not. I have copies of all our correspondence, including the envelopes."

Tony spoke again in a most urgent tone. "Let me get this straight. This man is coming here tomorrow night to sign the papers and leave for France?"

Carla spoke up. "That's right. He asked for an eight o'clock appointment so he could leave for Europe at twelve noon."

Tony, almost speaking to himself, said, "I'll bet he's planning on leaving Upton at least by tomorrow. That means he will go after Jen today!"

He looked at his watch. "There is a plane that leaves for Atlanta in an hour. Any possibility we could get back to San Antonio in time?"

Jeff stood up. "Oh yeah, I can get you there. José, why don't you take the rental car, and Tony and I can go in mine with the siren on. No one's going to bother us."

"That's a good idea. I'll also call and see if I can get the airlines to hold the plane. After all, this is a life-and-death situation, right Tony?" José said.

"Right."

In all of his cop days, Tony had never experienced such a ride as the one Jeff gave him to the airport. In fact, he was sure no New York cabbie could touch Jeff's ability to set a passenger's nerves on end. Some of the terrain was flat, some hilly and curvy, yet he never changed his speed. When they got into San Antonio, a cop came on the radio.

"Sheriff, you need any help? Going awfully fast."

Jeff explained, without slowing down, the situation.

"You are in a hurry; you are still thirty minutes away and the plane is to take off in fifteen minutes. Let me get right back to you."

In less than two minutes, the radio came on again. "The plane is waiting for you. The police have already called and requested a flight delay. We have dispatched some policemen to the airport so that they can get you through the airport and to the plane. Good luck."

"Thanks." Jeff answered back.

It took Tony less than five minutes to get his ticket and board. Unfortunately, because of the storm that hit Atlanta, the plane was rerouted to South Carolina and back to Atlanta. This three-hour delay, plus the fact that the phones were out, meant that no one could get to Jen. Would she put her trust in the wrong person? If she did, it would mean her death.

Chapter 27

The Great Stone House was quiet—too quiet—as the reality that someone was trying to kill Jen washed over Beth Anne and her.

Beth Anne spoke up. "We can't panic, and must act fast. Get some dark jeans on, and I will distract Mr. Reed. You have to get out of here."

While Jen hastily dressed, Beth Anne noticed her coffee.

"Jen, what is this?"

"Coffee."

"What did you put in it?"

"Nothing."

Looking angry, Beth Anne replied, "There is a white substance all in the coffee. Mr. Reed must have gone in and put something in the coffee. He was either trying to put you into a deep sleep or poison you. Do you feel okay?"

Mr. Reed or one of my "friends," Jen thought.

Jen then answered Beth Anne. "I'm okay now. I had a headache when I woke up, but it's almost gone. Fortunately, I couldn't drink but two sips before it put me to sleep."

Beth Anne fixed the bed to look as though Jen were still in it. She would often think back on this act and wonder what made her do this.

After she finished dressing, Jen suddenly remembered the secret. "Beth Anne, the man who built this house showed me something about

112

this room. Because I was not supposed to tell anyone, I forced myself to forget it, but now I know. There is a hidden entrance from here to the basement where there is a tunnel to the outside.

She looked around the room trying to recall where the passage was. "Oh yes, it's in the closet." The two women looked until Jen remembered.

"There is a panel behind the shelves." She pulled the shelves out and pushed on the panel. Finally it slid to the side, and there was a latch. Jen then pulled it, and a door opened.

"Oh, my." Beth Anne gasped.

As Jen crept down the stairs, she wondered if anyone else had discovered this place. She then noticed a switch on the wall. Miraculously, the light came on. The basement was dusty, covered with lots of cobwebs, and it showed no sign that anyone had been there in years.

"Where are you?" Beth Anne whispered.

"I'm trying to see if I can get the door to open." With much pushing it finally opened. On the other side was a tunnel. Jen would have to crawl, but she could see the outside. It was not closed.

"Beth Anne, I'm leaving. You be careful. And thanks."

Jen crawled through the tunnel and sneaked down the hill.

In the meantime Beth Anne closed the panel, and then went downstairs hoping to see Tom, but he was nowhere to be found.

Scot Reed knew he had to act fast. Earlier, while the others had been eating, he had found keys to all of the rooms, and made sure he could unlock Jen's door. Everyone was out except Beth Anne. He had seen her downstairs. It was now time to put his plan into action. The hall was clear. Scot quickly opened Jen's room and looked over at her bed. Obviously she was asleep.

This time you will not wake up. There was enough sleeping powder in your coffee to keep you out, and you will never even know, he thought to himself. He almost laughed as he started the fires.

After Scot finished the work, he quickly went back to his room to wait. Just minutes later, he could smell the smoke. For show, just in case someone had come back in, he ran out yelling, "fire!" He saw Beth Anne downstairs and screamed to her to get out.

With smoke billowing from the house, Tom, Smitty, and Kate came running up the hill.

"What's going on?" Tom yelled.

"Oh, Tom." Beth Anne said. "The place caught on fire, and Jen is trapped inside." She had to play this through for Scot Reed. Beth Anne was aware that Scot Reed had been talking to someone, but there was only Tom, Smitty, and Kate around. *Who was he talking to?* she thought.

"Trapped? We have to get her out!" Tom said in a near panic.

At that point, there was an explosion. Everyone hit the ground.

Trying to soothe him, Beth Anne said, "I'm so sorry."

Tom just sat there. Smitty didn't say anything, but felt like he was going to get sick, and Kate just turned her back.

Beth Anne tried to get Tom away from the others so she could explain what had really happened, but Scott Reed seemed to always be with them. She was concerned that he was a little suspicious of her. To try to buy Jen some time, Beth Anne began to ask Scot Reed questions about the fire. Though he knew he needed to get away, he enjoyed talking to the pretty, obviously very classy lady. *What's a little time?* the mechanic thought. *After all, my job is done and Jen is gone.*

Though she had escaped the fire, Jen was on a road to more danger than she had ever known.

∽ Chapter 28 ∽

Jen had hardly started her escape when she heard the explosion. She looked back to where the stone house stood, and saw flames everywhere. Watching the smoke billowing above the trees, she said to herself, "That fire was meant for me. I was supposed to be too drugged to escape." This thought sickened her to the point that her knees gave out and she just had to sit. While waiting to regain her strength, Jen thought back to a year ago. It was the last time the group had been together in happy circumstances. A shiver went up her spine as she remembered how at the end of the day, clouds had filled the sky. "That was an omen, and now the fire and smoke—our friendships and lives—have gone up with these flames, and we are being knocked to the ground just as is the great stone house." Momentarily Jen cried softly, but soon began moving as she realized that someone might see her. She had to get to a telephone.

Jen guessed that she had been walking about thirty minutes when she saw Kings Highway. Before the interstate, this had been the main thoroughfare, but tonight Jen was alone on the old road. She let out a sigh of relief; not too far away was a service station. The owner lived in the back. Jen knew him, and knew he would aid her in getting help. As her plans were forming in her head, a car pulled up.

"Jen, what are you doing out here? Are you okay? I thought all of you were at the Great Stone House."

"Oh, thank you!" Jen muttered to herself. "Mr. DePau, I am so glad to see you. I need a ride into town."

"Get in. This is no place for you."

Jen got into the car and, for the first time that night, felt safe.

Trying to calm down and gain some strength, she turned to Thomas and said, "Tom said you and Mrs. DePau went to Augusta for the weekend."

"That's right, but I had to leave early to take care of some business. I will rejoin Jean later. You never told me what you are doing out here."

Jen could not talk about what had happened.

"Please Mr. DePau, just take me to my parents' house. I'll tell you later."

"Sure" he said in a comforting voice. Do you mind if I stop by the house first? I need to get some papers, and then I am going to Atlanta."

"Of course not," Jen said in an unconcerned voice.

Thomas motioned for Jen to come into the house and wait in the library while he went upstairs.

Jen sat and looked around the big room. Its rich mahogany paneling and big windows gave it a majestic air. The large Queen Anne desk and the two leather wing chairs, along with the tapestry sofa, completed the look of old money. Feeling restless, Jen walked around the room. A large portrait of Miss Marie Antoinette hung above the fireplace. The picture dominated the room. With little thought, Jen began to study the painting. Tom's grandmother must have been about thirty-five when this was done. She was breathlessly beautiful. Her eyes almost gave the illusion of being round until you looked closely and noticed that they were slightly slanted. The dark hair and almost almond eye shape hinted of some distant Asian kin. One would think with these characteristics that the eyes would be dark, but they were blue. The light blue dress of satin and lace against her pale skin and dark hair gave Miss Marie Antoinette an almost mystical appearance.

Suddenly, Jen's heart began beating fast as she studied Miss Marie's satin dress with the lace appliqués. In Jen's mind she heard Miss Bessie say, "Laddie always said, 'I may have been born in rags, but I will live my life wearing satin and lace.'" Forcing herself to think back, Jen thought, *what was it Miss Marie Antoinette always said to us girls in charm school—satin and lace are the mark of a lady. That's what felt familiar at Miss Bessie's: the thing about satin and lace. It was also her eyes. When Mrs. Trotter took off her glasses, I noticed that she had the same odd-shaped blue eyes.* With her heart and mind racing, Jen now knew that Miss Marie Antoinette's roots were not those of a once-wealthy French family, and that she had not been killed in a train wreck. As the reality of all of this swept over Jen, she felt both panicky and weak—as though she would faint.

Cutting deep into her thoughts, she heard Thomas say, "She was beautiful, wasn't she?"

Without turning around, Jen whispered, "Yes."

"You know who she was, don't you?" Thomas said accusingly.

The comfort and kindness he had displayed earlier had now been replaced with coldness and anger.

"She had something to do with my father?"

"Yes, she kidnapped him." Thomas snapped.

Jen swirled around. This man, Thomas DePau, whom she had known all of her life, was watching her with the coldest, angriest eyes she had ever seen.

"Kidnapped? Why?"

"It was your grandfather's fault. Mama was in love with him, but he said no. He went and married a debutante. Your great-grandparents were rich, and wanted their son to keep their name high on the social list. They didn't think my mother was good enough for him. He needed someone with better social connections. Mama never got over the pain of being slighted."

As though he had been transported to another world, Thomas continued. "It was their fault. If it were not for them, Mama would have been a happy and rich woman, but no, she wasn't good enough for them, because she was poor. They ruined mama's life." Thomas then screamed, "And for that, they had to die!"

Jen was weak with fear, but in a strange way she was energized, and had to know the truth—no matter what her fate.

"Who had to die?"

"Who? Why your parents of course."

Thomas' face was contorted with the most evil expression Jen had ever witnessed. With his lip curled, he then said, "And now, you too must die."

Jen screamed at Thomas. "You killed my parents? Wealth, what are you talking about?"

Thomas shouted, "Shut up. It's time for you to join your parents. Won't that be nice to see them again?" he asked in an evil, sarcastic way.

He then raised his hand and pointed a gun at Jen. But just as he did, a noise came from the living room. Thomas turned to see who was there, and as he did, someone grabbed his arms. Tony and the sheriff had arrived. The two lawmen quickly wrestled the gun from this crazed individual, and in seconds Thomas was in handcuffs.

Jen's mind was reeling. "I don't understand," she said to Tony.

"I'll tell you the whole story later. Are you okay?"

"Oh yeah," she said sarcastically.

"Mr. DePau," Jen said, "I met your aunt several months ago. Of course at the time I didn't realize that's who she was. Mrs. Trotter told me how her sister—your mother—was hurt because she thought the man she loved dumped her for a wealthy woman. You see, someone mistakenly told Miss Marie Antoinette that my grandfather had married a debutante. Years later, Mrs. Trotter found out that my grandmother was really from a poor family; it was her cousin, who had the same name, who was wealthy. My great-grandparents did not care that their son was marrying a poor girl. They wanted him to be happy. Mr. DePau, my grandfather just fell in love with someone else."

Thomas crumpled and loudly sobbed, "Oh mama, oh mama, how cruel life has been to us," and the once-proud man was taken away in handcuffs by the sheriff.

Jen just sat and stared for a moment. She looked at Tony. "Where did you come from? What about the sheriff? Why was he with you? What's going on?"

Tony went over and sat next to Jen on the sofa. He looked shaken. "I thought you were dead. There is so much to tell you. The sheriff and I were on our way to the stone house to get you when we saw it in flames. We drove up and spoke to Beth Anne, and she told us about your escape. Scot Reed had just taken off. Fearing he would find you, we left to try and get to you first. We drove along the Kings Highway, but you were nowhere to be found. We thought maybe you had gotten a ride to your parents', and were on the way there when we saw Thomas's car parked outside of his house. Taking a chance, we stopped. We were looking in the french door when we saw him pull the gun. Fortunately, he had not locked the door, so we could easily get in."

"How did the sheriff get involved in this?"

Tony began his story. "Unknown to me, Harry started looking into the deaths of your parents several weeks ago. It seems there is a young man, James Thrice, who has the mind of a child but can work and does odd jobs around town. Thomas asked James to leave a package at your dad's clinic—told him it was a birthday surprise. James was told to go to the clinic late in the afternoon, fake sickness, and steal a key. Thomas knew where your dad kept spare keys. That night, James was to return to the clinic and leave a package and not tell anyone. Thomas told him it was a joke. The young man said this had always bothered him, but he had believed Thomas. Later, Thomas had James wait at the airport parking lot, and when he saw Thomas with a stranger, he was instructed to go up and talk to him as if he were Dr. Saxton—even call him by that name. All of this would have probably been left unnoticed, but about three weeks ago there was a revival at the Baptist church. One night, the preacher preached on the sin of lying. James became concerned about the things Thomas had asked him to do, so he talked with the minister and his mother after church. Remembering the rumors about your dad being involved in drug sales, his mother made him go to the sheriff's office the next day."

Tony stopped for a minute, and then continued. "According to what Sheriff Crenshaw told me, at first he had had a hard time believing that your accident and that of your parents' were connected, but he couldn't discount the fact that Old Jim had seen a person running from your house just hours before your wreck. After James went to him and mentioned the package being left at the clinic, Harry sensed that, for some reason, Thomas was trying to set your dad up. Sheriff Crenshaw then began an investigation. He found that the DePau business holdings were in bad trouble because of bad investments and gambling; most of the family money was gone, yet Thomas had been looking into buying property in Colorado and in Switzerland. Sheriff also found out that Thomas had been making trips to Texas. Harry had been in the business too long; he knew something was going on."

Feeling restless, Tony began to walk around the room before continuing his story. "Jen, I have been in San Antonio for two days. I wanted to see if I could find out anything about your dad's background. This afternoon I met your aunt, a very nice person, and realized that Thomas has been posing as your father. When I understood what was going on, I called Harry because it was obvious to me that you were in danger. He was out of town, but immediately started back to Upton after I explained the situation."

Jen held up her hands as a sign for Tony to stop talking. Looking frustrated, she said, "Wait a minute. My aunt? Mr. DePau was posing as my father? Why? What is going on?"

"As you know, Miss Marie Antoinette was really Laddie Tinley from Wesley, Texas. When she was a young woman, she fell in love with your grandfather."

Jen answered; "Yes I know."

"Well, probably out of spite, Marie Antoinette—I guess I should say Laddie—kidnapped your father and left him in Houston with her sister."

Jen answered in a confused voice. "She took my father just to get back at someone? That is crazy."

Tony shook his head. "Well, you haven't heard the whole story. Your grandfather always believed that someday his son, your father, would be found, and he left provisions in his will for the continuation of the search for Joseph. You have to understand, Jen; your grandfather was worth a lot of money, and he wanted your dad to have his share of the estate and to also know his family."

Tony continued. "Finally, some lawyers were able to track Joseph down. When they did, they sent him a letter about the possibility of his inheritance and true identity. However, Dr. Joe never received the correspondence."

Looking shocked with all of this information, Jen asked, "Why didn't he?"

"It was sent to Joseph Saxton, P.O. Box 2406."

"But his box number is 2046."

"That's right, and guess whose was 2406."

"Miss Marie Antoinette?"

"Right. Of course, all of these years, she knew your dad's true identity because everyone here knew the story of his being found at a hospital in Houston. Also, I showed your aunt his picture, and she said that he looked just like his father. So when Miss Marie Antoinette got the letter, and saw it was from Juarez, Texas, instead of returning it to the post office, she kept it. Seeing that they were trying to establish the identity of your father, I suspect that the old girl was afraid that if your dad got hold of the letter, somehow her true identity might be found out. Also, she knew there was a lot of money involved, so she and Thomas concocted this scheme of getting rid of your family and having Thomas pretend to be Dr. Saxton so he could get the money."

Jen was confused. "This doesn't make sense. Miss Bessie, Laddie's sister, told me that Laddie was killed in a train wreck, but she has to have been Miss Bessie's sister because they look so much alike, and I realize now they had many of the same mannerisms."

⤙

Looking into the distance as though he were trying to find an answer, Tony finally replied. "I don't know the answer about the wreck. It could be that Laddie has been in touch with her sister all of these years, and when Joseph's identity was found out, Miss Bessie concocted the story of the wreck to protect both her sister and herself."

Tony threw up his hands. "Hopefully some of these unanswered questions will be answered as Thomas is questioned."

"Tony, where is Thomas?"

"They are taking him to Atlanta where he will be booked."

"Why Atlanta?" Jen asked curiously.

"This has crossed state lines, and the FBI is involved. Speaking of Atlanta, we need to go. I know the Atlanta police will want to talk with you. I'm afraid you are in for a long night."

"Long night? Tony, it is 4:30 a.m. now."

The young detective smiled. "Well, maybe you shouldn't make any plans for today."

"Wait. Something is wrong."

"What do you mean?"

"There is at least one more person involved in all of this."

She told him she recognized Scot Reed—that he was really a mechanic who had worked on her car—and how Beth Anne had come to her room to say she heard this man plotting Jen's death with someone else, but that Beth Anne could not see the other person.

"Tony, the only others at the stone house were Kate, Smitty, and Tom. One of them must have also been in on this."

The elation that Tony had felt at believing that he had solved the crime quickly left. The thought that Jen had to face one or more of her peers as also having been involved left him discouraged.

Feeling that he and Jen needed a break before going to Atlanta, Tony made a phone call. When he got off the telephone he turned to Jen.

"Come on. We have to go to Atlanta. They want to question you, but I just talked with the Captain, and he said that we don't have to go immediately. Why don't we go and get some breakfast? That will give them time to talk with Thomas, and maybe we'll get the rest of the story when we get there."

When they arrived at the station, Jen was glad she had Tony to escort her. The scene was daunting, and she did not want to be alone. In one of the glassed-in offices, she saw Kate and Smitty, but they did not see her. Were they the ones Scot Reed had been talking to? She didn't think she could bear anymore horror.

Pointing over to the left, Tony said, "That's Captain Smith's office. Let's go in."

The Captain stood, and proper introductions were made.

The Captain motioned for Tony and Jen to sit down. Then he said, "Young lady, you are lucky. These men were out to get you this weekend."

With a calmer demeanor than she felt, Jen looked at the officer, "Sir, trust me, I know I was in danger, but would you tell me what you have found out about all of this mess?"

The Captain smiled. "Oh, I will be glad to tell you. Old Scot and Thomas have been singing like birds since they got here. Probably think that if they cooperate enough they will get a deal—fat chance!

"Anyway, to answer your question, Scot Reed is a mechanic from Atlanta. The plan was that he would get to the Stone House early, feign having work to do, and go up to his room. But before he went upstairs, he went to get a glass of water, and used that time to mix the powder from five sleeping pills in the coffee. Obviously, the fact that you always took a cup of coffee up to your room and were the only one to drink coffee was well known.

In the meantime, Thomas and his wife, Jean, had gone to Augusta on the pretense of getting away for the weekend. This was to be his alibi. The couple had their usual before-dinner drink, but Thomas slipped a sleeping pill into Jean's. When she went to bed immediately after she ate, he sneaked out and returned to Upton."

"So he was the other person at the Stone House?" Jen Asked.

"Yeah. Thomas had driven back to the Stone House, parked his car at the bottom of the hill, and walked up. No one saw him. Only Scot knew that he was coming, but Beth Anne heard them talking when she stepped out onto the screen porch. When the fire started, Thomas left immediately, thinking you were dead. His plan was to return to Augusta, get in bed, and when Jean awakened the next morning, she would have never known that he had left. He was going fast, but not so fast that he didn't see a woman walking alone approaching the King's Highway. After a few miles, he decided to turn around and just check to make sure you had not somehow escaped. Of course, when he came back and saw you he had to stop. It was then he decided to kill you at his house."

Jen could hardly absorb all she had heard. Weakly, she said, "I have to know; were any of the others at the house involved?"

"No. Not that we can tell. There is no reason to believe that it was anyone but Scot Reed and Thomas DePau."

Jen wanted to know more. "Captain Smith, do you have any information on why Laddie would kidnap my father? Was it just for spite?" she asked in a disbelieving voice.

"Oh yes," he said in a slightly exaggerated tone. "Seems that our Mr. DePau, from one of Georgia's oldest and finest families," he said with sarcasm, "talked all of the way to Atlanta. According to him, when Miss Marie Antoinette was dumped in favor of another woman, she would not let go.

Four years after your grandparents married, your grandmother got sick and died. Your dad was just a couple of months old. Laddie heard about the death and went to see your grandfather, believing she would win him back. He was so grief stricken that he did not even remember the young woman, nor was he interested. She was so full of hate that she aimed to get back at him."

Jen looked at Tony and said," I remembered that my dad had a box with the clothes he had on when he was taken to the hospital. The other night I was looking at them. Barely readable, the name Baby J. Bradford was written under the tag on his sweater. I don't even know if my dad had ever noticed."

About that time Kate and Smitty entered the office. Kate was the first one to speak, "Oh Jen, I am so sorry. You tried to tell us, but I was so wrapped up in my own problems that I didn't hear." As solicitous as Kate's words were, there was coolness in her voice.

Jen reached out and took Kate's and Smitty's hands, and hugged each one of them. Yet as she did, she felt them both slightly pull away. *Something is still not right.* She thought. *What is wrong? Maybe it's just fatigue.*

"What about Tom and Beth Anne? How are they doing?" Jen asked.

"Here they come." Tony said.

Tom and Beth Anne walked in. "I am so sorry," Tom said. He and Jen hugged. "I had no idea."

"I know. Beth Anne, thank you so much for your help. You saved my life."

"Oh Jen, we are so sorry." She was crying softly.

Almost to himself, Tom said, "My dad tried to kill her and my wife saved her life."

For a moment they all just looked at Tom and just let the incredulous reality set in.

Tom then turned and rather stiffly said, "We have to go to Augusta. I have to see about mom and tell her all of this. She's going to be crushed." With that they left. It would be many years before Tom and Jen spoke again.

Captain Smith returned. "Ya'll may go. Jen, I will be in touch."

He then took Jen's hand, and in a very sincere way said, "I am so sorry for all you have gone through, and you can be sure we will do all we can to see that these birds stay in custody."

"Thank you very much."

As they left, Jen's head was swimming. Though she was relieved that the murderers had been caught, she could not rid herself of the feeling that something was still not right with Kate and Smitty.

But what could be wrong? Wasn't the crime solved?

Chapter 29

The DePau family had lost everything. Thomas had always handled the money with no questions asked. Though Tom knew that there were serious financial problems in the business, even he did not realize that they were going under.

This lofty family who had kept company with some of the most important people in the United States and who could go back for generations and claim kin to those who helped build and shape the history of Georgia, was now broke. They could not even raise bail. The once-proud Thomas DePau was just another inmate.

In the beginning, Thomas thought that his name would get him out of trouble, but public sentiment was that of anger and disgust. Joseph and Virginia Saxton had been popular and well-respected people. Thomas's lawyer soon realized that his client would not get a fair trial in the state. He based the case on the precept that Thomas had acted out of insanity. The defense team asked for a speedy trial, and for the judge to decide sentencing. They believed that the judge in Upton would be more lenient. Jen was grateful for this turn of events. She did not want to sit through weeks of testimony.

The morning of the trial, Jen got up early. She was glad that Tony was going with her. They would go to Upton and pick up Toady and John and then go to the courthouse together.

When Jen sat on her couch to wait for Tony, she began to think about her life. The Big Four seemed to no longer exist. Tom had written a long and beautiful letter to Jen expressing his sorrow and shock for what his father and grandmother had done. He also told her that he and Beth Anne were moving to Houston, Texas, where he was going into business with a friend from college. Before closing he expressed his love for their friendship and stated that, at this point, he just could not face her. Lost in her thoughts, Jen almost didn't hear the knock at the door.

Jen opened the door. "Tony, come on in. Thank you so much for going with me today."

Tony stepped in. "Wouldn't miss seeing this bird put away. It is a pleasure trip." What Tony did not say was that there was no way he was going to let Jen go alone. He knew that in the two months since Thomas's arrest, Jen had called Kate and Smitty; but neither had seemed to want to talk, and had continued to ignore her. Their behavior worried Tony.

The drive to Upton was quiet, but when they got to the courthouse, all of that changed. News media from all over the state, and in some cases from elsewhere in the United States, were there to cover the story. Tony got Jen, Toady, and John through the crowd by way of the back entrance. When they were seated, Jen saw Tom, Beth Anne, and Tom's sister and mother arrive and sit at the front on the other side. Kate and Smitty got there within minutes of each other. They sat in the middle row. Jen thought sadly, *the Big Four are now truly divided—for ever and ever.*

Thomas and his lawyers came in and sat down. Instead of standing straight and tall and commanding an air of respect, Thomas was bent over with a crazed look on his face and his mouth slightly open. He was even drooling.

Tony whispered, "Thomas is trying to look insane so the judge will go easy—maybe even send him to a state hospital. That is what they are asking for."

"Oh, please, no. I saw what he was like when he tried to kill me. Believe me, Thomas DePau is not crazy; he knew exactly what he was doing!"

Obviously the judge agreed with Jen. He was not kind, nor was he impressed by the DePau name. Judge White called Thomas a ruthless and deplorable piece of humanity, and then sentenced him to life in prison without the possibility of parole. It was the harshest sentence he was allowed to hand down.

Jen was very happy, but she looked over and felt sorry for Jean, Thomas's wife, who looked devastated. *She is, in some ways, as much of a victim as I am,* Jen thought.

Outside the courthouse, many people stopped to give Jen their condolences and support.

As Tony and Jen approached Tony's car, they heard Kate.

"Jen."

Jen turned around. Kate and Smitty were walking toward her.

"Are you okay?" Smitty asked.

"I guess," Jen said in a noncommittal way.

The four stood and talked for a few minutes. As they did, they saw Tom's car turning the corner.

"They are leaving for Houston today. What am I going to do?" Kate said softly.

Jen looked at her and thought, *What do you mean, what are you going to do? This isn't about you.*

Breaking into her thoughts, a young reporter came up. "Ms. Saxton, this is off the record. What are you going to do now?"

Jen thought a moment. "Hopefully rebuild my life."

The reporter held out her hand and said, "I hope you will be okay."

"Thank you," Jen said.

As they all parted, Kate looked at Jen and thought, *Oh yeah, she'll be okay. The great Jen. She always lands on her feet and everyone thinks she is so wonderful. If they only knew what I know.*

TV reporters were everywhere. Smitty heard one say, "Well folks, it's all over now.

Smitty took a deep breath and thought, *I wish this were over. For me it's just begun because now I have to learn to live with the guilt.*

Part 2

Shattered Lives
Broken Dreams

❦ *Chapter 30* ❦

Two Months After the Trial

Though her arm was hurting, Kate put her hair back in a pony tail and put on her "grubbies," as she called them, and began to clean house. About 10:00 a.m. there was a knock at the door.

"Oh, hi Mom. Come on in."

Sara Katherine, who was worried about Kate stopped by every day for coffee. Kate had changed, and Sara Katherine did not like what she was seeing. Her vivacious and fun-loving daughter had now become withdrawn, and seemed forever sad.

"Just thought I would come by and beg for a cup of coffee."

Kate just smiled.

They talked for a while though there was a certain awkwardness about the conversation.

Finally, Sara Katherine said, "Oh, I saw Toady yesterday. She said that Jen is having a hard time. Have you by any chance called her? I am sure she needs your support."

Oh, I'm sure she is fine, Kate thought, but she didn't say anything except, "Oh, really? I'm sorry she is not doing well," and then quickly changed the subject. The last thing she wanted this morning was to talk about her old friend. This was not lost on Sara Katherine, who could not understand what had happened to Kate's friendship with Jen.

The two talked for a while. When Sara Katherine stood to leave, the phone rang. "You get that. I'll let myself out."

"Okay, see you later."

"Hello."

"Yes, this is Emily Frasier with the personnel department at Addington Industries in Atlanta. Is Ted Stroud there?"

"No he is not. This is his wife. Can I give him a message?"

"Yes. Tell him we want him to start to work a week from tomorrow rather than a week from Monday. That is if it is possible for him to do so."

"Start to work? Oh, you know, I think you have the wrong number."

"Is this Theodore Jackson Stroud's residence, 428-668-0880?"

"Well, yes it is. But—" Kate was feeling confused and sick. "Let me have him call you back."

The woman gave Kate the number and then said, "Okay. I'll be here until five thirty, but I need to talk to Ted as soon as possible."

When she hung up, Kate just stood there, confused. A feeling of doom settled in. Trying to shake it, she went into Ted's so-called office. Actually, for the last few years, this had been the room that he retreated to so he would not have to be with the family. Many nights, he slept there. Kate decided to look around the office.

"Kate?"

Kate looked and saw Ted standing in the door. "I didn't hear you come in, but I'm so glad you are here."

She told him about the call, just waiting for Ted to say it was a mistake.

Instead of relieving Kate's concern he answered, "Okay, I'll call her back."

"Wait. What's going on? You'll call her back? You have a job in Atlanta."

"Yes I do." Ted said rather defiantly.

"You mean we are moving and you didn't even tell me?"

Ted took a deep breath. "I just resigned at you father's business because I have accepted this job in Atlanta."

"Why?"

"Just let me finish. *We* are not moving to Atlanta. I am."

For a minute, the meaning of what he had said did not sink in. Kate just looked at him, and then realized that he was going to move without her or the children.

Kate could hardly comprehend what Ted was saying. Finally, in a shocked tone of voice, she said, "You're leaving me and the children? Why?"

"Why?" Ted exploded with anger. "Because I can't take this any longer. Look at you. You look sloppy all the time, and you are boring to me. Kate, I want a wife who cares about herself. One who is interesting and fun. You have changed. Once the children came, you just became a mommy and forgot about me and our marriage!"

"Forgot you!" Kate screamed. "Funny, but I felt the same way. For ten years I have been trying to raise two children, and, I might add, by myself. What do *you* do? You haven't been much of a father. Instead of being here for us, you stay out many nights until the wee hours of the morning. You don't think I hear you come in, but I do!"

"Look, those children were your idea."

"My idea? I don't think I got pregnant alone."

"You knew I didn't want another child when Anna Kate was born."

"Ted, I was on the pill. I don't know how I got pregnant. Those things happen."

"Yeah. You wanted another baby. I'm really sure you were on the pill."

"I was!" Kate was really mad at being called a liar.

"Look, what's done is done, but I'm moving on. I will continue to provide for the children and see them. It's not the children I'm leaving— just this dull marriage, dreary town, and boring life." Ted slammed his hand down on the table to make his point, and then walked out to go into his office. Kate followed.

In a little calmer voice, Kate tried to reason. "Ted, wait. You can't just suddenly walk out after being married for eleven years. We can work this out. Please let's talk."

"Kate, you are pathetic! We may have been together for eleven years, but our marriage ended a long time ago as far as I am concerned! Face it; it's over!"

"Won't you go for counseling?"

"Won't you go for counseling?" Ted said, mocking her.

He then stopped, spun around and looked at a cowering Kate.

"Hear what I have to say. I am bored with this marriage, this small town, being married to a woman who can't let go of high school, and being expected to live up to your dad. I am out of here, and never plan to come back, so don't even believe there is hope for us!" With that, Ted reached in the closet and pulled out his suitcase and a hanging bag that were already packed. Obviously, he had planned this exit for a long time. Within five minutes he was out of his house and out of his marriage.

When he left, Kate just sat slumped at the table. She was in shock and could not move. Nothing seemed real.

It was not too long, though, before there was a knock at the door.

"Mom?"

"Kate, what's going on? Your dad just came and said that Ted resigned and was moving to Atlanta. Why didn't you tell me?"

"I just found out. He left me." Suddenly, the enormity of what had happened hit Kate and brought her back to reality. She then fell into her mother's arms and sobbed uncontrollably.

Seeing her daughter in so much pain saddened Sara Katherine to the core, but oddly, she realized she was not surprised.

Sara Katherine stayed with her daughter that day and helped to explain as best as possible to the children what had happened. Sara Katherine was stunned that they were not more upset than they were.

She wondered about that, but figured that when the reality that Ted was not coming back set in, the children would then show more sadness.

For two weeks, Kate stayed in bed. Her mother would come over and cook for the children and do what she could to help, but Kate just wanted to be left alone. She thought about everything she could concerning her marriage and wondered what she could have done to save it.

About three weeks after Ted left, Kate finally made herself get up, fix breakfast, and get the kids dressed. When they were out of the house, she sat at the table and began to think. *Will Ted ever come back? What can I do?* she thought desperately. *Will I ever be happy again?* And then the secret that haunted her seemed to answer back, "No, you don't deserve happiness. This is it for you."

∽ *Chapter 31* ∽

Three Months After the Trial

Karen was thinking to herself as she prepared supper. *I wonder what's going on. Smitty's mother calls for the kids to come over for the night just after Smitty makes sure I am going to be here. It seems too convenient. Oh, how I wish it would be one of those romantic evenings we used to have when the parents took the kids. Romance. sure. Oh, that went out a year ago. What's wrong with Smitty? What's wrong with us?*

Interrupting her thoughts, Smitty appeared in the door. "Is supper almost ready? I will set the table."

"Great. Everything will be prepared in about five minutes."

Without saying anything more, Smitty began to set the table. Karen watched him, remembering how in the past when they were working on a project, whether it involved working on the house or making a meal, they would talk and laugh. Now, the silence and the absence of humor was the norm.

The couple decided to watch a TV program as they ate. This made the deafening quietness a little less painful, and helped prevent stilted conversation. The tension in the air was stifling for both Karen and Smitty. Once the meal was finished and everything was cleaned up, Smitty suggested, "Let's go into the living room. There are some things we need to talk about."

Karen had decided at a very early age that she wanted to marry Smitty, and though it would be years before they got together, she never worried that she would lose him to anyone else. But now her heart began to beat fast, and she had a sick feeling in the pit of her stomach. Smitty had changed. Was he going to leave her just as Ted had left Kate? Karen braced herself for the worst.

The living room was small, with two comfortable chairs and a sofa. It reflected the tastes of a young couple who had to work for everything they had. The walls had some framed posters, and on the tables were pictures of their different family members. The room was decorated in colors of white and a soft gray. It was comfortable and inviting.

The two adults sat opposite of each other, Smitty in a wing chair and Karen on the sofa. Karen's throat began to feel very dry, as it always did when she sensed trouble.

Smitty leaned forward in his chair as he began to talk. "Look, I know that I have been less than an ideal mate and dad lately, and I am sorry."

As Karen listened, she was mystified. These words did not sound like Smitty. It was obvious that he had been practicing this conversation for a long time.

Smitty got up and started to pace. "I really wanted to go into law, help people and make a difference, but it hasn't happened. We are not making enough money to do anything or put away funds for the children's education."

"We have more than we ever have had in our lives," Karen countered in an upbeat voice.

"You are right. We do. But Karen, this is not good enough for me. I was embarrassed when we went back to the Law Review reunion. Those guys are making big bucks, and here we were in an eight-year-old car, and very little money in the bank. Something has to change—I am working day and night with nothing to show for it. You know how people just call at all hours and expect me to see them as well as represent them for nothing or very little. The Mill people seem to think I owe them. It's too hard. These are the same individuals who always encouraged me, but I can't carry them forever, nor can I turn them away. I have to make a change."

Karen could stand this no longer. She jumped up from the sofa and in a demanding and somewhat angry voice shot back, "What are you saying Smitty? That you can't take our life any longer and, like Ted, you want to leave us and find something better?"

They just looked at each other for a moment. Karen could not believe what she had just said. The silence between the couple was deafening.

Smitty was tempted to retort with a, "You would be better off if I did leave if you only knew what I have done."

But he said in a rather soft voice, "No, Karen. I don't want a divorce, but I do want to close my practice and try something different."

"What do you want to do?" Karen asked in a calmer and relieved voice.

"I don't know, but I would like to stay in Upton."

Karen had always admired Smitty's ambition, and was proud of his accomplishments; however, at this moment she realized that the most important thing was not what he did for a living, but that they were together.

She went over and put her hands on his shoulders. "Smitty, all I want is for you, for us, to be happy, and if that takes you closing your law practice, then so be it."

Smitty took her in his arms and held her close. But instead of feeling happy and relieved, he was consumed with guilt. *If you only knew the truth of why I am quitting law.* Not being honest with his wife gave him a feeling of extreme sadness and shame.

If only I could go back and change the past, he thought, as Karen rested her head against his shoulder.

Chapter 32

Three and One-Half Months After the Trial

After the trial, Jen retreated to Atlanta, and life had not been easy. The grief over losing her parents coupled with the psychological reaction she had to the fact that her parents were murdered and that she almost lost her life had caused deep depression. As if this was not enough, it was obvious to Jen that any ties to the Big Four were forever broken.

She had tried several times to approach Kate and Smitty only to be rebuffed. When she last called Kate, they had talked for about two minutes and then Kate had told Jen that someone was at the door. Though Kate had promised to call back as soon as the person left, Jen hadn't heard from her since then. It was always like this with Kate, and Jen realized that the friendship was over.

Smitty had been a similar story. He had been her dad's lawyer, but after her parents' deaths, he suggested to Jen that she get someone else for legal representation since he was closing his law practice. He recommended two people in Atlanta, one of whom she started using. Jen knew the old Smitty would have stood by her until all the legal matters were solved.

Even if Smitty felt she needed to get another lawyer, why was he continuing to ignore her? One day, Jen was in downtown Atlanta when she saw Smitty at a distance walking toward her. He pretended not to see her, and abruptly turned and crossed the street. In her heart, Jen realized that, for whatever reason, her old friend was avoiding her.

She had received another long letter from Tom expressing his sorrow and disgust for what had happened. It was a beautiful affirmation of their friendship past, but made it apparent that any kind of present or future relationship was now impossible.

The one bright spot in Jen's life was that her aunt, Rachel DeGeorge, and her two sons and their wives and children had taken Jen into their family. Rachel, whose sons were about ten years older than Jen, was spending a lot of time in Atlanta trying to help Jen through this experience. Rachel also had many social connections and was working on eventually getting Jen more involved in literacy programs. This was to give Jen something, other than herself, to focus on.

On this particular morning, Jen dragged herself out of bed. Her aunt had had to go back to Colorado the day before, and Jen was on her own. She was hardly able to put one foot in front of the other, much less dress and make financial decisions, but she had promised to meet with her financial planner, Richard Nottingham. He was an up-and-coming partner in the very prestigious CPA firm of Wilson, Sterns, and Wilcox. John and Toady had pushed this meeting. They knew that with Jen's wealth and fragile emotional state, she needed someone to look after the financial side of her life. It had taken several months for all of the papers to be drawn up and signed before the bulk of the property and money that was due to Jen was turned over to her.

While walking through the lobby of the swanky downtown office building known as Peach Tree Towers, Jen caught a glimpse of herself in the mirror in the lobby. It was a cold and dreary February day, and though her spirits matched the climate, it was not evident outwardly. She had an off-white cashmere coat and under it wore a dark purple skirt with a silky mauve blouse. With her long, dark hair and large green eyes constrasting her outfit, Jen looked striking.

Richard Nottingham seemed nice enough—he had even expressed sympathy about her situation—but Jen felt angry. Why had all of this happened to her? This man who was now going to be in charge of her money could not begin to understand what her life was about—not that he would care.

Jen watched him, and had to admit that, underneath his attention to business details, he seemed like a decent guy. If he would just do something with that slicked-down hair and those horn-rimmed glasses, he could be nice looking. In spite of her anger, Jen almost laughed. *He looks like a dork*, she thought. *Oh, and look at the picture on the desk. The perfect family: wife, husband, boy and girl. Who are you to express sorrow to me? You have the world by the tail. There is no way you could ever comprehend what I have been through.*

Jen felt so angry that she just wanted to scream at this person who was going to take care of her money.

Shaken from her thoughts, she heard him say, "So this is the figure that we came up with for your monthly allowance. This is based on interest. You will not have to touch the principal, which, of course, is what you always want to avoid. Do you think this amount will be enough for you?"

"Enough! My gosh, that is just under what I made in one year of teaching. Oh, I think I can live on that," Jen answered in a rather sarcastic tone.

Richard looked at his client. They were obviously about the same age. *This has got to be hard on her.* He truly felt sorry for Jen, and understood some of her anger and frustration.

As they stood and shook hands, Richard said, "Feel free to call me at any time if there is something I can do."

Jen thought, *With what you are being paid for this job, Buster, I will feel free. Oh well, at least I have Tony to see next. Lunch will be a joy. What would I do without my detective friend?*

Jen did not realize that she might find out the answer to this above thought sooner than she wanted.

Chapter 33

Beth Anne walked in the door and saw that it was seven thirty. Since it was raining, she had driven the children to school. Tom had left for work two hours before. She now sat down for a second cup of coffee. When they had moved to Houston one year ago, the couple decided to buy a house in Briargrove near the Galleria. Here, the children could walk to school, as it was only two blocks away, but Beth Anne always walked with them to make sure they got there safely. The family liked their home and Houston, but the move had been hard on them.

Tom and Beth Anne had both been products of privilege, which always assured them of acceptance. Yet in Houston, no one knew or cared about their past social life. Tom never mentioned his family. He had made it very clear to the children that they were not to ever talk about their grandfather. Beth Anne felt concerned for her husband because he now felt totally on his own with no familiar cushion on which to fall. This concern was punctuated with a sense of uneasiness.

The oil business was booming, and the swinging single scene was evident all over Houston, from the singles classes in the churches to the single clubs sponsored by businesses for their employees. It was a time when being single, independent, and doing one's own thing were "in," and being married with a family was "out." Beth Anne called it the "era of me, my, and mine." Many marriages were falling apart as people sought to find a greater happiness in being free and finding themselves. Beth Anne wondered if perhaps her family was in some kind of danger.

Tom and his partner, Bo, had seemed to hit on the right thing by going into the computer business. They were making money, and working hard. While Beth Anne understood that they had to be dedicated to make the business work, she did not like what she was seeing. Tom and Bo's secretary, Carla Sue, a former Dallas Cowboy cheerleader who was very good looking, was mildly hostile whenever Beth Anne was present. Also, she was becoming more aware that anytime she and Tom did go out, some woman, usually young and very attractive, would sidle up to her husband and flirt. Tom would turn on the old charm when this happened, but around the house he was becoming more and more detached and sullen. Tom's leaving so early in the morning and coming home later and later at night was getting to Beth Anne. That morning he had left angry at her because she was trying to get him to get away for a family weekend. He just walked out of the door saying he was tired of her always pushing him.

"How much longer can we go on like this?" she said to herself as she poured out her coffee and started to clean.

Chapter 34

After the divorce was final, Kate and Ted sold their house. By the time they paid their debts, little money was left over. With the urging of her mother and dad, and feeling terribly alone, Kate and the children decided to move in with her parents.

One afternoon Kate was sitting alone at the table when her mother walked in. "Hi. Well, our shopping trip to Atlanta was quite uneventful. Oh, think I will join you for a cup of tea." As Sara Katherine sat down, she noticed that Kate had been crying.

"Honey, what's wrong?"

Taking a deep breath, Kate answered. "Oh mom, I just feel awful. My divorce has been final a little over a year, and it's been almost two years since the trial, and the Big Four all went different ways. It just seems that everyone but me has moved on. Smitty is teaching. Look at this picture of Jen in the Atlanta Constitution—she is co-chairing a charity event. Me? I'm just sitting and doing nothing but going to work every day.

"It really hit me today when Ted came to get the kids. It's so hard to see him drive away with his girlfriend and our children. They are going to Six Flags Over Georgia. Anna Kate and Todd were so excited. Mom, that should have been me in that car, not some other woman! I don't know what to do. I just want my family back.

Sara Katherine looked at her daughter. This once-vibrant woman had become withdrawn, and though still pretty, she did a minimal amount of work on her appearance. *What do I say?* Sara Katherine thought as she took a deep breath and plunged ahead.

"Kate, I know that for some reason you and Jen have not talked lately, but she has called you. Why don't you go and see her? The two of you were such good friends."

Kate gave her mother a hard look, and with an agitated voice said, "Look, I know we were good friends for a long time, but some things happened, and I won't discuss it. Please don't bring up Jen again. That's all I need is to start thinking about the past and feeling guilty. Anyway, with all of her money and new social life in Atlanta, how interested could she be in a childhood friend? But that's really not the point right now. I feel as though life is passing me by. I couldn't even hold my marriage together. All I really want is for Ted to come back to me. I just don't know what I did to make him leave."

Slowly, Sara Katherine responded. "Kate, you are taking all of the responsibility of this divorce on your shoulders. What you need to do is to get mad. Ted left you!"

"Please mom, I am painfully aware of that. You just don't understand."

"I understand better than you think."

Something about her mother's tone of voice made Kate curious. "How could you?"

Taking a deep breath Sara Katherine started. "You know how sometimes your dad will say, 'You are just a pearl of a girl,' and we will both laugh?"

"Yes. I remember asking you why Dad always said that, and you said it was just a joke between the two of you."

"Well it wasn't always funny. In fact, for a while it was quiet serious. Pearl Gravel grew up in Homer Community with your dad and me. We all went to school together though they were a year ahead of me in school. The two of them went together. Pearl was pretty, and, we thought, very glamorous. Right before her senior year, her dad died, and her mother, who didn't like living in a country community, took Pearl and they moved to Hollywood. Pearl's mother thought she could get into acting. Your dad was hurt because Pearl broke up with him before leaving. During his senior year, Fred and I became friends and did things together. I knew that he was still heartsick for Pearl, but we had a good time. Two months after graduation, Pearl wrote back to a friend that she had married an up-and-coming movie star. She even sent pictures and talked of their very glamorous and exciting life of movie sets and movie stars. I suspect all of this was a product of her imagination. In the meantime your father went to war and we wrote regularly. At the beginning of 1942 he was sent home after being injured. While Fred recuperated, he and I became even closer and our love grew. We married in 1943. A year later, Pearl returned and lived with her aunt. It was rumored that she had divorced. Your dad was working hard to get his construction business going. After Fred and I had been married a little over two years, he started acting withdrawn, but when I asked him about it, he just said he was tired. I didn't think anything about it. Even though I knew Pearl was back in town, I trusted your dad.

"The night of our third anniversary I fixed Fred's favorite meal. I even had been able to get some champagne. Everything looked so nice. We usually ate at six thirty. Well, six thirty came and went. I called him at work but there was no answer. Finally, at seven thirty, your uncle Jeb came over and he told me that he had seen your dad and Pearl eating at a restaurant that used to be out from town. He also told me that she had been hanging around Fred's business."

"What did you do?" Kate asked in a shocked voice. She could not believe what she was hearing.

"At first I cried and then I got mad. I thought, look at this beautiful meal that I worked hard to prepare. Who is he to act like this? So I called Aunt Maggie in LaGrange and asked if I could come and stay with her. She said of course.

"Next, I packed my bag and asked Jeb to take me to the restaurant where the couple was eating. I walked in with my head held high. Your dad looked scared to death when he saw me. I spoke nicely to Pearl, gave your father the key to the house, and told him that I would not need it because I was moving to LaGrange."

"What did dad say?"

"He jumped up and tried to get me to wait, but I just told him not to worry, just stay and enjoy our anniversary dinner with Pearl—I could tell he had forgotten. I then left with my head up, and Jeb took me to LaGrange that night."

Kate was astonished by this story. "What happened next? Obviously you got back together."

"Obviously, but it took a while. This all happened on a Friday. Your dad called three times the next day, but I would not talk to him except to tell him to go on with his relationship with Pearl. He swore there was nothing between them that she only wanted him to eat supper with her and talk. Anyway, I just decided I was not going to live like that. On Monday I found a temporary job. Mr. Anderson, who owned a large store, needed someone to work for six months. He didn't much want to hire me—said I would go back to my husband—but I promised to stay if he would just let me work.

"After three weeks, I finally agreed to see Fred. We began to talk, and he was begging me to come back, but I would not leave the job until my time was up, so your dad would come to LaGrange on Saturdays and leave on Sunday nights. Before I came home, I told him that the next time not to even bother to call. He knew there would never be a second reconciliation. Kate, you and I are both alike. We are nice and very patient with people, and sometimes they think we are weak or can be walked on. Your dad saw that underneath this niceness is fire, and he respected that."

"So maybe if I could just get mad enough and show Ted another side of me, he would come back?"

Sara Katherine looked at her daughter for a moment. "No. When you truly get mad and move on, what that other person thinks is of no consequence. The most important thing becomes self-respect, no matter what anyone else does. It just so happened that your dad and I got back together, but if he had not persisted, and I had not been very sure that Pearl was out of the picture, I would have stayed in LaGrange and never come back."

"Oh mom, I wish I could get to that point. But right now, I would take Ted back in a New York minute."

In a short time, Kate's attitude toward Ted would change drastically.

Chapter 35

In a groggy state, Kate reached to answer the phone and noticed that it was 2:00 a.m.

"Hello."

"Mom?"

Kate sat straight up in bed; she could tell her daughter was upset. "Anna Kate, what's wrong?"

Softly crying, in a small voice, the child replied, "Todd is sick."

"Sick. How?"

"He is throwing up and his stomach hurts."

"Put your father on the phone."

There was a long pause. Kate was getting agitated. "Anna Kate, go get your father."

Very hesitantly she answered. "He's—he's not here."

"Where is he? Did he go to get some medicine?"

"No ma'am. I don't know where he is."

Kate couldn't believe what she was hearing. "When did you see him last?"

"Well, we came in from the movie about ten o'clock, and daddy told us we could watch TV until he got back. He was going to take Tracy home."

Trying to stay calm, Kate asked, "How long has Todd been sick?"

"About thirty minutes."

"Do you have a number for Tracy?"

"No ma'am."

"Can Todd talk to me? Let me speak to him!"

"Hello."

He sounded terrible. Kate tried not to let him sense the fear she was feeling. "Hi Partner. How ya feeling?" She asked in an exaggerated tone of voice.

"Sick. I feel so bad. I'm scared." Todd was now crying.

"Honey, I am going to get help to you right away. Put your sister on the phone."

Kate was alone. Her parents were in Florida. She had to get someone to Todd fast. Jen was her only hope.

"Anna Kate, honey, I am going to call Jen and ask her to come over, then I'll call you right back."

I may not be worth much, but I don't deserve this, Kate thought as she phoned her former friend. *Oh please answer, please be home.*

"Hello," came a sleepy voice.

"Jen! It's Kate. Please, can you help me?"

"Kate, what's wrong?"

Hurriedly Kate explained the situation. "Would you please go over and see about them?"

"Sure. I am only about seven minutes away."

Kate's voice rose a little as she said in a somewhat accusatory tone, "Oh, you know where Ted lives."

"Yeah, I ran into him at a party and he told me."

"Oh."

Seemingly not to have heard Kate's accusations, Jen answered, "Let me get dressed and I'm on my way now. I'll call you when I get there."

"Oh thank you, thank you, Jen."

Kate then called Anna Kate. "How is Todd?"

"Throwing up. Mommy, I'm scared. Please come now!"

"Anna Kate, I am going to leave here soon. It will take a while for me to get there, but Jen is on her way."

"Okay. Thanks, mommy."

"Whatever you do, don't open that door for anyone but Jen. Do you understand? Wait, I will just stay on the line with you until Jen arrives."

"Okay." Anna Kate sounded relieved.

The two talked about many different things. Kate was just trying to keep her daughter calm. In about five minutes there was a knock at the door.

"Make sure that is Jen. Does your dad have a peephole?"

About that time Anna Kate heard Jen.

"Anna Kate, it's Jen."

"Mommy, it's Aunt Jen." The child put down the phone and let Jen in.

"Mom wants to talk with you."

"Kate, I'm here. Let me check on Todd. Hold on a minute."

After a few agonizing minutes, Jen reported; "He's vomiting, but no food, just liquid now. I'll call my doctor, Dr. Cason, and get back with you immediately."

After conferring with her doctor, Jen called Kate.

"Dr. Cason said to meet him at the hospital—Peach Tree General."

"Okay. I'm on my way. Jen, thanks so much," Kate said with genuine meaning.

Kate made the seventy-mile drive in fifty minutes, and literally ran to the emergency room after parking the car.

The people at the admissions desk called a nurse who came out and announced, "Mrs Stroud, your son is with the doctor back here." The nurse motioned to a room. Anna Kate and Jen were also with him.

When Kate saw Todd, it was all she could do to keep from breaking down.

She then turned to the doctor. "What's wrong with my son?"

"Acute case of Ptomaine poisoning. I'm afraid he got dehydrated. That's the reason for the drip. Your daughter was smart to call you; if she had not, Todd would have been very seriously ill. He should be okay-- just not very hungry for a few days."

Kate put her hand to her face; "This has been a nightmare."

The doctor gently patted Kate on her shoulder. This physical contact made her almost jump at first. "He's going to be okay. In fact, he will be ready to leave in about an hour."

Kate then turned to Jen. "Jen, thank you so much for your help. I don't know what I would have done without you." While she truly felt what she was saying, her manner was distant.

"Kate, I would have been horrified if you had not called."

"Well, I do appreciate it. Look, it's been a long night. Why don't you go on home? We will be okay."

Jen wanted to stay with her friend, but she knew that tone of voice. Kate was dismissing her.

Ignoring her hurt feelings, Jen answered, "Whatever you want. But please, if anything ever happens, or you need anything, feel free to call."

The two young women stiffly hugged, and Jen walked away. She hardly noticed Ted rushing in.

"What happened?" the disheveled young man asked. "There was a note saying to come here, that Todd was sick."

"What happened? Let's see if I can reconstruct the events." Kate's voice was one of extreme sarcasm. Then, with anger spitting from every word, she continued. "I'll tell you what happened. These two children were left alone while their father gallivanted around with his girlfriend. In the meantime, your son got very bad food poisoning. According to Anna Kate Todd got hungry about ten thirty and ate some pizza in your refrigerator."

"Oh, no," Ted moaned. "I am so sorry; I forgot to throw that stuff out. It had been there for a long time."

"How could you leave these children alone all night? It is 3:30 a.m. and you are just getting here, meaning that you just got home at five o'clock. You are despicable!"

"Now wait a minute, Kate," Ted said, trying to get his ex-wife calmed down. "I know it looks bad, but I did not mean to be gone so long. It's just that I took Tracy home and one thing led to another—you know how it is."

"Well, I know how it will be." Kate's voice was rising in anger. "These children will not spend the night again with you until they are old enough to stay out all night and you are too old to care. And if you don't like those arrangements, meet me in court. I am sure the judge would love to hear a story like tonight, especially since I know now that this is not the first time they have been left most of the night alone. The kids just didn't say anything; they were trying to protect you. Well, mister, the cat's out of the bag, and it's now time to protect those two children. I really don't think the new arrangement will upset them."

Ted stared at his wife for a minute. The anger in him was rising. Sensing this, Kate stepped back, but stood her ground. Instead of saying anything, Ted walked away, visited with Todd for a minute, and left the hospital. As he got in his car, he was thinking. *I have never seen Kate so angry; she was really kind of cute. That's the last of having the children for the weekend. Oh well, now my weekends are mine. I'm sorry about tonight, but I will not worry about it. Well car, let's see if Tracy would like an early breakfast.*

As Kate drove back to Upton, she knew that she had never felt as much anger or fear in her life as she had that night, and that any desire to have Ted back was gone forever.

As most people were getting up for church, Kate and the children went to bed. It had been a long night. It was late in the afternoon when Fred and Sara Katherine got home. Fred decided to go to the business to pick up some things.

"Hi, where is everyone?" Sara Katherine called out.

"Oh, hi mom. Well, Anna Kate went with a friend to church tonight. I am just too tired, and besides, Todd is sick."

"What's wrong?"

Kate related the story to her mother just as it had happened.

Sara Katherine was appalled, but not really surprised, at Ted's actions.

"Mom, good did come out of this. I realized that I have always taken my children for granted—just believed they would be here. For so long I have looked back to high school as the time when I was happy. I did not realize until last night when I didn't know what was wrong with Todd how much more my children mean to me than any homecoming crown. How could I be so stupid?"

"Well, your life was so happy in high school. Maybe things were not as good as you wanted after the children came."

If she only knew, Kate thought.

"Well whatever," Kate answered. "But that marriage is behind me and I am ready to move ahead. I have been thinking all day. I'm going to talk with dad about how to get more involved in the business. I enjoy working there, and now want to make it a career; after all, I have two children to raise."

"Oh, Kate, I am so glad to hear you talking like this. Now maybe you can find happiness."

You don't understand. I can never be happy—not knowing what I know. But I will work hard for my children and pray they never fall into the trap I did.

Chapter 36

Jen was delighted when she checked with her answering service to find that Tony had called. She had not seen him in two months. With her traveling so much and him working on his growing business, it seemed as though neither one had much spare time for the other. She had returned to Atlanta late the night before from a three-week trip, and was looking forward to meeting her friend for lunch.

On the way to the restaurant, Jen thought about Tony and their relationship. *I don't know what I would do without him; he is the only constant in my life. Even though I have met so many people over the last two years, I feel an emptiness. Neither Kate nor Smitty ever call nor will have anything to do with me. I just don't understand what has happened, but at least I have Tony.*

The parking lot at the Green Frog was crowded, but Jen noticed that Tony had not arrived. When she walked in, the Maitre'd recognized her and led her to a table. She had not been seated long when Tony walked up. They were obviously glad to see each other, but after about five minutes, Jen began to sense that something was different. Tony was his usual jovial, witty self, and was happily telling her about his business, which she knew was growing beyond belief. In fact, he had just hired his third detective, and was expecting to look for another person in six months. Yet, there was a reserve—a distance that she had not noticed before. *What is going on?* She thought.

"Okay, my friend. What's up?"

Looking a little startled, Tony replied, "What do you mean?"

"I mean that I know you, and today you seem maybe a little different."

Tony smiled and looked down at the table for a few minutes. He waited to speak as though he was choosing his words carefully. Instinctively, Jen braced herself.

Tony looked at Jen, and began to speak. "You have always reminded me of Susan. Like you, she never missed a beat and would call the person out on it. Actually, there is nothing wrong. In fact, I have some good news that I hope you will like, but I wanted you to hear it from me. I met someone."

Jen's heart was beating fast, and she was thinking, *this can't be happening.* But she said, "Oh. Tell me about her."

"Well, her name is Molly McGuire—a pretty, red-headed Irish Catholic. Anyway, she is a librarian at the city library where I do a lot of my research. She was always polite, thoughtful and especially helpful. One day we began talking and discovered we have a lot of the same interests.

"For a while we would just talk when I would go to the library, which became more frequent, and then about six months ago I asked her out. We just clicked. Things progressed quickly, and, well, we are getting married. You will like her."

No I will not! Jen thought. Weakly, Jen said, "You are getting married?"

"Yes." Tony then rushed on to say, "Jen, you have always been special to me, and you always will be, but I know that you are not ready to settle down, and when you do, you don't need someone whom you met as we did. I would always be a constant reminder of a horrible experience."

"I know, Tony. As much as I think we could have a good life together, I can't deal with a love relationship yet."

Tony seemed relieved. Jen felt that he truly loved Molly.

Mercifully, someone came over to talk to Tony. It gave Jen a chance to slip out and go to the restroom. Once there, she stood with her hands on the vanity and softly cried. She mumbled to herself, "I can't go through this again. What will I do? I am all alone." Realizing someone could come in, she quickly regained her composure. "Okay, get a hold of yourself. Tony was ready to marry; you are not. But be honest with your feelings." Jen put some water up to her eyes, dried them, and made sure they did not look red before she returned to the table.

"Tony, I really am happy for you, and with all of my heart hope that you and Molly will be happy. I also don't want to lose your friendship. There have been too many losses."

"Hey, you've got me for life—that's a promise." He squeezed her hand.

"Thanks. I needed that. Now, tell me about Molly other than she is a pretty redhead."

"Well, she grew up here in Atlanta. Her mom died when she was thirteen, and her father passed away a year ago. He was successful, but when Molly was twenty, her dad was hurt in an accident. His inability to work ate away at their savings, and Molly helped to support and take care of him until his death. Her half sister and half brother both live out-of-state. They were twenty and twenty-one when she was born. The three don't have much contact. They were Molly's mom's children. Molly is really a special person and is looking forward to meeting you."

"When is the wedding?"

"In one month, and we want you to be there." It was more of a statement than a question.

Though Jen was not sure of her calendar, she made a mental note to break any engagements on that day. It was important to Tony that she attend the wedding.

"I would not miss it for the world."

"Good. Now we have to get you and Molly together. When do you have some time?"

"What about tomorrow night? I will cook a special meal."

"Hey, that's an invitation I won't pass up. What time?"

"About seven thirty."

All of the rest of the day, Jen thought about Tony and what might have been. She searched her feelings to make sure she was not ready for a commitment, and then remembered her mother's words about how being replaced by another person makes us hurt. This introspection helped, and by the next day, Jen was truly looking forward to meeting Molly.

It did not take long for Jen to understand why Tony had fallen in love with this redhead. They seemed so suited to each other. His outgoing nature was offset by her quiet but confident demeanor. As Tony had predicted, Jen and Molly took an instant liking to each other. Before the wedding, the two women spent time together shopping and having lunch as a natural friendship began to grow.

When Molly walked down the isle, Jen saw a happiness and joy in Tony's face she had never seen before. As Jen watched them make their vows, she wondered if she would ever again feel the wild abandonment of happiness and the joy of true love.

Chapter 37

Beth Anne looked at the clock when she came into the kitchen. *I can't believe it—only seven thirty and it's already hot. These Texas August days are unbelievable.* After bathing, she ate breakfast alone. Tom always left for work about six or earlier, and the children were getting in one last visit with their grandmother in Atlanta. Just as she was finishing her coffee, there was a knock at the door.

"Beth Anne?"

Unlocking the door, she replied, "Hi, come on in." It was Joanie, her next-door neighbor. "Wow, you look happy."

"Oh, I had a talk with Jim last night," Joanie answered with a smile.

"Judging by your demeanor, I would say that things worked out very well."

Joanie and Jim were from West Virginia, where mining was a way of life. They grew up in a small town where couples married after high school and the men were expected to work in the mine. College was not the norm, but Jim felt differently. He wanted to get away and try for a better life. He and Joanie had been high school sweethearts, and had married right after graduation. They left for New York immediately, where he got a job in the mail room of a large corporation. Jim was ambitious and worked very hard. With time, he caught the eye of one of the executives, who took him under his wing. Through this person's help, Jim began his climb up the corporate ladder; he even finished his college degree. Lately, Joanie had worried that her husband was leaving her behind and that he found her boring compared to the women with whom he worked.

"I told Jim how I was concerned that I was not keeping up with him, and that I know this is dangerous in a marriage. I also suggested that even though I don't have too much time, I want to start to college as long as I could manage that and take care of the children. He was so sweet, and assured me that he could not ever imagine finding me boring, but thought college was a great idea! We discussed the fact that if anything happened to him, the children would not want to move. By continuing my education, we are ensuring the kids of a better life. Anyway, we are going to make this a family affair. Jim has promised to help with the children, and they are going to have to take some of the cleaning responsibilities—which will not hurt them. I am going out to the University of Houston this afternoon. Oh Beth Anne, please go with me. I have a meeting with one of the deans at three o'clock, but I need support."

"Sure I will go. That might be fun. Let me just call and see what time Tom is coming home."

Joanie watched her friend make the call. *Poor thing. Tom is never home before nine thirty, and I doubt he is working all of those hours,* She thought.

Beth Anne got off of the phone. With a dramatic, heavy Texas drawl, she was mimicking Tom's secretary, Carla Sue. "I'm sorry, Tom is in a meeting. He works very hard." I am so tired of that woman! Anytime I call I can't get through, and I swear, she is always so condescending. I will go, and if Tom gets home and there is no supper, he can just blame his sweet secretary!

The dean of students had been called to an emergency meeting and Beth Anne and Joanie had to wait until four fifteen to see him. At the last minute, Beth Anne had decided to take her transcripts. They did not get away from the campus until about five o'clock. Jim was out of town on a business trip, and when Beth Anne finally got through to Tom at work, he told her he had a meeting and would not be home until late, so the two women decided to go to an early movie to wait out the traffic and then to go for supper.

"I know where we should go. TGIF on Richmond is supposed to be a real swinging place. Have you been there?" Joanie asked.

"No, let's go. Sounds like fun. I could use some excitement in my life right now," Beth Anne answered a little wistfully.

While the two women were eating and visiting, Beth Anne realized that she was having a good time. For the past year, she had either eaten supper alone or with the kids because Tom claimed he was constantly in business meetings—even on the weekends. She shook her head just a little as if to ward off the worry that lay just beneath her consciousness at all times.

As the two women were leaving, Beth Anne glanced into another dining area and saw Tom, Carla Sue, Bo, Tom's partner, a woman she did not know, and two men. Instinctively, she and Joanie walked over. As Beth Anne approached, she noticed Carla Sue leaning in toward Tom in a very suggestive and intimate way. *Meeting my eye!* Beth Anne thought.

When they got to the table, Tom looked up, but did not say much. Carla Sue just shot Beth Anne a triumphant look. It was Bo who stood, introduced the women, and then got them chairs. Beth Anne was very polite to everyone. It did not take long, however, for Bo and Tom to turn to the other women and ignore Beth Anne and Joanie. Beth Anne turned her attention to the two men who had been introduced as Cliff Swenson and Jerry Potter. She talked to them at length about their business in Dallas, and the business they were doing with Bo and Tom. She could not help but notice that Jerry seemed to be hostile towards her, even though he tried to cover it, and that Cliff was a charmer, but did not seem to have a lot of substance. After about thirty minutes of talking with the clients and being ignored by Tom and Bo, Beth Anne and

Joanie excused themselves and left. Though Beth Anne had remained very cordial, she was fuming.

Neither woman spoke as they drove home. As Joanie pulled into the driveway, she turned to her neighbor and said, "When the realtor sold this house to you, she was so excited—told us about this elegant Atlanta debutante who would be living here. I will never forget Jim turning to me and saying, 'well, this is one neighbor who will not be interested in us.' When I saw you with your pageboy and simple but elegant clothes, I just figured that you would snub our family, as we don't exactly come from the same background. Your friendliness and kindness caught us off guard. I guess what I am trying to say is that you are a wonderful person.

Your full hair and the new clothes are pretty, but the simple elegance with which you always dressed before is outstanding and it is you. Don't get on Carla Sue's playing field. You don't need that."

"Thank you," Beth Anne said sincerely.

Beth Anne was almost sick. Seeing her husband with Carla Sue was more than she could handle. Finally, too tired to think about it anymore, she went to bed, but hardly slept. She heard Tom when he came in about two thirty. *Late meeting, sure!* She thought.

Tom had slept on the couch, which was something he did more and more often, claiming he did not want to awaken Beth Anne; of course, he was gone when she got up at six. After breakfast, Beth Anne's hurt began to turn to anger. *Who do they think they are? My dad would have never taken that, and no one would have ever just ignored him as I was last night. This is no marriage! It is a survival contest. And those clients. They were the sleaziest people I have yet to meet. Okay, now what?*

Beth Anne recalled a conversation she had had with her father shortly before he died. She wanted to know what his secret for business success had been. The business had been left to him by his father, who was killed in an accident when Beth Anne's dad was only twenty-two. Fearing that at such a young age he would lose the company, two of his uncles tried to buy him out, but he would have none of that. In answering Beth Ann's question, he said, "There were five things that I always followed: hard work, honesty, integrity, continuous planning, and following my hunches. There have been times when I had to wait to make money, but in the long run, it was these characteristics that made the company a success. It also ensured that I could look at myself in the mirror and like what I saw. There was one other thing that has always guided me and that was when something that has worked stops working, study to understand why, and then, if necessary, let it go." He also reminded her that in order to have integrity toward others, you must have it for yourself.

It was now time for Beth Anne to make her own plans. She thought for a long time about her marriage. In the last year, communication with Tom was nil. He was either sullen or gone all the time, claiming that he had to work, but last night had confirmed her fears—there was too much mixing of business with pleasure. His relationship with Carla Sue looked too cozy, and this was more than Beth Ann could bear. She decided to try one last time to get Tom home to talk with her. She called around and found a beach house they could get at Galveston for the weekend. Next Beth Anne phoned the office with the determination that she would get through to Tom. Oddly enough, it was he who answered.

"Hi, how would you like a getaway weekend to the beautiful shores of Galveston?" Beth Anne said, trying to keep things light.

"Please," Tom said with an annoyance, "I have to work. Don't you understand that's what it takes to get this business going?"

"Don't you understand that if you want to keep your family together, you need to be present sometimes?" Beth Anne tried not to sound hurt nor accusing, but matter-of-fact.

"Look, if you can't take this, that's your problem, not mine. I have to go." With that, Tom hung up.

Beth Anne was hurt and angry, but not surprised. She knew she had gone as far as she could with Tom. The marriage was spiraling out of control, and she had to look after the welfare of her children. Her dad always said that he played out his hunches because he believed that they were signs from God. Beth Anne decided to do the same. The two men, Jerry and Cliff, did not seem to be the type of men who would be heading a firm. They seemed sleazy, and she was going to find out what was going on.

At nine o'clock, which was ten o'clock Atlanta time, Beth Anne called Tony.

After they exchanged pleasantries, she said, "Tony, I know I am one of the last people you ever thought would call, but I need your help. Tom and his partner, Bo, have started a computer business here in Houston and they are doing well, but I am concerned. I won't pretend that everything is great; the crime has eaten away at my family, and, possibly, Tom's good sense. Last night I met two of his clients, and just don't have a good feeling about them; they just seemed seedy, as does his secretary, Carla Sue Blanton. Do you think you could find out something about these people and let me know?"

"I'll be glad to try. Give me any information you have about them."

Beth Anne told him all she knew. Luckily, the other night at the restaurant, Cliff had dropped a business card without realizing it. When no one was looking, Beth Anne had reached down and put it in her purse. By doing so, she was able to get their address.

"It probably won't take too long. Will a couple of days be okay? I will call you." Tony said.

"Sure, but I may not be here. Why don't I call you?"

"That's fine. Call around 10:00 a.m. your time."

Beth Anne was sure that she did not want to sit around waiting for this call. Besides, she really needed to think, and did not want to see Tom until she had made some decisions. Not wanting to call the office and talk with Carla Sue, Beth Anne left a note:

Decided to go to Galveston alone for a couple of days and spend some time at the beach. I am staying at the Galvez Hotel if you need to get in touch. B.A.

She then called to let Joanie know where she was going.

As she knew he wouldn't, Tom did not call her at the beach, but Beth Anne made the best of it, as she needed to get away and think. The salty air did her good and helped to clear her mind.

Precisely at 9:00 a.m., Beth Anne called Tony. She was not surprised at what he told her. After their talk, she left Galveston and thought about her plan all the way home.

"Joanie. Hi. Do you have some time to come over?"

"Sure. How was your trip?"

"Very good. It gave me a chance to think things through. I will tell you more when you get here," Beth Anne answered in an almost-excited voice.

"I just put a cake in the oven. Will thirty minutes be okay?"

"That's great. It will give me time to wash my hair."

"Wow, you look great!" Joanie said as she walked through the door.

Pleased with herself, Beth Anne answered, "Well, thanks to you, I realized that I need to be me, and that does not include the big hair. Anyway, I like my pageboy.

"But this isn't all there is. I need your help. Carla Sue does not know your voice; would you call Tom's office and pretend to be the secretary to a Mr. Clay Serraton of Miami, Florida? Tell them that he is in town just for today and wants to meet with Tom and Bo about buying software from them. Ask for a meeting to be set up for about two o'clock. I'll tell you why later."

Joanie was animated and thought this was all great. She called, and was very convincing. The meeting was set for two o'clock.

Beth Anne laughed. "Joanie, you scare me. You do this too well."

"I always aim to please," Joanie said, "but what is this all about?"

Beth Anne sat down and told her friend her plans.

Joanie looked very serious. "You know these are strong measures."

"I know that I can't go on like this." Beth Anne's voice was strong and emphatic. "Watching my husband with another woman was too much. Besides, I am going to protect my children's and my future."

Joanie looked at her watch. "Look, I have to go pick up the kids. Call me when you get home."

Beth Anne walked her to the door. "Thanks for your help."

⌢

As Beth Anne approached Tom's office suite, she felt very confident. With her linen navy suit, white blouse, and a simple but expensive gold pen, she looked both businesslike and very classy. When she walked through the door, Carla Sue noticed the change, and Beth Anne saw a quick look of fear cross her face; however, the look was so fast that most people would have missed it.

"Well, Beth Anne, what brings you here? Out shopping or having lunch?"

Beth Anne knew that the question was not one of interest, but one that was meant to remind her that she was just a housewife, as she had heard Carla Sue refer to her.

"Actually, I am here to meet with Tom and Bo, and you."

Carla Sue gave a little laugh which covered up an uneasy feeling that was unraveling within, and in a very condescending voice, she said, "Beth Anne, we are busy. Tom and Bo have a client coming in at two. It is a very important meeting."

The condescension made Beth Anne want to hit Carla Sue.

With a little smile, Beth Anne replied, "Yes, I know all about the meeting."

Bo was at his desk working. He had seen Beth Anne come in, but he was busy preparing for the meeting. Also, he was very embarrassed about the way they had acted in the restaurant and he wanted to avoid her. He finally decided he better go out and find out what was going on.

"Beth Anne, hi, it's good to see you," Bo said with his usual charming voice.

"Bo, can you please convince her that we are all busy getting ready for a meeting?" Carla Sue said.

"Do you need something?" Bo said in an almost condescending voice. Beth Anne stood motionless for a moment, and then she turned, faced Bo squarely, and with a drop-dead look, said in a low but very commanding voice, "I know about your meeting. Because I can never get through when I call here, I had my neighbor set up the two o'clock appointment. I guess you could say, it is *my* meeting with the three of you."

With a sneer in her voice, Carla Sue started to say, "How could you do this?"

Bo's demeanor almost became subservient. "I'm sorry you have had trouble getting through. That won't happen again. Do you want to meet in the conference room?"

"Please."

Carla Sue was getting very anxious. She saw how Bo had gone from charming to very businesslike in an almost subordinate way. *What is going on?* she thought.

About that time, Tom came in the door. He had been down the hall talking with someone.

"Beth, what are you doing here?" he said in an annoyed voice.

Quickly, and with a look of seriousness, Bo added, "The other meeting has been canceled, but Beth Anne wants to meet with the three of us."

"Is this something we can discuss at home?"

"No."

Beth Anne was now walking toward the conference room. Carla Sue was confused. Why was Bo acting as he was, and why did they both stand aside and let Beth Anne sit at the head of the table?

They all sat except for Beth Anne. She stood to address the group in a very confident and commanding manner. "I wanted to meet with you for several reasons. First, I apologize for having my neighbor to call and set up a fictitious meeting, but my calls never get past the front desk." She looked at Carla Sue as she said this. Carla Sue was still too confused to be bothered much by what was being said. She saw the look of concern on Bo and Tom's faces. *Why were they scared of this woman?* she wondered.

Beth Anne continued, "The urgent needs for this meeting are several. First, Carla Sue, do you know what a silent partner is?"

In a chirpy voice, the secretary answered, "Oh, I guess a partner who doesn't talk much." Her quick wit usually got her laughs, but not today. Bo and Tom just stared straight ahead with solemn looks on their faces.

Not acknowledging the attempt for humor, Beth Anne continued, "A silent partner is someone who invests in a business but has nothing to do with the running of it. Up to now, I have been just that. You see, I own 55 percent of the shares of stock."

Tom was watching his wife. He had never seen her so commanding. Where was she going with all of this?

Carla Sue's mouth was getting dry. She had misjudged Beth Anne. She had taken her politeness as weakness, but this was no dumb or weak woman standing before her.

Beth Anne looked from Carla Sue to Bo, and then to Tom. "Do any of you know who Carl Johnson and Jay Platter are?"

Tom could stand it no longer. He was not comfortable with his wife coming in and taking over. "Beth Anne, what is going on?"

Not deterred by Tom, Beth Anne continued. "Do you know who they are?"

She then looked at Carla Sue, who now felt miserable and scared. "Why don't you explain to Bo and Tom about Carl and Jay?"

Kind of laughing, Carla Sue tried to undo the momentum. "I have no idea who these people are."

Beth Anne continued. "I didn't like their looks and had a feeling there was more to this duo than met the eye, so I played out my hunch and had them checked out. Turning to the other woman, she said, "Should I finish or do you want to?"

Scared, but hoping that Beth Anne did not know the whole story, Carla Sue tried to sound tough. "Please, I don't know what you are talking about."

"That's interesting. Carl and Jay have both spent time in prison for swindling money and are now under investigation for selling pirated software. It seems they get into companies, make friends with the people who run them, and act as clients; however, what they really want is to get their hands on the company's computer programs, copy them, give them a different name and sell them cheaper. Carl is Carla Sue's brother-in-law, and Jay is their cousin. You know these men as Cliff Swenson and Jerry Potter."

The two obviously shocked men looked at each other and then accusingly at their secretary.

Trying to maintain her poise and calm, Carla Sue denied knowing about the men.

Beth Anne then continued. "This morning I called Tremor Curtis in Dallas. This is the company where Carla Sue worked before coming here. She was fired because she was caught giving their programs to Cliff and Jerry. Though the company fired her, they did not press charges. They did, however, contact the police, who closed in on the two men just as they were about to market the software. I talked to the lieutenant who had been in charge of the investigation and he said that all of these people had left the Dallas area.

Realizing she had to work fast, and being confident that she could beat Beth Anne at her game, Carla Sue began to defend herself. "Look, I admit that I made a mistake. I had gone to Las Vegas one weekend and lost a lot of money. Cliff had approached me about letting them see the software so that they could copy the program, but I had said no. It was only when I needed the money that I let them have a copy. I was sorry as soon as I did that and was going to quit, but as you said, I was fired first." She delivered this speech with the most doleful and sexy look at Tom and Bo that she could give.

She is good; I have to give her that, Beth Anne thought. She almost laughed out loud at the performance.

Beth Anne then said, "You mentioned feeling bad about giving the men the software and that you were going to quit. It was six months before the company caught up with you. When were you going to make your exit? In fact, unknown to you, they set up cameras in the offices and you were caught getting other programs and putting them in your purse. The security guard, who had been watching the camera monitors, came in and demanded you put the programs back. He told you he would not tell the company officials, but he went back on his word. If necessary, I can get hold of that tape."

"Look, I was trying to find a job. I didn't have a rich daddy to give me money," Carla Sue said accusingly.

There was a moment of silence. Bo and Tom were too stunned to say anything. Carla Sue still hoped to get out of this and keep her job.

Finally, Beth Anne said slowly, "When trust is broken, so is the effectiveness of the relationship." She looked at Tom and Carla Sue as she said this. "Sometimes it can be rebuilt, but in this case, there is no need. I want a person in your place who will connect me to the party I am calling and someone who does not have a checkered past. We will give you two weeks' severance pay, but no recommendation. Bo, I want you to escort Carla Sue to her desk and let her get her purse, and then see that she leaves the building."

"Bo, Tom, surely you are not going to let this woman come in here and just fire me. Okay, I made a mistake in the past, but I have been an excellent secretary."

"You also have lied. You did not tell us that you knew Cliff and Jerry, I mean Carl and Clay. If you were trying to get a new start, why did you let them in?" Tom asked.

Trying to sound innocent, as though she were a victim of the two men, Carla Sue answered, "Because they threatened to tell you about my past. Look, I need this job. Bo, come on. We grew up together and knew each other until our sophomore year in high school. Where is your loyalty? Do you really think I would try to cheat you?"

Looking down and then directly at Carla Sue, Bo answered, "Yes I do. Beth Anne is right. The trust is broken. Also, Tom and I need this business, and we can't afford for people to get hold of our software and pirate it."

"Bo, you have forgotten your past. You are just being loyal to these people because they are rich."

Bo stood and said, "It is time for you to go." The two left the room. Beth Anne just stood there for a moment. Tom had a miserable look on his face. "You could have told me this at home."

"No, I could not. Tom, I have tried all I know to keep this marriage together, but the other night at T.G.I. Friday's was too much. I don't have the ability to watch my husband go out with another woman."

"What are you saying?"

"That I give you the freedom you want. I am going to go back to school and make a place for myself and the children. If you want to be a part of that you may, but if not, you are free to go."

Tom looked at the floor for a while and then said, "I'm sorry things didn't work out between us."

With that, Beth Anne turned and left. She went straight to the university and registered.

It was only when she got home and saw that Tom had been there and had packed his clothes that she began to cry. "I still love him, but I can't go on like this."

Beth Anne walked over to the window in time to notice the man across the street returning home from work. She knew that Tom would never do that again. Their marriage was over.

Chapter 38

The next two years marked changes in the lives of the members of the Big Four .

Beth Anne and Tom divorced.

Smitty continued teaching, but his work ethic was nothing like it had been. His idea of conducting a class was to have students read from the book and then answer the questions at the end of the chapter. He would leave school, go home, and bury himself in a book. Karen was losing respect for Smitty, and wondered how much longer their marriage would last. Oddly enough, he and Kate had nothing to do with each other.

Kate worked hard in the family business. Her father, Fred, was surprised and happy to see that his only child would have the ability to run things when he retired. For her part, Kate was enjoying building her career and her reputation as a savvy businesswoman. This also helped her feel good about herself, and at times helped her to forget the dark secret she carried within herself.

Jen was deeply involved in Atlanta's society as she worked hard for literacy. Most of her time was spent chairing and co-chairing events. She also traveled to other cities in which she would attend parties, saw her new aunt in Colorado, and visited with Toady and Charles, who were now living in a retirement community in Florida. Jen had given up any hope of a continued friendship with Smitty and Kate. After losing her parents and friends, she found it hard to trust most other people, but her friendship with Tony and Molly continued to grow. She also met someone special.

New Beginnings

ᑐᑍ Chapter 39 ᑐᑍ

Four Years After the Trial

As the phone rang, Kate noticed that it was 7:30 p.m. "Hello."
"Hi there, this is a voice from your past."

"Tom DePau! How are you! Where are you?"

Tom laughed. "Which question do you want answered first?"

Laughing, Kate said, "Oh, it doesn't matter. You choose."

"Well, for starters, I am great, and I am in Atlanta. The Warden called. Dad is sick, and I came to check on him. Say, do you always work so late?"

"No, but the kids are with Ted this weekend."

With a little bit of a sigh in his voice, Tom answered, "Oh yes, I know about weekend parenting."

"Ted lost his rights for a while. It's a long story, but since he regained his privilege of having the children overnight, he has been careful. Also, my parents are out of town, so that just leaves me to run things here at the business."

"Kate, it sounds as if you have turned into quite a businesswoman."

"I am getting that reputation," Kate said with some pride in her voice.

"This seems odd, talking on the phone to you on a Friday night. It seems like I should be out on the football field and you cheering."

Kate sighed. "I know. Life sure changes."

"I am not going back to Texas for a couple of days, so what about dinner tomorrow night?"

"Oh, Tom, I would love that."

"I hate to ask you, but do you mind coming to Atlanta? I still can't bring myself to go to Upton."

"Sure. It would be fun to get away."

The two old friends made plans to meet at seven on Saturday night.

Fred always closed the business at noon on Saturdays. Just before closing time, Peggy dropped by the store. Peggy was a thirty-eight-year-old widow who had become a close friend of Kate's.

"Wow Kate, you look happy; you are even humming."

"Well, my singing may not be good, but I am happy."

"What's happening?"

"How about going across the street and getting a sandwich and I will tell you?"

As soon as the waitress took their order, Kate began. "Guess who called me last night."

"I give up. Who?"

"Tom."

"Tom DePau?" Peggy said in a surprised voice.

"Yes. He is in Atlanta and invited me to meet him for dinner tonight."

"Kate, that sounds like fun."

"It's not like I get to go out all the time. Anyway, when we finish, I am going over to the Smart Shop and buy a dress I have had my eye on. It will be my first new dress in two years. I think it's about time."

"Hear, hear," Peggy said as she raised her water glass in a mock toast.

That evening, Kate dressed carefully in her new dress. On her way to Atlanta, she felt carefree and happy for the first time in years.. When the Maitre d' asked her about seating, she told him she was meeting someone. Kate then stepped just inside the dining room and saw Tom at a table. In her blue dress which was accented by a strand of pearls and her almost shoulder-length blond hair, Kate looked more beautiful than Tom remembered. He stood as she started toward the table, and for a moment, time seemed to stand still as all eyes were on the beautiful couple; it was as though they were back in high school and the envy of all. Tom and Kate hugged briefly and then sat. At first they talked incessantly, as though there was not enough time to get everything said. However, after a while the conversation slowed. *This is normal*, Kate thought to herself. She tried to deny the backing away that she felt coming from Tom.

For twenty-four hours now, Kate had imagined Tom and herself finally getting together. Wouldn't it be romantic if after all of these years the two everyone had always imagined as being right for each other finally became a couple? In her dreams, Kate had seen Tom thinking about moving his business back to Atlanta. After all, he and Beth Anne were divorced, and he was a Georgian, not a Texan.

Kate decided that she had to know how Tom felt about living in Atlanta.

"Tom, do you ever think about moving back to Georgia?"

Tom looked at Kate. When he had lived in Upton, he had taken for granted his popularity. He had also enjoyed being known as a DePau, a member of an important family. In Houston, no one cared who he was, and he missed the prominence he had always known. It had been Tom's dream to once again experience this headiness, and for about twenty minutes after Kate arrived he did. But as the two talked, something happened. It became clear to him that Upton and all the good that came from it was in his past. The present held different experiences, but he realized that he liked his life and what he did. His place was now in Houston, not in Upton, and it was now up to him to build his own name, as had others who had lived before him. This understanding and mission gave him strength, purpose, and the ability to let go of his cherished childhood.

"No. I like Houston. My business is doing better than we ever expected. The children love it, and besides, I am getting married."

"Married!"

"Yep. Here, I have a picture of her. Her name is Debbie. She is only twenty-eight, but very nice, and will make a good stepmother." He handed Kate the picture.

"Do you know who she looks like?" Kate asked in a surprised voice.

"Who?"

"Jen. She has that same long, dark hair and green eyes."

"Now that you mention it she does."

Kate tried to rebound and make the best of the rest of the meal, but on her way back to Upton she could not help but cry a little as she mumbled, "Another dream busted." She hit the steering wheel in anger.

It was only nine forty-five when Kate got back to Upton. She was restless and needed to talk, so when she drove by Peggy's house and saw the lights on, she decided to stop.

Peggy opened the door. "Kate, hi, come on in."

"I'm not intruding on anything am I?"

"No, I have just been sitting here reading a book. Come on in. How was you dinner?"

Sinking down on the sofa, Kate answered, "Oh, Peggy. When did things stop working out?"

"What are you talking about?"

"I know you are going to think this sounds silly, but after Tom called, I began to think about how wonderful it would be if we could get together and eventually get married. It was sort of like—I have worked hard at learning the business and growing as a person, and now—"

Peggy interjected, "And now Tom was going to come and rescue you and take you away to the never never land of happiness?"

"Well, not quite that dramatic, but something like that. What's wrong with my wanting to find someone and get married? I liked being part of a couple."

"Did you?" Peggy remembered hearing rumors of Ted running around. She always wondered if Kate had known about any of this.

"At first it was wonderful. I'm sure there are men out there who would love to be in a good marriage; of course, they just never come my way. I just want to be happy again."

"I understand about your wanting to remarry—so do I, but we can't just wait around for something to make us happy and then life will begin. That's like high school."

"What do you mean?"

"Well, think about it. When you were in school, you lived from event to event: the Friday night games, the dances, the breaks, the dates. Those were the things that made us happy. What I'm trying to say is that we learned to look for a particular experience to bring joy."

"I don't understand."

"Okay, being a cheerleader brought you happiness, then it was becoming the homecoming queen and all your other honors. Next it was off to college, your wedding, your children, the Upton celebrations. Now that you don't have a particular event to look forward to, you don't know how to be happy."

"Well how do you?"

"You make it yourself?"

"How?"

"By living as much as you can—finding joy in what you do and doing things that bring you joy."

"Living. I do that. Each day I get up, go to work, work hard, come home, parent my children, go to bed. Some joyful life!"

"Maybe it could be better with a different attitude."

Kate was getting angry. "What do you mean?"

"Look Kate, I don't want to hurt your feelings, but when I have been with you, Sara Katherine, and Anna Kate, I get the distinct feeling that your mom is the real mother and that you are sort of the big sister."

"I'm doing the best I can," Kate replied defensively.

"I know. But think about this: If your daughter or son ends up divorced, what are they learning from you? To be a good worker for sure, but what else?"

"Wow, I really feel attacked."

"I'm sorry. I really didn't mean to come down on you so; it's just been on my mind. What you are going through happens to us all."

Somewhat disgusted, Kate got up. "I have to go. This has been a long night."

"Please don't leave angry. Just think about what I have said. You know me well enough to know I would never purposely say something to hurt your feelings."

Kate knew that. Peggy was one of the nicest people she had ever known, and that fact kept her from barking back with some choice words.

"I will think about this."

Kate went home, put on her robe, fixed a cup of tea and sat up much of the night mulling over the things her friend had said. Though she had not admitted it at the time, Peggy's comments were the very things that had been on Kate's mind for several months. She just was not sure where to begin making changes.

The opportunity for this would come soon enough.

Chapter 40

Karen watched Smitty and Dick grill the hamburgers. It was a Friday night in late July. Patty, Smitty's sister who was six years his junior, and Dick had come over to eat. This was a frequent occurrence. Karen was grateful that soon after the trial, the couple had moved back to Upton. Patty was a nurse, and Dick had bought out John's CPA firm. They were hard working and fun to be with. Their company was the only thing that seemed to have a positive effect on the morose personality Smitty had displayed in the five years since Dr. and Mrs. Saxton had been killed.

Karen sighed as she thought about the upcoming school year. It would be Smitty's fourth year of teaching, and he was not trying to do anything but get by. Students complained about his boring classes, and parents were beginning to get upset. Karen was not only frustrated with this, but she was also embarrassed by his lack of work ethic and knew that the only thing that kept him from getting fired was that Mr. Sneed, who had been their principal, believed that one day Smitty would come out of this stupor. But Karen could tell that even Mr. Sneed was becoming weary from waiting.

Patty interrupted her thoughts. "Here, let me take the potato chips out. I will get the children." Karen took ice out to the already-set table. She sort of forgot her concerns about Smitty as everyone ate with gusto.

About ten o'clock, the couples retired to the living room to watch the news.

"Let's see the beginning of the news and then we had better go. I go on duty at six thirty in the morning," Patty said.

Dick chimed in, "Yeah, and I have to go into the office. I have a ton of work to do."

"I have to be in Atlanta at nine for a conference," Karen interjected.

Karen noticed that Smitty seemed relaxed until the news anchor announced, "Tonight we have a special segment. We are interviewing Jen Saxton. Ms. Saxton's parents were killed by Thomas DePau from the once-very-influential DePau family. She will discuss living as a victim of crime. We will bring this special to you right after the commercial."

Karen watched Smitty. For a moment he just stared at the screen with a pale and troubled look. Then he jumped up.

"Where are you going? Don't you want to see Jen?" Patty asked.

"Sure. I am just going to check on the dog. I will be right back." But he did not return for about fifteen minutes. Karen knew that he had timed this to safely miss the interview. For reasons which she could not guess, Smitty would have nothing to do with his old friend.

"Did I miss the interview? I could not find the dog and got worried," Smitty asked, trying to sound nonchalant.

"Yeah. She was great," Karen answered.

Obviously trying to change the subject, Smitty said, "Well, I am sorry. By the way, Dick, when are we going to get some fishing in?" The two men talked about a fishing expedition, and then the couple left. After they walked out the door, Smitty snapped, "I am going to bed!"

Early in the morning, Karen was awakened by noise. *What's going on?* she thought. It was Smitty. He had tossed and turned all night, and now he was talking in his sleep. Karen froze as she realized what he was saying.

"I'm sorry Dr. Saxton. It is my fault that you were killed. I really didn't mean for that to happen. I'm so sorry. I wish it had been me." He then stopped talking, settled down, and fell into a relaxed sleep.

This talk disturbed Karen. She looked at the clock and saw it was five thirty. Quietly getting out of bed, Karen went into the kitchen and fixed a cup of coffee. Though usually calm, she was almost losing it. "Calm down," she said to herself. "You need to sit and think this through." Willing herself to be composed, Karen sat at the table, and by trying to understand what was happening, she allowed herself to think thoughts she had repressed for a long time. *Ever since Smitty and I started dating, we had made it a point to be together when there was a problem, yet he insisted that I not return when Dr. and Mrs. Saxton were killed, and when I did, he had changed. At first I just thought it was the sorrow of losing someone so close. Then there was the moment after the trial. I will never forget walking down the courthouse steps with a strong feeling that this was not over. What did Smitty mean when he said it was all his fault? Okay, I have known for several years there was something terribly wrong. Now it is up to me to find out what happened.*

Karen checked on Smitty. She could tell by his breathing that he was sound asleep, and that he had no idea of the confession he had made. She then went into the kitchen and made a call.

"Hello," came a sleepy voice.

"Julie," Karen whispered. "I'm sorry to call so early, but I must talk to you. I'm coming to Atlanta today. Can you see me?"

By this time Julie was wide awake. It was not typical of Karen to call at this hour of the day, and Julie sensed that her old college roommate was in trouble.

"Of course. Do you want me to come to Upton?"

"No. I will come to your place."

"When will you be here?"

"Well, it's six fifteen now. Probably around eight. Is that too early?"

"Of course not. Are you okay?"

"I've been better. I must go. See you around eight."

Karen quickly dressed. She did not want to awaken Smitty or the children. They were expecting her to be gone, so her absence would not arouse any suspicion. Karen decided to go by Dick's office to see if he was in. Thank goodness he was. Maybe he knew something or could give her some information. She had to know what was going on.

Karen knocked on the door. "Hi, what brings you here this early? Did we leave something at the house?"

"No. I need to talk with you."

"Sure. Come on in." Dick noticed a frightened look on Karen's face. "Here, sit down. Can I get you some coffee?"

"I would love some coffee. Dick, I must tell you something, but you have to promise me you won't say anything to anyone. Not even to Patty."

"Sounds serious. Is it about Smitty?"

"Will you not say anything?"

"Of course not."

Karen then told him about her feelings after the trial, the way Smitty had acted in the last few years, and then what he had said in his sleep just a few hours earlier.

She had hoped that maybe Dick would say something that would calm her down and give her some hope that she was blowing things out of proportion. That didn't happen.

For a long moment, Dick said nothing. He just cupped his hands over his mouth and stared into space. Karen's heart was beating wildly. She knew the news was not going to be good. Finally her brother-in-law spoke up.

"I wish I could give you some support—tell you that your suspicions are unfounded—but I can't. The day Dr. and Mrs. Saxton were killed, I was in Atlanta for a meeting. As soon as I heard the news, I left to come here immediately. I knew that you were out of town, and I felt that Smitty might need family around him. As I drove past the church I saw his car, so I stopped and went in. Smitty was kneeling at the altar and crying. He kept saying over and over, 'I'm so sorry; it's all my fault.'"

Karen thought her heart would stop beating. "Did he see you?"

"No. And I never said anything because I figured that he just felt guilty for some reason. You know he and Dr. Saxton had had a huge disagreement concerning the selling of the drug store."

"Yeah, but I am sure Dr. Saxton did not hold it against him. Smitty wanted him to sell the drugstore. He felt it would be a good thing for everyone. It would have also meant money for us because Smitty would have handled the legal end."

"I knew all about that," Dick said. "Anyway, I just sort of forgot it. Chalked it up to grief. I have to admit that it has bothered me a bit that he seemed not to have anything to do with Jen. And then last night. I don't know Karen, but something seems to be very wrong. What are you going to do next?"

"Julie, my ex-roommate, is expecting me about eight this morning. She has worked with a lot of criminals in her counseling practice. I'm hoping she will guide me."

"Do you want me to drive you to Atlanta?"

"No. I need to be alone to think. Besides, driving relaxes me. Just don't say anything. I can't believe that we are seriously thinking that Smitty had something to do with the Saxtons' deaths."

Dick closed his eyes tightly for a moment and then said, "It's almost too horrible to think about. I have to ask this: are the kids safe?"

"Yes. I am sure of that."

With a very heavy heart, Karen left for Atlanta.

Chapter 42

The high-rise in which Julie lived was evidence of both her success and the good fortune she had of being from a wealthy family. The inside, which never had anything out of place, was decorated in neutrals from white to a pale peach. It was elegant, and a testimony that no children lived there. Yet, as different as their lives and backgrounds were, Julie had always been the best friend Karen had ever had. Julie was a wonderful and kind person.

With one knock at the door, Julie was there. "Karen, come on in."

The two friends hugged. "Are you okay?" Julie asked, with obvious concern.

"Let's just say it's been a long morning." Karen answered in a matter-of-fact voice.

"Come on and sit down. I will pour us some coffee. I figured you had not eaten anything, so I fixed some cheese straws and fruit."

Karen smiled. She had never heard of these wonderful cheese delectables until she went off to college and Julie's mother sent them some. Out of fear of losing her scholarships, Karen could rarely eat anything during exams except for the cheese straws and fruit, so Julie's mom kept them in strong supply. This morning, upset as she was, Karen found the food a welcome treat.

After giving her a minute to get something into her stomach, Julie began to question her friend. "What's going on? Is it Smitty?"

Without hesitation, Karen answered. "Yes." She then told Julie about the early morning confession and what Dick had told her.

Julie, who thought she had heard everything, was not prepared for this. She thought maybe that the couple had decided to divorce or separate, but never had she expected that Karen was coming to her with a belief that her husband had been involved in the deaths of Dr. and Mrs. Saxton. Julie knew that she had to be very careful about what she said. She wanted to get the facts, but did not want to alarm her friend unnecessarily.

"I must admit that you have caught me off guard with this."

"I'm sure I have."

"Do you believe that Smitty is guilty of this crime?"

Karen looked at her friend. Julie had a way of asking questions that got right to the point; this was what made her good in her work and in demand. "I would love to think that he has snapped and is confessing for some reason; however, reality is that in the five years since the Saxtons' deaths, Smitty has changed. He went from someone with an impeccable work ethic to an individual who just gets by. This was once a fun person, but is now sullen and angry. And forget our sex life. It has almost become something little more than a memory. I also understand that though he made confessions, at neither time did he realize that anyone heard him. Secret admissions are sometimes different from those made to the police. I have known for a long time something is wrong; I just didn't know what. As horrible as it sounds, what I heard this morning makes the most sense."

"What do you want to do now?"

"I'm not sure. I know I could never harbor someone who has committed such a heinous crime. What would you do?"

With an understanding that her answers had to be right, Julie stopped and thought for a long minute. "Before I made a decision about what must have happened, I would first gather as many facts as possible. Tony Antone, the detective who broke this case, is someone I know well, both socially and professionally. Let me call him and see what information he can give us."

Karen agreed with this course of action.

Julie picked up the phone and dialed. "Molly, how are you?"

"Hi Julie. I am fine."

"Listen, I really need to talk to Tony, is he there?"

"You caught him just as he was walking out the door."

When Tony answered the phone, Julie explained to him about Karen's concern. "Could you possibly see us today?"

"Sure. I'm leaving for the office now. Can you meet me there?"

Julie gave a thumbs up to Karen and said, "We are on our way."

The office was only about fifteen minutes from Julie's condominium. When they arrived Tony was already there and waiting. One look at Karen told him that they needed to bypass any social interactions and get right to the point.

Karen told Tony everything she could think of that might shed some light on what had happened. When she finished, Tony spoke up.

"I know that it took a lot of guts for you to come here and that you must be suffering. However, I always warn clients, when necessary, about steps they are considering taking. I have talked with Thomas DePau several times, and will tell you that he is a very smart man who only cares about himself. He is also very aware of how to use the legal system. If anyone other than Scot Reed, who pulled the trigger, had been involved, you better believe Thomas would have had the presence of mind to work out a deal with the DA to implicate the others. However, it could be that the old boy has some love in him. What I am trying to say is that if Smitty is involved, probably the only thing that has kept Thomas from talking is that his son, Tom, is also guilty. Understand that if you are right, you will probably tear apart at least one other family."

Karen didn't hesitate. "I would hate to destroy anyone, but if these two were involved in murder, they don't deserve to live as free people."

Tony then answered, "One thing is on our side. Scot Reed is dying of kidney failure. I understand that he has found religion and is trying to clear his conscience. He had surgery yesterday, so Monday will be the earliest I can talk with him. It will probably take two days. He is really sick. Plan to meet me here on Wednesday morning, unless I let you know differently. There is one more thing; Smitty may be close to breaking, and you might not be safe with him. I would encourage you to get the children and leave for several days."

Almost defensively, Karen stated, "I don't feel that we are in any danger."

Tony hesitated before answering. Many times he had seen women like Karen, who could never imagine their husbands would harm them, end up either dead or hurt. Carefully he said, "I have a saying: 'Desperate people are dangerous people.' Trust me on this, and find somewhere to go."

Julie spoke up, "Karen, I was planning to go to our lake house for a few days. Call your mom and have her pick up the kids and meet us there."

"Yeah. I am sure you had planned to take a few days off to be with three children," Karen answered with an almost sarcastic tone.

"Look, this is no time to play heroine. Besides, I enjoy your family. There would be lots to do that would keep you busy, and your mother always enjoys the lake."

When the two got back to Julie's, Karen called Smitty and then her mother.

"Smitty, I ran into Julie at the conference today. It was not a very good meeting, so we left and got some coffee. Anyway, she wants me to get the children and go to the lake with her for several days. If you don't object to the trip, I am going to call mom and see if she wants to join us, and if so, she can come and get the kids."

"Sure. This is sort of sudden isn't it?" Smitty asked accusingly.

"Yeah. But it seemed like a fun thing to do."

"Fine. When is your mom coming?"

"I don't know. I will call her and one of us will call you right back."

"Okay."

After Karen hung up, she looked at Julie and said, "I have never lied to my husband before. This is horrible."

Karen then put in a call to her mother. "Mom, I am in Atlanta and ran into Julie. She wants you, the kids, and me to come to their lake house for a few days. Is there a possibility that you could pick up the kids and get some clothes for me and meet us there?"

A sixth sense told Helen there was more to this invitation. She had been worried about Karen, and did not hesitate to help out. With an enthusiastic voice, Helen said, "Of course, hon. That sounds like fun."

Wednesday morning finally arrived. In one sense, it seemed to Karen that time had passed very quickly as she had waited to hear from Tony, and on the other hand, it had seemed to drag.

Karen was so nervous that even driving back to Atlanta was too much, so Julie took the wheel. As they drove along, Karen put her head back and began to talk about the past.

"I've known Smitty all of my life, but I will never forget one Friday afternoon when I was in the seventh grade. My dad came in and said we were all going to the football game at the high school. Said that Paul Jarvis' son was playing and that everyone was talking about that even though he was only in the ninth grade, he was one of the best. Many of the people from Mill Town decided that they needed to support Smitty by going to the game.

"Julie, this was a night that changed my life. It was the fourth quarter with two minutes to go, and we were behind one point. The opposing team was on their own thirtieth yard line with a first down. Their quarterback reached back and passed. Before his intended receiver could touch the ball, Smitty jumped up, intercepted the pass, and ran seventy yards for a touchdown. The crowd went wild. Those of us from Mill Town experienced a special pride; he was one of us—the first to star at the school. Listening to the cheers was intoxicating. At that moment I knew that this young boy had shown everyone that people from Mill Town could be successful, that we, too, had what it took. It was like a shot in the arm to me. I had never really cared about school, but I started working hard, making good grades, and getting involved in activities by joining the school choir. In my eighth-grade year, the choir director asked me to sing in the girl's quartet. Of course, I was the only one from Mill Town, and I was proud of my accomplishment. But at the end of the year, she took us to Atlanta for a day of fun. I just wore what I wore to school, but the other three girls had new Villager dresses. They were the 'in' thing. It was obvious that they had gotten new outfits for the occasion. I felt so embarrassed and dowdy looking. When I came home, Mother was anxious to hear about the day, but I just went straight to my room. I knew we could not afford to go out and buy new clothes. I just told her I didn't feel good. She finally got the truth out of me, and vowed to help. One of the new managers of the Mill was young. His wife was real sweet, and dressed beautifully in clothes she made. Mom cleaned for them some when the Mill would close.

"Anyway, his wife agreed to help me learn to sew in exchange for my babysitting for them. That's how I started making all of my clothes. I was never again embarrassed about how I looked, and always fit in. Julie, I know all of this sounds like I am rambling on, but what I am trying to say is that knowing Smitty helped me to do more than I ever dreamed. Whether it was academics or sports, he was the best and our hero, and now I am on my way to find out if this star is also a murderer." Too overwhelmed to talk, much less think, Karen put her head back, and did not speak again until they reached Tony's office.

Chapter 43

Tony ushered Karen and Julie into his small conference room.

He wasted no time with small talk. "First, the good news. I talked with Scott Reed who assured me that Smitty knew nothing of the plan to kill the Saxtons. Said that if anyone knew, it would have been from pillow talk, so to speak. Seems that Thomas had a thing for young women. So you can take comfort in that your husband is not a murderer. However, Reed's confession was not enough, so I did some investigating and came up with some information that you need to know. Do you remember Dayton Thomas III? He is an inmate at the prison here in Atlanta, and is waiting in my office—got permission to bring him here."

Before she could say anything, Tony was gone.

Julie turned to her friend and said, "Do you know Dayton?"

"Yes. He was in Smitty's study group in law school. He's from a very wealthy, old family from Savannah—very smart, but spoiled. Daddy pulled him out of all the messes he created for himself. After graduation, Dayton decided to stay in Atlanta and work. Smitty was working with him when Dr. Saxton was killed."

"Karen."

"Dayton. How are you?"

Trying to make light of a bad situation, he answered, "Well, enjoying some moments of freedom."

"What happened?"

Dayton walked over to the window and looked out. "It's a long story and one I am not proud of. You always told me that I needed to become more responsible and focused. Well, I am afraid that it has taken me all this time and a few years in prison for that very good advice to sink in. But enough about me; you want to know about your husband."

Karen's mind was spinning. *What could this man know about my problems?* Dayton continued. "Remember, at the Law Review picnic, I talked with Smitty about a potential client. I needed someone with his negotiating skills and he said ya'll needed the money a large case like that could bring. So we agreed to work together as a team. We met with the company. These people liked what we offered them and paid us a big retainer."

Breaking in, Karen said, "I recall all of this, but what does this have to do with the present situation?"

"If you will remember, Smitty would come up early every Thursday and we would work all day Thursday, Friday, and Saturday. The third week we worked our usual Thursday through Saturday afternoon. Man, I was dying—never worked so hard in my life—and finally persuaded Smitty to take a break. You know that husband of yours. He was skeptical about stopping for too long since the job was nowhere near being finished. I talked him into going out to a nice restaurant to eat. Afterwards, I told him I had to stop by this warehouse to meet with a client. This was a lie. The truth was that this was a gambling joint and I wanted to gamble—my usual Saturday night activity. I sat down and played a hand. Tried to get Smitty to play. He said no. Finally, I told him to just a play a hand or two and I would leave and we could get back to work. At first Smitty was totally against it—said that gambling was illegal.

Finally, he agreed to play one hand. He won a lot of money, so he played another hand and won more. Smitty kept playing and kept winning. But before the night was over he had lost all his money. Anyway, we ended up being two gambling addicts. Smitty was obsessive about trying to win back all he had lost. Every week we would promise ourselves that we would play just a few hands and then get down to preparing our case. The work never happened. Even though we had been paid a large retainer, we were not taking care of our client. When their case went to court, we were obviously unprepared and lost. The company that hired us wrote to the bar and complained. One Friday afternoon when you and the kids were out of town, Smitty came to Atlanta. He had received a letter from the state bar association revoking his license for five years for accepting a retainer and not doing the work. I had also just received my letter. We were both distressed, Smitty more so than me. Anyway, to soothe our feelings, we went over and began some heavy drinking and gambling. There was a fight, and someone called the police. The cops arrested everyone, and we spent the night in jail. Tom, Smitty's friend from Upton, came and bailed him out about ten the next morning. For that stunt, the bar added an extra two years for the suspension of our license.

"After he got home, Smitty called and told me about the doctor and his wife. The business of our licenses being suspended, being arrested, and then finding out that his friends had been killed were almost too much for him. The reality of how far he had strayed from his own code of ethics had set in. I was really concerned that Smitty might try to commit suicide."

Karen could hardly take in what she was hearing. "You mean to tell me that Smitty had his license to practice law suspended because he didn't work on a case, started gambling, was involved in a fight, and thrown into jail!" This was too much. She continued in complete bewilderment, "When was Smitty going to tell me all of this?"

"Don't be too hard on him. He was horrified when he realized all he had done—kept saying that if you knew, you would leave him. Smitty really loves you, Karen. The old boy just felt so bad about losing everything he had worked so hard to get. He was a mess."

Karen looked at Julie. "I don't understand. Help me here. I have a husband who was making secret confessions to being involved in a murder, so I came to find out what really happened. Now I am being told that he was not involved in the Saxton's death, but that, in reality, he had his law license suspended. When was he going to tell me? I don't understand this. What is really going on?"

Julie held up her hands slightly. "I think I understand. We all know that it is not unusual for someone to confess to a crime he or she didn't commit."

"I realize that. But why would a person do such a thing, especially someone as smart as Smitty?" Karen asked.

"Look at what was going on in his life—for some inexplicable reason, he had completely gone against a strong work ethic, lost all he had worked so hard for, ended up in jail, and then found out a man and woman whom he considered a second set of parents had been brutally murdered. The guilt and shame were too much. He needed to be punished—didn't live up to the expectations. The Saxtons would have lost all of their respect for him when they learned of his indiscretions. In his mind, he did kill a part of his relationship with them, so the guilt just took over."

Dayton asked, "This doesn't make sense. I mean I know he didn't kill Dr. Saxton. We were in jail. If I know he didn't have anything to do with their murders, how could a smart guy like that think he could? You would know if you killed someone."

Julie answered. "It's complicated. We are learning more about this type of behavior. Most of us believe that it has a physical connection to the person. My experience with clients who suffer from this type of problem is that they get into stressful situations that, I believe, cause a chemical imbalance. They start obsessing and lose the ability to reason."

Dayton could not believe this explanation. "No. Smitty is too smart for this."

Julie continued. "Not necessarily. First of all, some smart people are very inclined to get into this kind of thinking because their minds work in ways that someone of average intelligence would never think of. Also, the rational Smitty would know what he had and had not done. But when a person gets into this thought pattern, he loses the ability to trust his instincts. This is not as unusual as you may think. People just don't have a tendency to talk about it."

Looking at her college friend, Julie continued. "Karen, what was going on in your lives at that time? Anything unusual?"

Taking a deep breath, Karen began. "Smitty had been practicing law for eight years. We had three children by then and made very little money. I didn't realize there was a problem because we had more than we had ever had. However, he did confess to me later that he had been embarrassed when we had gone to the Law Review picnic. It bothered him that we had so little to show for our work while the others were obviously making a lot of money. I just didn't comprehend that it troubled him so much. It had been our dream to return to Upton and work for those from Mill Town. However, as I think back, I remember Smitty was getting discouraged. People thought nothing of calling us at all hours of the day and night asking for help, but when Smitty would try to charge them, they would get angry. It was as if we owed them. What they didn't realize is that we had to pay our bills and college loans. Though we had had scholarships, we had still had to borrow money for our education."

"Were you in debt?"

"Yes, but who isn't? I guess to me it didn't seem like a big deal."

Julie broke in. "Okay. Look at the situation. Smitty had gone through school the star. He returns to his hometown not only as a hero, but as the one everybody could look to for help. He got stuck. Not only could Smitty not take care of all of the problems of Mill Town; he could not even provide, as he wanted, for his family. I suspect he was frustrated, angry, and probably a little scared, but Smitty always had to be the star. He couldn't admit such human feelings. Without realizing it, his world started spinning out of control. He got the opportunity to make some money, but slipped into gambling, got arrested, his friends were killed, and then his license was suspended. All of this was proof that he must be a horrible person."

Karen interjected. "But how could this make him believe that he was responsible for the deaths of the Saxtons?"

He couldn't live up to others' expectations, so he saw himself as not being good. I suspect guilt overwhelmed him and the obsessive thinking kicked in. It's hard to understand. People can become so frustrated and confused that they can believe they have done something horrible. Truth and fantasy become entangled, and a person in this state does not have the ability to discern which is which. I have seen it happen more than once. Why do you think people make false confessions to the police? This is not as unusual as you might think."

"You mean that for five years, my husband may have really thought that he actually had something to do with the Saxton's murders, and he didn't?"

"That is right."

"But Julie, why couldn't he tell me?"

"I don't know, but I would guess that ego played a big part, and, of course, I suspect he was extremely scared. Smitty knows what happens to convicted murderers. He has probably lived in fear of being taken to jail."

For a moment, Karen put her hands up to her mouth and just sat quietly. Softly at first, she said to Julie, "I can't imagine what he has felt like these last five years, believing that he was part of a murder and that he could be incarcerated. No wonder his teaching has barely met the standards. How else could he have lived?"

"I have had several clients who experienced this, but one patient stands out in my mind. She said that concentrating on anything else but the concern of what you have possibly done is virtually impossible."

"I'm trying to understand, but it disturbs me that Smitty could not tell me about having his law license revoked. Yet, I feel so badly for what he has gone through. Oh, Julie, this is so hard."

"Karen, I have known you and Smitty for a long time. Though I understand the dishonesty hurts, go easy on him. With all that was going on, there is no way that he could possibly have been thinking clearly."

"But I am his wife."

"I realize that. Would people have expected him to play football as well as he did if he had had a broken leg?"

"I get the picture."

When Karen and Julie got to Karen's car, Julie spoke up. "Karen, I have an idea. Why don't you take me to my condo, and I will get my car and drive back to the lake house? That will give you a chance to go on to Upton and talk with Smitty while there are no children around."

"Thanks. I'll do that."

Julie was concerned about Karen. "Are you feeling better?"

"Well, I am terribly relieved that Smitty was not involved in the Saxtons' deaths, but I am very hurt he could not be honest with me. The truth is, our marriage is in a lot of trouble."

Julie reached over and patted her friend's arm. "You will work it out. I know you two."

Karen did not say anything, but thought to herself, *I hope it's not too late for us.*

Chapter 44

Smitty did not hear Karen drive in or unlock the door. When she stepped into the living room where he was reading a book, he was surprised.

"Oh, hi," he said. "I didn't hear you come in. What are you doing home? I thought you were coming tomorrow."

Karen looked at Smitty. He looked as though he had not shaved, and it was obvious that he had not cleaned any of the house. *He was probably going to do that today,* she thought.

Before she could say anything, Smitty spoke up. "Sorry about the mess or how I look. I just got involved in my books. Thought I would have today to straighten up."

"Don't worry. Smitty, we have to talk."

A weariness quickly fell over Smitty as he noticed the seriousness in his wife's face.

Karen had thought this through all the way home. She quickly got into the counselor mode so as to keep the emotions at bay and to not sound judgmental or accusing. "Do you think that you had something to do with the murders of Dr. and Mrs. Saxton?"

His response was extremely intense and emotional. With a look of total fear and desperation, Smitty responded, "Why do you ask that?"

Smitty was now standing, and very agitated. Karen felt a little frightened as she remembered Tony's remark: "Desperate people are dangerous people." Suddenly she wished that she had asked Julie to come with her.

Making herself appear calm, and taking a deep breath, Karen answered his question. Speaking very softly and soothingly, she began. "Hon, early Saturday morning I awakened and you were saying, 'Dr. Saxton, I am very sorry. It was all my fault.'"

"Oh my gosh. I said that?" Smitty was suddenly pacing the room like an agitated caged animal. "Did you go to the police?" He asked with a voice full of anxiety and fear.

Realizing that she had to calm him down quickly, Karen responded, "Smitty, you did not have anything to do with the murders of the Saxtons."

"You don't know that. How would you know? You don't know everything that I do." He was almost screaming.

"That is true, and that is the reason why I went to Tony Antone, the detective who broke the case."

Stunned, Smitty stopped pacing, faced Karen and softly, in an almost defeated tone said, "You went to Tony? What did he say?"

"I had to, Smitty. I had to know what was going on." Karen then told him everything Tony had found out about the murder. She did not mention the law license at this time.

"But, I felt so guilty. Karen, those people had always been wonderful to me, and I loved them like my own family, but I was so mad when Dr. Saxton would not sell the drug store. We could have made money, and I really thought it would be a good thing for the town. Of course, it turns out that the owners of this chain do not service the community like they said they would."

Smitty looked down at the floor for a minute, then faced Karen. She saw a strength begin to return to him. "There is more. I started gambling."

"Smitty, I talked to Dayton today."

"You did what? He is in jail."

"I know, but Tony managed to get him out long enough to take him to his office and meet with Julie and me. When he told us about your losing your law license and the gambling, Julie was able to understand what had happened."

Looking almost scared, Smitty asked, "Are you so angry that I did not tell you about the law thing that you are going to leave me? I know how you feel about honesty."

After a pause, Karen answered. "I thought about it, but then I realized that I promised for better or worse. This time I will stay, but we have to get help. I must understand why you couldn't tell me the truth."

Sounding very relieved and remorseful Smitty responded, "I truly am sorry I deceived you and will do anything to make it up to you."

Karen assured Smitty that she loved him and would also do anything to make the marriage work.

Sensing he could leave the subject, Smitty turned to the Saxtons. "It feels like I must have had something to do with the murders. How can I feel so guilty but not be?"

She then explained how it is not as unusual as he might expect for a person to become obsessed with a sense of false guilt. "Look, I have never worked with this sort of thing, but Julie has. Julie's at the lake house by now, but told me that she would stay in tonight, so if you wanted to call her, I think she could better explain what possibly happened to your thinking."

Karen dialed her old roommate's number and gave the phone to Smitty.

"Julie."

"Hi Smitty; How are you doing?"

"I feel better than I have in a long time, but still don't understand how I could feel so guilty about something I had nothing to do with. Karen said you could help me."

"We don't understand everything about this illness, and it is an illness, but there is a school of thought that believes this type of thinking happens as a result of an inward chemical reaction that occurs to some outward stimulus such as extreme stress. I even believe it often happens in people with body changes such as in young people when they reach puberty. Can you tell me what was going on in your life at the time of your arrest?"

"Well, I *had* already gone through puberty."

Julie laughed, and was glad to see that Smitty's humor was returning. It meant that he was thinking rationally.

Smitty continued, "I believe that sitting in jail overnight was the worst experience of my life. Julie, I don't know what happened to me. I have always believed that gambling is not only wrong, but a very stupid thing to do with your money and time, yet once I started, I couldn't stop."

"What else was going on in your life?"

"I had always been successful in everything I did, but things changed, and nothing worked. My law practice was becoming a nightmare."

"Why?"

"I couldn't make any money. This didn't bother Karen because we did have more than we ever had, but I wanted to move beyond struggling. Even with scholarships, we both still had student loans to pay off."

"Why do you think you couldn't move ahead?"

"The people from Mill Town were my main clients. In some cases they were not able to pay the going rate, but in many instances, they believed I should work for little or nothing or for free. I would get phone calls all hours of the night and be expected to go to the jail or wherever and get these people out of trouble. All of this was really getting to me. When we went to the Law Review reunion, I felt so embarrassed and hopeless. My classmates had something to show for their success. Here Karen and I were in our old station wagon. It was horrible. I felt so angry and frustrated, which I now realize made me feel totally hopeless.

For some reason when I got a chance at a big case, I gambled it away. I will never understand this."

Based on some of my studies and patients' experiences, I do have some thoughts that might help to begin explaining what went wrong. There were several things going on at the time that could make you go into this type of thinking. I remember when we were all in school; you and Karen would talk about helping these people who had meant so much to you. However, somewhere you confused the concept of help with that of saving these individuals. Smitty, you were their hero—their hope—and they also saw you as their savior. You were in an impossible situation which led to the feeling of hopelessness. The gambling became an outlet because it anesthetized your mind, and for a moment you could forget the reality that all of the plans you had made for your life were falling apart. Also, there was the excitement that maybe through the next hand you would win a lot of money. However, the arrest, the loss of your law license, and the death of the Saxtons proved too much. You, the hero, could not even save this couple who had meant so much to you. The guilt was probably made worse by the fact that when they were killed, you were in jail for something you did not even believe in doing. I suspect that you thought if only you had been there, you could have saved their lives."

Softly, Smitty said, "I was supposed to have had a meeting with Doc the morning they left for Atlanta."

"And you would not have found them. After I got back to my place, I called Tony to ask a few questions. According to what he told me, the Saxtons were killed about 4:00 a.m. and put in the car. The killer then drove the car out of town and pushed it over the embankment. He had planted an explosive to make sure the car burned. So there was nothing you could have done."

"Julie, you don't understand. Soon before dad died, he reminded me of how good the Saxtons had been to the family and that I should always do what I could for them."

"He did not mean for you to give your life for them. Smitty, it is a blessing that you were not around. The man who killed this couple would have shown you no mercy. My gosh, you are a husband and a father. There is a limit to what you can do."

"I hadn't thought of that."

Look, this sort of illness is not as uncommon as you may think. Unfortunately, people often become so frightened of their feelings they just suffer in silence. I would advise you start getting help soon. My suspicion is that you have some chemical reaction that happens with stress, and it would help you to learn how to deal with this. It's not that hard. Also, you must understand that this is not the result of weakness or stupidity. I suspect a lot of this has to do with your belief and desire to help others have better lives, which is probably your calling. However, you will have to learn the difference between being a helper and a savior—a hero."

After he got off the phone, Smitty looked at his wife, and with a partial smile on his face, he said, "You cannot imagine how free I now feel. I have been so scared. I could just imagine the police coming to the door and arresting me. It all seemed so real."

"Karen, I am so sorry for what I have done to the family. Please don't let it be too late for us."

Softly, she answered, "I love you, and am committed to our marriage. There is nothing that I want any more than to get our lives back to normal, but we do have to find out where the trust broke down."

Smitty agreed to do what it took. The couple immediately sought counseling for their marriage and for Smitty's stress. They both had to learn to let Smitty be real. Yes, he had been a hero in school, and had set an example and given hope to others from Mill Town, but he came to understand that he was still a mere mortal, and that because of this, he would never to be able to be anyone's savior.

The marriage and family life returned to normal, as the two were very committed and worked hard to make their union work. In many ways it became better than it had been as they learned better communication techniques.

After some therapy, Smitty felt more confident, so he called Jen and set up a lunch meeting. When they got together, he explained what had happened to him and how he had felt too scared and guilty to be around her. Fortunately, Jen knew of someone who had a similar disorder, and immediately understood. The two old friends renewed their friendship, and Smitty and Karen again became very much a part of her life.

With the understanding of what really happened, Smitty felt a freedom he had not known for a long time. His teaching career took off. In the next couple of years he won many teaching awards. With time, he got back his law license, but that was just for his own self-satisfaction. The education bug had bitten him, as he realized that it was in this arena where he could do the most good.

Two years after he and Karen talked, he started working on his Ph.D. When the principal retired the next year, he became the principal of Upton High School. However, Smitty had no idea how his and Karen's passion for education would change Upton and the surrounding towns.

Chapter 45

As Treavor and Jen were leaving the bank, she heard someone call out. Jen turned and saw Mrs. Tripper Stone waving.

"Mrs. Stone. How are you? I would like you to meet my fiancé, Treavor Gaylor."

"How do you do, young man? Are you from around here?"

"No. Actually, I am from New Mexico."

Jen smiled to herself. At about seventy-two, Mrs. Stone was one of the richest women in Atlanta. She was from old money, but with her straw hat and old cotton skirt, you would never know she had a penny to her name. Actually, at parties and when she felt the need to dress, Tripper was a very attractive woman, but that was only when she believed that getting herself up was necessary. She once told a columnist that everyone knew she had money, and that she shouldn't have to dress to prove it. This woman was a character, and very smart. The three stood and exchanged pleasantries for a few minutes.

After they left the bank, Treavor went back to his meeting.

Jen was driving home, but felt restless. *Hum, one o'clock,* she thought to herself. *I'm just a couple of blocks from Molly and Tony's. I never drop in on people, but I am so close, and would really love to talk with Molly.*

Who could that be? Molly wondered to herself as she answered the doorbell.

"Jen! It's great to see you. Come on in."

The two old friends hugged. Jen then offered, "Molly, I'm sorry to just drop by, but I was only two blocks away. It's been so long, but if I am catching you at a bad time, don't hesitate to say so."

She is always so polite about not wanting to intrude. "No, you are not interrupting anything except housecleaning. Trust me, this is no intrusion—it is a welcome break. Besides, the children are taking their naps, so we can visit."

The two friends sat in the living room.

"Jen, it is just so great to see you. We haven't talked to you in about three months. What's going on?"

"Oh, I have been busy. Actually, I met someone."

Molly was delighted. "Great. Tell me all about him. I want details."

"Well, he is nice looking; about my age. He is an international investment banker and real estate dealer."

"Where did you meet him? Here in Atlanta?"

"No, actually he is from New Mexico. I was there for a gala for literacy when I met him. We have actually gotten to know each other on the phone more than in person. With his business, he has little time. We talk for hours. I hate to say what my phone bill is. Anyway, Treavor had to come here on business. Came in yesterday, but had to work today. We did go to dinner and a movie last night."

Molly observed Jen's countenance. She seemed happy, but reserved.

With some concern in her voice, Molly asked, "Are you in love with him?"

Sighing slightly, Jen answered, "It's not that great Hollywood love. I really like him, and I know that I am tired of being alone. It's not the same as it was with Mike."

"Is Mike the guy you dated in college?" Molly asked.

"Yeah, he was killed in Vietnam. Our relationship seemed to easily fall in place. There was always a joy and excitement. This isn't the same. Maybe it was because Mike and I were so young. Anyway, Treavor, his

name is Treavor Gaylor, is anxious for us to get married, but I'm—
I'm just not so sure. For one thing, we have not spent too much time
together. Treavor thinks we know each other well enough from our
phone conversations and that I am just afraid to take a risk. I guess I feel
just a little confused. Maybe I'm expecting too much at my age."

"Jen, I have a great idea. Why don't the two of you come over for
dinner tonight? That will give him a chance to meet some of your friends
here in Atlanta, and for you to see him in a different situation. Perhaps
that will help you sort out your feelings."

"I would like that. Molly, it's so confusing. I don't want to miss out
on an opportunity to marry. At thirty-seven, my time may be running
out, but I don't want to make a mistake. He would like to marry within
the next two months. I just don't know. Treavor says he is not going to
wait forever."

Molly did not like the fact that he was rushing Jen, but she did not
want to say too much before meeting him.

Jen left Molly's at two, did some shopping, and got home about four.
She had not been home long when the phone rang.

"Hi." It was Trevor.

Jen was glad to hear his voice. "Hi. How was your meeting?"

"Things are going my way, so I am happy. I'm just taking a break, but
we should be finished here soon. You feel like a good meal tonight?"

"Actually, a friend of mine invited us over to eat. Both she and her
husband, Tony, are close friends of mine."

Treavor sounded disappointed. "Honey, I wanted to spend time
with you."

"But Traevor, every time we have made plans to be with my friends,
you have had business come up. I want people I am close to to meet
you."

Trevor realized that this was important to Jen and that she was not
going to back down, so he decided that he might as well go along.

"Okay," he said sweetly. "Oh, by the way, is Tony the detective you told me about—the tall, dark, and handsome one?"

"Yep." Jen answered sweetly. " But he is just a friend. I promise."

"Okay. If you promise," Treavor laughed.

About six thirty Jen's phone rang. "Hon, I'm still at my meeting. Why don't you give me directions to Tony's and I will meet you at their house? That way we won't both be late."

Though she tried not to show it, Jen felt bothered by this turn of events. "What time will you be there?"

"Maybe at seven or a little after. I'm trying to wrap this up. Just thought it would be quicker if I could go straight from here."

Jen relented. "That's true. Okay. I'll see you there."

At six forty-five, Jen left for Tony's. The anticipation of dinner with her friends almost made her forget that nagging feeling that something was wrong.

As it happened, Treavor arrived only about five minutes after Jen.

When Jen introduced her friend to Tony and Molly, she observed Treavor's demeanor. She noticed that he was more subdued than usual. When asked about his work, Treavor said very little, and changed the subject. *Maybe he is cautious about what he says, or maybe he feels a little shy. After all, these are not people he has known for more than thirty minutes,* Jen reasoned to herself. *He seems friendly enough. I need to stop judging him and have a good time.*

Molly had gone in to check on the children. When she was coming down the hall, she could see that Tony and Jen were headed to the kitchen to get some food to take outside, where they were going to eat. Treavor was trailing behind, checking his watch. Molly was concerned that he was not feeling like he was a part of the group, so she went out of her way to make sure he was not being left out of the conversation. However, when she noticed him checking the time again, she became annoyed. *I realize that this entertainment must seem very humble compared to what you are used to, but we are nice people, and this is good food. If you can't be happy here, I really don't believe Jen is the person for you,* she thought.

The couples were in the middle of the meal when the phone rang. Tony went to answer it. He came back. "Treavor, it's for you. There is a phone in the den, so you can have some privacy."

"Well, I'm glad it's for Treavor and not you." Molly said as she looked at Tony. Explaining to the others, she continued, "We almost have to have a rule here not to answer the phone during meals. Tony gets so many calls."

Treavor returned. Jen noticed that he looked more relaxed than before. *It must be good news,* she thought.

"Folks, this is great, but I am afraid that we are having some business problems, and I am going to have to fly out to England tonight."

"Can't you wait until tomorrow?" Jen asked.

"I wish I could, but my office has a ticket for me on tonight's flight. That way I will have a little time tomorrow with our people there and the next day I will have the whole day to work with our clients. I really am sorry. This is just one of the headaches of international business."

"You mean you are leaving now? We have not even finished our meal. Can't you at least catch a later flight?" Jen asked in a shocked tone of voice.

"I'm so sorry. Wish I could stay, but I've gotta run."

Almost before Jen could say goodbye, he was out of the door and in his car.

After Treavor left, Jen was feeling upset and confused. "Would you be offended if I didn't stay long? I need to be alone."

Molly spoke up. "Of course not. I'm sorry Treavor had to leave so early."

"Yeah, me too," Tony said.

After Jen left, Molly and Tony cleaned up the dishes and then sat outside for a while.

"What did you think of Mr. Gaylor?" Molly asked in a rather sarcastic tone.

"Not too much. I don't think he is all he says he is."

"Tony, do you want Jen to find someone?"

"Of course, why wouldn't I? Wait a minute. You don't think I have something going with her do you?" Tony asked, his voice rising a little.

"No. But I know that the two of you liked each other very much."

"Yes, we did. Molly, I liked Jen. Meeting her told me that I could open up to a woman again. However, there have been two women I have loved—Susan and you. If Jen and I had been in love, we would have gotten together. She's our friend—that's all."

Molly smiled and squeezed Tony's hand. "I guess I needed to hear that."

"Okay. Why didn't you like him?" she continued.

"I think he's a fake. I'd bet money that phone call was a setup. He didn't seem to want to be here. How convenient that Jen was in her own car. He didn't have to take her home. I have questioned so many people that I have a second sense when they are trying to hide something. I want to go and visit with Jen tomorrow and talk with her. Would that be okay with you?" he said thoughtfully.

"Sure. If it helps, I didn't like him either."

This surprised Tony. Molly always found good in people. This strong admission added to his mistrust of Treavor. "Why?"

"Twice I noticed him looking at his watch. It made me feel that we were boring and he just wanted to get away. I'm like you—that phone call was planned. It got him out of here. I think, though, that you need to wait and let Jen call you about this. She may not be ready to face the truth."

"Okay. Point well taken. I hope she calls soon; this man is bad news. The big question is, who is Treavor Gaylor?"

Chapter 46

When Jen arrived at home, she was feeling very confused, so she fixed a cup of coffee, turned the lights down low, sat on the sofa and tried to talk out her confusion to herself. "What is the problem? Treavor is a nice person with a good job, and we have a good time together. What do I want? And why did it bother me so much that he was called away on business? That happens all the time." After a while, too tired to think, Jen crawled into bed with a book. At 7:00 a.m. the next morning, she awakened with the book on top of her and the lights still on.

"I must have been out of it," she said to herself as she got out of bed. After breakfast, she fixed another cup of coffee and went out on the patio to think. "I must make a decision about Treavor. Maybe I will call Tony and Molly to see what they thought of him. Why is this so hard?"

She then jumped up and said to herself, "Oh my gosh. I almost forgot my meeting with my new accountant. It's at nine thirty. I need to hurry."

The meeting with Elizabeth Grimes, the Financial Advisor who was taking Richard's place, did not take too long. Though Jen liked Elizabeth, who seemed personable and knowledgeable, she sort of missed Richard. Underneath that slicked-down hair, horn-rim glasses, and stiff-as-a-board demeanor, Richard seemed to be a very nice person, but he had left to start his own business. Though she had offered to take her business with him, Richard felt that it would not be ethical to take such an important client from the company that, in his words, "had been so good to him."

After leaving the firm of Wilson, Stevens and Wilcox, Jen decided to go shopping and then to a movie. She knew that she was just escaping, but she was not ready to think about Treavor. By the time she arrived back at home, it was five o'clock. The phone was ringing when she walked in the door.

"Miss Saxton?"

"Yes."

"My name is Clarice Gibson. We have not met, but we both attended that gala for literacy in New Mexico about three months ago."

"Yes, Mrs. Gibson. I have heard that you have done so much for the literacy foundation." Jen had seen Mrs. Gibson from a distance on the night she had met Treavor. He had pointed Clarice out. Supposedly she was one of the wealthiest women in that part of the country.

"Miss Saxton—"

"Please, call me Jen."

"Jen, I did not call you to talk about literacy. Last night I received a call from a very good friend of mine here in Atlanta, Tripper Stone. We go way back. We were roommates at Stevens."

"Oh yes, I ran into her yesterday at the bank."

"That is the reason why I am calling. She said that you introduced her to your fiancé, Treavor Gaylor, is that correct?"

"Why, yes it is. Is there a problem?" Jen's heart was beating very fast. She instinctively knew something was wrong.

"I'm afraid so. Tripper said that Mr. Gaylor mentioned that he is an investment banker."

"That's right."

"Jen, Treavor Gaylor does some modeling and odd jobs here in Santa Fe. He also works for an escort service. You see, I am not like you young folks of today. I was taught that a lady always has a male escort when she goes out at night. Anyway, I hired him to go with me to parties. He made a very nice companion, and I could depend on him, or so I thought. The reason Treavor was in Atlanta was because I was there at the medical center having some tests made. I needed someone to help me get to and from the doctor's each day and he agreed to accompany me. While I was having my tests, and at night, Treavor was free to do as he pleased. It so happened that Tripper was joining me last night for dinner. When she arrived, she saw me in the distance talking to Treavor. He did not see her. Tripper asked me about him, and told me that he was passing himself off to you as a very successful professional. I'm sorry to tell you this, but I feel you deserve to know the truth."

Feeling embarrassed and mortified, Jen said, "Oh, Mrs. Gibson. I really appreciate your telling me this. I feel like such a nut!"

"Jen, don't worry; life is too short. By the way, I may be getting old, but I do have a sense of humor. I decided to give Mr. Gaylor a taste of his own medicine. I told him this morning that I needed to go to New York to do some shopping and asked him to go ahead and make arrangements at the hotel. He readily agreed. I got him a ticket. He just assumed that when I got to the Big Apple I would get our return tickets. She then laughed. After he left Atlanta early this morning, I came on back to New Mexico. Let's just let Mr. Gaylor figure out how to get back home."

"Mrs. Gibson, you didn't," Jen said, laughing.

"I did. It makes me angry that he escorted me to parties and took advantage of someone. Let him stew in New York—have a taste of his own medicine. Oh, if he hasn't gotten back in a few days, I will send some money. Anyway, Jen, Tripper says that you are a very nice person and that your parents were lovely people. She was horrified when this happened. You deserve much better."

"Thank you Mrs. Gibson," Jen sighed.

After she hung up, Jen had a good cry. However, she also admitted that she had always had a feeling that something about the relationship was not right, and knowing the truth about Treavor gave her a peace.

She called Molly and Tony. Tony laughed heartily at what Mrs. Gibson did to Treavor.

"Couldn't have happened to a better person," he said.

After Jen hung up, she thought, *well, that's the end of Treavor, and probably my last chance for marriage.*

❧ *Chapter 47* ❧

Kate sat at her desk and reread the note that had arrived that morning:

Hi, just wanted to say I enjoyed seeing you in Atlanta. I broke my engagement. Decided that I am not ready for that commitment again. My business is doing great, and I am making new friends. Wish we could all be together—Tom

It had been a year since their dinner in Atlanta. *Did this note mean anything? Was there a special reason Tom wanted her to know he had broken his engagement? Was he looking for a certain type of response?* Kate wondered.

"Wait a minute," Kate said to herself. "Stop the dreaming. It was obvious that any possibility of a relationship with Tom was not going to happen, and the truth is, I just wanted someone to pull me out of my misery."

Kate walked over to the window of her office. She looked down on the streets of Upton and began to think. *This place has changed. I used to feel loved here; life was a victorious and a fun experience. That all changed. Will I ever be happy again?*

All of our lives were torn apart, but somehow the others seem to have moved beyond the loss. Tom has his business, the kids can't stop talking about what a great teacher Smitty has become, Jen's name is in the paper

constantly with all of her traveling and charity events, and Ted never seems to want for a good time. Unlike the others, I am stuck with just getting by. It's as though my joy is in the past. As a child, teenager, and young adult, I won elections and honors with ease, but now—nothing. Why?

And then it was as though the light began to shine as Kate continued mentally psychoanalyzing her life. *Wait a minute. Do I believe I only have a right to happiness if I win it? Life is not an election; it is a free gift. The others took their present and built on it where they were, even though none of them liked their circumstances. What am I doing, waiting for a contest to take place to see if it is okay for me to move on? If that doesn't happen, am I looking to be rescued, as though that is the only way to find happiness? I may not be much or deserve any better than I have, but my children warrant the best.* In that moment Kate resolved that she would move forward so that Anna Kate and Todd would learn how to survive in the face of loss, and so that they too could know a childhood of joy and happiness. She knew what she had to do first.

Kate told Annice, the administrative assistant, "If anyone is looking for me, tell them I will be gone for a little while." With that, she left and went to Carl Hastens's office.

"Kate, what brings you here? Come on in," Carl said in his friendly, salesmanlike voice.

"Well, I wanted to talk to you."

"Sure, come on back into my office."

When they were both seated, Kate began. "Carl, I noticed that the old Anderson place is up for sale. That has always been my favorite house in Upton. I believe that if it were fixed up, it could be a beauty. Would you mind telling me the price, and, if it is in my range, showing it to me?"

Carl was pleased at Kate's attraction to the old place. "Actually, it is only going for $22,000."

"Why so little?"

Carl leaned back in his chair as he easily answered Kate's questions. "In small towns, people are still looking for the smaller, ranch-style houses. However, in the cities, these old post-Victorian homes have caught on, and I think it is just a matter of time before that happens here. To be honest, though, that place is going to need a lot of work. Do you want to go over and look at it?"

"If you have time," Kate said in an excited tone of voice.

As the two got up to leave, Kate turned and said, "Listen, no one— meaning my family—knows that I am looking for a house. So if you don't mind—"

Before she could finish, Carl interjected. "I understand. Mum is the word. I'll tell you what; why don't you go ahead, and I will meet you there."

"Okay."

The Anderson house had been owned by a couple. When they died, they left it to a nephew who was basically a recluse. He had lived there as long as Kate could remember. After his death last year, it took a while for any relatives to be found. His only living kin turned out to be a cousin who was now living in England. He inherited the house, but put it on the market as soon as he could.

As they walked up to the house, Kate saw that she loved the porch and the gingerbread features, and when they walked in, she was still impressed. It was a typical house built at the beginning of the century with a hall down the middle and large, high-ceilinged rooms on either side. She noticed, however, that though this place was old and obviously in need of work, it had beautiful heart-of-pine floors. Kate had learned enough in the construction business to see that there also didn't seem to be any obvious structural problems. She commented on this to Carl.

"Yeah. I noticed that too. I think that Mr. Anderson was sort of a jack-of-all-trades type of guy, and knew how to fix things properly."

"What about the plumbing?"

"I have checked this out as well as possible. Everything seems to be working, but you will need to get this examined by a professional. Kate, let me be honest with you. I understand that you are probably anxious to get your own place, but take your time. You don't want to get stuck with something that is no good. On the other hand, if this place is in good shape, you would have a very nice house if you are willing to put the time in to fix it up." The two talked for a minute, and then decided to go have a cup of coffee.

Carl told her about the other houses on the market, but it was only the Anderson house that interested Kate. Then Carl said, "I hate to bring this up, but sometimes it is hard for a woman alone to get a loan. Have you checked this out?"

"This should be no problem. Oddly enough, about a year before Ted and I divorced, I opened my own account with the bank and borrowed eight hundred dollars. I paid it back regularly, was never late with a bill, and have gotten other loans from them."

"Were you looking to divorce Ted at the time?"

"Not that I realized, but something just seemed to push me to get my own credit rating. Was that a smart move or not?"

"Think about the house, but I am going to tell you that a couple from Atlanta has expressed an interest in this place. They are coming here Saturday; that gives you a three-day jump on them."

"Why are they interested in a place in Upton?"

"They are in their late forties and are looking for a house in a small town. They can get it paid off before retirement. Also, this would be somewhere they could come on weekends until they move here permanently. They seem to be tired of the city."

That night after supper, when the kids were in their rooms doing homework, Kate asked her parents if they could talk.

As the three sat around the kitchen table, Kate started. "Mom, dad; I am so appreciative for all you have done for me since Ted and I divorced."

Reaching over and patting her hand, Sara Katherine said, "Dear, it has been a joy to have you three here."

"Well, it has meant a lot to the children and me, but now I feel it's time for us to get our own house and start rebuilding our family."

Sara Katherine looked surprised and a little hurt. Fred replied in a loud, disgusted voice, "Get a house; rebuild your family. That's crazy. You have a place right here."

Calmly Kate continued. "No, dad; it's not crazy. For a while I needed the haven of my childhood home. I was hurt, in shock, and hoping that Ted and I would get back together. This is never going to happen, and now that I feel better about everything, it is time to get on with my life."

"Look, Kate," Fred continued in an excited, mildly angry voice, "houses are expensive. You need to hold on to the money you got from the sale of yours. You don't know what could happen in the future."

Sara Katherine interjected, "Dear, do you have a particular house in mind?"

Fred looked at her as though she were a traitor, but before he could say anything, Kate replied, "The old Anderson place."

"Kate, that house has been empty for over a year, and no telling how long it's been since anything was fixed there. It is probably so run down," Fred said angrily.

"I met Carl Hastens there today. He took me through the place. Actually, it looks to be in pretty good shape."

"How much are they asking for it?" Sara Katherine asked.

"Twenty-two thousand."

"Why so low? Probably knows it's in bad shape," Fred snorted. "Anyway, you and the children don't need to move. Your mother is here when the kids come home from school, and you are safe here. How are you going to take care of yourself over there? What would you do if someone broke in?"

"Jen has lived alone all these years, and she seems to do well, as do thousands upon thousands of other single women."

"Well, that's different. This is out of the question," Fred stated as though the discussion were closed.

Understanding where both her daughter and husband were coming from and wanting to defuse a big argument that she knew was brewing, Sara Katherine said, "Kate, I would like to see the place." Then she laughed a little. "I have always been curious about how it looks on the inside. So have you. Even as a small child, you loved that place."

Kate smiled at her mother, then turned to Fred. "Dad, I am sorry you don't understand. I don't want to make a mistake by overlooking something important. Would you just go over and give me an honest opinion about what you think of it?"

"No. You don't need to move. I'm going to bed." Fred abruptly got up and left the room.

Kate looked at her mom, who whispered, "Don't worry dear. I will talk to your father and we will all go have a look tomorrow. I hate to see you move, but I understand. Women generally want and need their own homes."

Fred was clearly unhappy when Sara Katherine walked into the bedroom. "I cannot believe you didn't support me out there. Listen; Kate needs to hold on to the money she got from her half of the house; she doesn't know what is going to happen in the future; she might need that money."

Sara Katherine sat down in a chair and began to calmly speak to her husband. "Honey, do you remember when we had to move in with your mother after our house burned?"

"Of course. How could I forget?"

"Well, do you also remember how happy you were when we had saved enough money to get a place of our own?"

"That is different!"

"Why?"

"Because a man is supposed to provide for his family—that is what we do."

"What about me? I was ecstatic."

"Sara Katherine!" Fred retorted impatiently. "Couples want their own places to live. That is normal."

"Dear, adults, especially women, want their own homes. Just because Kate is now single does not mean that she has become a child. She is a young woman with two children. The desire to have a house in which to raise her family is normal." With more force in her voice, Sara Katherine proceeded, "Now, what is the real problem here?"

Fred sat down on the edge of the bed. He knew he was defeated. Wearily, he answered, "It's just hard for me to understand the world today: women being left with children to raise; men, and women too, out there doing who knows what. It just makes me mad that Ted left her in this situation. Kate should have a husband to take care of her. What if she bought that house and someone broke in? What would she do? It's not safe for them to live alone!"

"Most parents want to see their children happily married, and Ted, in a way, broke all of our hearts. But sometimes I think that maybe he did Kate a favor by leaving."

"Why?" Fred shot back.

"I don't know. Perhaps it's a mother's intuition. Anyway, do you want to keep punishing Kate for Ted's actions? Do you want to stop her from living her life to the fullest just because of what could happen?"

"No, of course not. I just wish things had turned out differently for her."

"So do I, but this is the way it is, and we have to deal with truth, not fantasy."

Fred looked at his wife and smiled. "I always know when I am going to be defeated. You just have a way of saying things so that I eventually understand. Thanks."

The next morning Kate was fixing breakfast when Fred came in.

"Kate, I am sorry about last night. Why don't you call Carl and see if we can go over and look at the house sometime this morning."

Kate smiled at her father and then walked over and hugged him. "Thanks, Dad."

About 10:30 a.m. Carl met Kate at the house. Fred and Sara Katherine arrived about five minutes later.

As Fred walked up onto the porch, he was surprised that he saw no rotted wood and that the steps did not squeak. They seemed strong.

While her husband went off to inspect the wiring, pipes, etc., Sara Katherine walked around looking at the architecture. Behind the faded and peeling wallpaper, she imagined a home that once held large, lavish parties for the young elite of the county. Kate, who had been with her father, walked up.

"What do you think, mom?"

"Oh, I believe this place could be made back into a beautiful home. My goodness, they must have miles of molding around the ceiling. It is so beautiful. And this hall. I love the wainscoting and the beautiful chair rail."

I love it too. I also like these big rooms. It would give the kids a place to call their own."

As the two women were talking, Fred appeared.

With a slight smile on his face, he said, "In spite of last night's conversation, at which time I will admit I overreacted a bit, I have to say that this place is in good shape."

"You really think so, Dad?"

"Yes, I do. Old Mr. Anderson took good care of it. Well, he seems to have kept the basics well—can't say much for his sense of style." Fred gestured around. "But that can be easily remedied."

Kate then asked, "What about the roof?"

I don't like climbing up in high places any more, but I called Jim Skaines to check it for us. He is up there now. He is one of the best in the business, but it should be okay. We put one on here about 6 years ago, and there is no sign of roof leakage. Kate, I hate to see you move, but I do understand why you want your own place. If this were fixed up,

I believe you could probably have one of the nicest houses in this town. If I were your age, I would grab it."

"You really feel that way?"

"Absolutely."

Carl walked in and called Kate over for a minute. As she stepped away, Sara Katherine turned to her husband.

"You have really changed your tune. What happened? Was it just our talk?"

"I thought about this house after I went to bed. I remembered that several of the older homes—the Thomas' home, the Goldstein home, the Crawford place and this one—were built by a builder who lived in these parts for several years. He went on to build some of the best homes in Atlanta. Had a fine reputation. I was afraid that old Mr. Anderson had just let it run down, and that Kate was jumping ahead of herself. I'll tell you what, Sara Katherine, that daughter of ours has learned a lot more about the construction business than I ever realized. She knew this place was in good condition. Listen, I have an appointment with some salesmen, so I have to get back to the office. Get Kate to take you home." Fred kissed his wife goodbye.

Kate told her mother, "Carl wanted to tell me that he had another appointment. I told him I was interested, but before I made a total commitment I wanted to bring the children over after school. He gave me a key so we could come in this afternoon. Oh, I almost forgot, last night I made sketches of how I thought the rooms could look. Want to see them?"

The two women discussed the sketches and talked about how they could bring these rooms back to life with their sewing skills.

Kate spent the next hour at the bank filling out papers. Later that day, she picked up the children at school and took them to get some ice cream.

"Wow, this is a treat," Anna Kate said.

"I wanted to talk to you two. It is time we got a home of our own. Todd, you are almost ready to start high school and Anna Kate, you will be there before you know it. You need a place where you can bring your friends, play your music, and not worry about keeping your grandparents up."

"Where are we moving?" Todd spoke up.

"There is a house I want you to see, but first look at these sketches. How would you like rooms that looked like these pictures?" She showed them her drawings.

"Cool." Todd said in a matter-of-fact voice.

"Wow. When can we move?" Anna Kate responded enthusiastically.

"Well, first things first. I want you to see the house. I have not bought it yet, but am very seriously considering it. Before we go, I must warn you that it does not look good now, but we will fix it up. This is how the outside would look."

Kate showed them all of the sketches and told them that they would paint the outside and fix up the bedrooms before they moved in.

"Mom, let's just go look at it." Todd said impatiently.

Kate was sort of nervous. She wanted the kids to like the house, but also knew it would be hard for them to truly envision how pretty it could be. When they got there, both of the children said in unison. "Oh, no way!"

"Guys, come on now. Just get out and look. Remember the pictures I showed you. It will be a great-looking place. We will fix up the outside before moving in."

"It looks haunted," Anna Kate shot back.

Todd started acting silly and making ghost sounds.

"Stop it," his sister said as she hit him.

Kate continued selling the idea to the kids. "First, we will have to get the yard cleaned. This is going to be a family affair. But I want you to see how big the rooms are.

The group moved into the house. "Anna Kate, this could be your room, and yours would be over there, Todd. Look at these pictures I drew, and try to envision how they would look."

The children liked the idea of the large rooms, and Kate's sketches helped.

Trying to keep up their improving moods, Kate then said, "Come look at the back yard. See, there is a nice fence. You have wanted a dog; we could put a doggie door here in the kitchen, and then the dog could go in and out as he pleased.

"You mean we could get a dog if we moved here?" Todd was obviously excited, but was trying to sound calm and cool.

"Absolutely." Kate said enthusiastically. "Even a large one. In fact, Grand Daddy would be pleased about that. He is kind of worried about us living here alone, and having a watchdog would help his feelings."

"This place is getting better all the time," Todd said.

Anna Kate had gone outside. "Mom, come out here. What is this?"

Because the bushes that had grown up around it, Kate had never seen the little one-room house with French doors. Some of the glass was broken.

Kate was overjoyed. "Oh my goodness. This is what they called a party room. They were popular years ago. Then, getting more excited, Kate began, "Oh, this is great. We could fix this up so you could bring your friends out here if you wanted to get away from the house."

By the time they all left, the kids could not wait to move. Two days later, on a Friday, Kate had signed all of the papers, and she was now the owner of her own place. That night, Kate, the children, and her parents took supper over to their new home and had a picnic.

As Kate sat and watched the children explore the place, and as she and her mother talked about changes they could easily make, she felt a joy. Yet, she was still haunted by the deep secret and shame that had haunted her since before the Saxton murder.

Kate thought, *Maybe I should not expect happiness, but the children deserve the best, and even the past will not hold me back.*

Chapter 48

B eth Anne sat in the living room drinking her coffee. It was 4:30 a.m.—her favorite time of the day. The early morning was a chance for her to plan and reflect. This morning she was in a somewhat melancholy mood as she thought back over the three years since the divorce. So much had happened: Bo and Tom had settled down and built a very prosperous business, Beth Anne would receive her master's degree in just two weeks, and Tom would marry Patty in three weeks. The upcoming marriage bothered Beth Anne, as Patty and Tom had only known each other for three months. They had opted to marry in the minister's study, and there would be no formal wedding. Beth Anne was glad of that. At the same time as this wedding, her mother would be taking the children to the Swiss Alps for a month. She would miss them, but they had not been too happy about their father's wedding plans, and the trip would do them good. For herself, Beth Anne had planned a cruise, and hoped to be having a good time while her ex took his vows.

Beth Anne closed her eyes. The thought of her children having another parent was hard. Patty was nice, but only twenty-seven, which made her ten years younger than Tom. She knew that there would be stepbrothers and stepsisters. Her prayer was that Tom would stay committed and close to his two biological children.

231

Beth Anne and Tom saw each other frequently both because of the children and because she met monthly with Bo and him when they went over the business. They had remained as good of friends as could be expected when there is so much hurt between two people. She was so lost in thought that she almost did not hear the phone ring. She felt breathless as she answered. This time of morning usually meant that something had happened. *Please let my mother be okay. I can't take anything else right now.*

"Hello."

"Beth Anne."

"Tom. Are you okay?"

"Yes. I'm sorry to call so early, but figured you would be up. I am in Atlanta. The warden called me last night. Said that dad had had a heart attack. They didn't think he would survive. I just had time to get to the airport and catch the next plane out. He died as I was en route."

"Oh Tom, I'm so sorry."

"Thanks. Listen, I am at the place—Tom never said prison; always "the place." I know this is a lot to ask, but would you consider bringing the children and meeting me in Florida. Since mom is living there now, that's where we are taking the body. I really need family." He then quickly added, "I want the children here."

"Sure. We'll get the next plane out."

"I hope I am not hurting any of your school plans."

"No, don't worry. I am finished with everything except one test, but I can take that when I get back. It's no big deal."

"Good. I was counting on your saying yes to coming. There are three tickets waiting for you. There is a plane that leaves at nine thirty. Is that too early?"

"No. I'll get the children up and packed and we will see you later today."

"We are leaving Atlanta in about thirty minutes. I will meet you at the airport in Tampa."

"Okay."

"Beth, thanks. I owe you one."

"We will be glad to be there."

Beth Anne hung the phone up and went into high gear. Once she and the children had gotten on the plane, she fell asleep. About ten minutes before landing, Beth Anne awakened. It was then she began to think, *what have I gotten myself into? This is going to be great: Tom, Patty, the children, and me. I don't know how much of this I can handle.*

There was little time to worry. The plane quickly landed, and Tom was there to meet them. Since it was lunchtime, they decided to leave the airport and find the closest good restaurant. Everyone was so busy talking that Beth Anne momentarily forgot Tom's fiancé. It was when they sat down to eat that Jeff piped up. "Where is Patty?"

Tom looked a little funny. "Uh—uh—she is not coming. I don't think this is the time for her to meet the family."

"Why not?" asked Liza.

In a flustered voice, he answered, "It just isn't." He looked at Beth Anne with a pleading look for help.

"This is a stressful time, and your dad would rather the family meet Patty when they can enjoy her visit," Beth Anne told the children.

"Well, it seems weird to me," Jeff commented.

Me too, Beth Anne thought. But she said nothing, and the subject was dropped.

As they walked to the car, Tom came over to his ex-wife.

"Thanks for helping with the children in there. This whole thing of having to go to the place, make plans for dad's body to be flown back here, and try to have a funeral—hopefully before the press finds out he has died—is almost too much for all of us. Unfortunately, they will not release the body until tomorrow morning. The funeral will be tomorrow afternoon."

Beth Anne, Tom and the children went out to Jean's house after lunch.

Later that afternoon, Tom took the children on some errands with him so the two women could visit.

"How are you doing?" Beth Anne asked.

"I'm okay. At one time I loved Thomas, and this death would have devastated me; however, the man I married died when he committed that heinous crime," Jean answered in a strong voice.

Beth Anne wasn't quite sure what to say next, but her ex-mother-in-law continued.

"I was crushed after the trial, and visited Thomas once a month. There was no way I would have missed one of those visits, and would have continued had he lived; after all, I was his wife. However, after I got over the shock of the crime, I began to see the type of person Thomas really was. He never asked how anyone was doing or seemed to care. All he did was rant and rave about his living conditions and blame everyone but himself for his predicament. In all of this, I began to realize that Thomas didn't love any of us, and probably never had. Somewhere in that understanding, I guess that some, or maybe all, of my love for him died. Thomas and his mother were mean to me. They constantly reminded me that I was not good enough for them."

Beth Anne found that this information did not surprise her, but she was curious. "How did you survive all of this—the move, seeing your husband go to prison?"

Jean thought a moment. "At first not very well. I grieved for Thomas, and for what he had done. I was so embarrassed. For a year I just sat around my daughter's house. Nothing she said made a difference. As it happened, I needed to see a lawyer, so Gretchen took me to hers. When I met him I was shocked. You see, when I was single I worked in a bank in Atlanta with a law student. I also became friends with his fiancée, Dorothy. We would all sometimes go to the picture show. Gretchen's lawyer is their son. Well, he got me back together with his parents and they were a great help. Dorothy decided to take a course at the Junior College. I went with her just for something to do, but quickly got hooked. I thrived on going to school and decided to take a nine-month business course. As I was finishing up, the college started a department dedicated to people returning to school, and they hired me—first as a secretary and now I am the Assistant to the Registrar for that department. It's been a wonderful experience. I loved raising my children, but in some ways, this is the happiest time of my life. I don't have a husband or mother-in-law telling me daily that I am so lucky to be in their lives."

"Oh my goodness, Beth Anne, I didn't mean to rattle on so."

"No. I am so happy that things have worked out for you." Beth Anne felt relieved and happy for her ex-mother-in-law.

Then Jean asked, "What about you? Oh, I hate that crime; if that had not happened, you and Tom would still be together."

With a sigh, Beth Anne answered, "I don't know. It seems that if you are not divorced these days, you are not "in". At least in Houston, it's like that."

Jean seemed outraged. "Well, it's not right."

About that time, Tom and the children returned. Beth Anne was glad she and Jean had had a chance to talk.

Jean then took them out to the college to see her office and to meet her friends. It was obvious that she was well-thought-of there.

The next couple of days were bittersweet for Beth Anne. Except for the sleeping arrangement, she and Tom were once again a couple. They did things together, talked about the crime—something Tom had refused to do—enjoyed each other's company, and made funeral arrangements. When she got on the plane to fly back to Texas, Beth Anne sat back in her seat and thought, *These two days have been the happiest I have known since moving to Houston, and it makes it harder to think about the fact that within two weeks Tom is marrying someone else. I have two options: constantly relive the past forty-eight hours, or think about and do the things I need to do in order to proceed with my plans.* She chose the latter.

SIX WEEKS LATER

As Beth Anne approached Tom's office building, butterflies in her stomach threatened to upset her calm demeanor. She began to think about the last six weeks. *It seems like years ago that we were in Florida for the funeral. It has been a month since I have spoken to the children. They will get in tomorrow. I also have not talked to Tom since his wedding. I am more positive than ever that the announcement I will make today is right. I don't want to have to see my ex any more than necessary. It's just too hard.*

She was still deep in thought when she entered the building. The fact that no one was in the front office totally escaped her. Beth Anne was brought back to the present when she opened the conference room door and everyone yelled, "Surprise!" The room had been beautifully decorated, and excellent food waited to be tasted. Shocked, she looked around and saw the sign.

Congratulations Beth Anne on Your Master's Degree—Suma Cum Lauda.

Oh, this is for me. I can't believe this.

"Thank you everybody," Beth Anne said in a surprised voice. "This is so nice." People filed by to speak. Tom approached her, but as he did, so did several other people, and one had a message that Tom had an emergency call waiting. There was a crisis with some of the computers in their London office, and he was trying to help them clear up the problem. Beth Anne was relieved that she did not have to talk with him.

After the party, there was a short board meeting. When that was coming to a close, Beth Anne stood. Tom had missed most of the meeting because of the problem in their other office, but slipped in just in time for her speech.

"I have decided to return to my original position as a silent partner. These meetings have been very helpful in helping me to learn about the everyday running of an organization and should help me in the future. I plan to start an organization for people who are victims of crime (She had mentioned this to Tom in Florida and he thought it was a great idea.), be it the person against whom an act was committed, family members, or family of the criminal. We live in a time where we spend money on protection, but very little on those who have been directly involved, against their own will, in heinous acts. I feel it is time for someone to step forward and pursue such an organization and I plan to be that person. Stop The Violence—STV—will open its doors in just two weeks at 5841 San Felipe. Thank you for all of your help, and know that I will miss the meetings and seeing you, but I will keep in touch." On the verge of breaking down, she quickly sat down.

Tom stood and turned toward his ex-wife. "Beth Anne, there was a day when I would have applauded your decision not to meet with us." He, Bo and Beth Anne all laughed as they remembered the infamous meeting with Carla Sue and the anger that came forth. "But your insight and wisdom have been strong factors in the phenomenal growth of this business, and I speak on behalf of the board in saying that you are certainly welcomed back at any meeting you care to attend. There is one more thing. You used to say that one day you hoped to deserve your own glass slipper. If anyone does, you do." He then handed her a beautiful glass slipper and gave her a brief hug.

Too overcome to say much, Beth Anne just said a brief thank you.

At that moment, Tom was again called out of the room. Beth Anne, feeling she could not keep her composure much longer, took that time to quietly slip away, and cried all the way home.

Feeling exhausted, she sat on the couch and put the slipper on the table in front of her. *Oh Tom, it is so beautiful,* she thought. *I have accomplished a lot, except I can't seem to terminate my love for you. I guess I will always have to live with that.*

Jarred by the ringing phone, Beth Anne decided she was too upset to talk to anyone, so she let it ring. She would never have guessed what the caller had to say and how it would have changed her life.

⤶ *Chapter 49* ⤷

It had been two years since Kate had bought her house. Remodeling the place had given her a lift and confidence she had not known since high school. Her newfound assurance had affected other parts of her life. Because fixing up her place was a complete do-it-yourself project, she became more aware of the growing trend toward individuals doing much of their own work. She also realized that many people who traveled to Atlanta for merchandise had to go through or by Upton. With her information in hand, Kate approached her dad and persuaded him to add a do-it-yourself department. Fred had been so impressed with Kate's business acumen in the last couple of years, that he turned this aspect of the business over to her. She not only added popular new products, but each week she also offered classes on different how-to projects. Within the year, business had more than doubled.

Kate was also a member of the Chamber of Commerce, and was now heading one of their committees called Love Our Town. The group held an annual fall arts festival and this year is was under her leadership. Because magnolia trees were so prevalent in the town, they decided to call it the Magnolia Festival. This year's event had been a smashing success.

It was 5:00 p.m. when Kate walked into her dad's office. "Wow, I feel like I can finally catch my breath. That festival took it out of me, but I am pleased with the results."

Kate became aware that her dad had his head in his hand. The strong, fast-moving Fred never sat like this.

"Dad, what is wrong?"

He looked up at his daughter. "Oh, I don't feel well. Probably something I ate," Fred said, trying to convince himself as well as Kate.

Kate was alarmed. "Your color looks horrible. I am calling the doctor right now." When Fred did not object, she knew that something was terribly wrong. While she was talking with the nurse, her father fell forward on his desk.

"Dad!" Kate yelled.

She went over to her father, but he was not conscious. Kate ran back to the phone. "Bring the ambulance quickly. Daddy is unconscious."

"Annice, could you come in here?" Kate shouted.

Annice had worked for Fred for thirty-five years and was like a member of the family.

"What happened?" She listened intently as Kate explained. Moments later, the ambulance drivers ran in. They performed CPR and put oxygen to Fred's mouth and then put him on a stretcher. He was barely conscious.

"Annice, would you go and get mother? I will ride in the ambulance with Dad."

"Sure."

The three women who meant the most to Fred waited while the doctors worked on him, and they cried when Dr. Walker walked out and said he had tried, but he had not been able to save him.

⤳

Fred had been a respected businessman and community leader. People turned out in numbers to pay their respect. For the first week, Kate was in and out of the store while she also tried to help her mother. Each day, another person would come by to see if they would be selling the business. Finally, out of desperation, Kate put up a sign that read: This Business Is Not For Sale! This stopped some of the inquiries.

Fred left everything to Sara Katherine. At first she was too much in shock to even think about the business, but after a month's time she told Kate they needed to have a talk.

The two women were sitting in the living room. "It's strange, but in some way I believe that your father had some type of premonition about his coming death."

"Oh mother, don't say that."

"Well, it's true. Oh, I don't mean that he felt that his days were numbered, but I do suspect that he felt an urgency about getting details cleaned up. That is the reason I wanted to talk with you. Two months ago we were sitting in this very room. I can hear him now, 'Sara Katherine, I know you don't like to think about things like this, but I need to talk about the future of the business if something should happen to me.'"

"Kate, when your father would bring up such topics, I would usually steer him to another course. The thought of living without him was too much, but that night I was very calm, and felt the need to let him talk. Anyway, he said, 'When we were young, I thought maybe we would have a son and he could follow in my footsteps. Then Ted came along, and I assumed that one day the place would be his and Kate's. I will tell you something though, no son, and certainly not Ted, could have had any more business sense than our daughter. She is a natural, and even though I am leaving everything to you, I hope you will name her as the president of the company. You might want to make Calvin the vice-president because he knows the construction end so well.'"

"Dad said that about me?" Kate asked, feeling a pride never before experienced.

"He certainly did. Oh Kate, he was so proud of you. We both have been. How do you feel about being in charge?"

"I would love it," she answered, with deep conviction.

The next day, Sara Katherine met with all of the employees and announced that though she would remain on the board, Kate would be the president, and Calvin would move into the position of vice-president of construction. Calvin had come to work with Fred when he was seventeen and had been there twenty-seven years.

Because Annice had unofficially been over all the books and knew the inventory like the back of her hand, she was named business manager. The business had grown so large that these more important positions needed to be filled.

Kate was excited, even though she knew the job would be tough. There were people who still questioned whether a woman had what it took to run a building and construction company. A few vendors required more payment ahead of time than they had with Fred, but that only lasted a short time. However, Kate knew that though she and Calvin got along well, he had a hard time thinking of her as a boss. *One day my authority will be challenged, and I hope I can rise to the occasion,* she thought.

The day she had known would eventually come started off innocently enough.

"Kate." The voice was so soft that she almost missed it, but she looked up.

"Nettie Lou. Come on in."

"Thank you," the obviously shy young woman replied.

Kate gestured to a chair as she thought, *Dad always said that the sun did not shine very often on Nettie Lou, which was too bad because she was a nice person.* Though she was about twenty-five, she seemed almost like a little girl. She was the product of an abusive father and an alcoholic mother.

Though Nettie Lou had been a good student, she had dropped out during her senior year when she had learned she was pregnant. Her marriage had lasted just long enough to produce two girls. Kate suspected that the government helped her out with food.

"What can I do for you, Nettie Lou?" Kate asked in a friendly and gracious tone.

"Well, I don't know if I should be here, but I feel funny about what happened yesterday. Last night I couldn't sleep, and decided to tell you."

"Tell me what?" Kate asked.

"My furnace went out yesterday morning, so I called here to see if somebody could fix it. It was too cold. They sent Bobby Joe out. He said I needed a new furnace. I was surprised, because your daddy put in one for me just three years ago. Bobby Joe said he was probably not feeling well and just chose one that was not any good. Kate, your daddy always helped me out. If I couldn't pay all at once, he would work out a payment plan that I could handle. He always said, 'Don't go without food to pay this bill. Just let me know, and we will work it out.' He was so nice. Anyway, Bobby Joe said he had a rebuilt furnace, but not to tell anybody, and he would sell it to me at 60 percent off. He tried to make it sound like a good deal.

"I made him tell me everything that was wrong with my furnace, and I wrote it all down. Here are my notes. But Kate, there is something else. He backed me up in a corner and grabbed and kissed me. Said there was more where that came from and if I played my cards right, he would take a little bit more off of the cost of the furnace. He then squeezed my arm and threatened to hurt me if I told anyone about this." She then showed Kate the bruise, which was still evident.

For a moment Kate was so angry she could not say anything. She just sat there. Nettie Lou misunderstood her quietness.

"Kate, I swear it is true."

"Oh, Nettie Lou, I believe you, and am so sorry this happened. Just leave everything to me." She reached out and touched the woman. "Will you be there later today?"

"Sure."

"I'm going to send Calvin out. I want him to look over that furnace. Would that be okay?"

"Oh, yes. Kate, I just finished paying for it. I really don't think that I should need a new one so quickly."

"Look, you don't worry about anything. If, after only three years, that furnace needs to be replaced, we will do it."

After Nettie Lou left, Kate had to take an aspirin to ward off a headache. She then began to read the copious notes that the woman had made. *She is meticulous about details,* Kate thought to herself. After about twenty minutes, Kate had calmed down. She called Calvin at his office, which was housed in the construction building.

"Calvin, come over to my office please," she said in a terse voice.

"Sure."

As Calvin put away some things before leaving his office, he felt a sense of annoyance. Though he knew that Kate was a superior businesswoman while his expertise lay in construction, it still rankled him somewhat to work for her. Fred had been a great boss, and so was Kate, but he still saw her as a cute cheerleader. For the last three months they had coexisted more or less on an equal basis, but today it was obvious that she was in charge.

"Kate, you wanted to see me?"

Kate was rereading the notes and did not see Calvin walk in.

"Oh, yes. Close the door please and have a seat."

Calvin was feeling a little concern. Kate was obviously tense, and having him close the door meant that something serious was happening. He noticed that when he sat down, Kate did not come around the desk and sit in the other chair as she usually did.

"What's going on?"

Kate then relayed the story that Nettie Lou had told her.

"I want you to go out to her house and check out the furnace. First of all, I will not have anyone from this business going out and acting inappropriately with our customers. I also don't believe that after three years she needs a new furnace."

"Wait a minute, Kate. You only have Nettie Lou's word on what Bobby Joe did. You know Nettie Lou; she is not too bright," Calvin answered in a slightly agitated voice.

Raising her voice somewhat, Kate answered, "You don't know that she is not bright. I happen to think she might be a pretty smart person, but that is beside the point. It does not take a rocket scientist to know if someone has come on to you."

"Look, for me to go out and check behind my men will only make them angry at me. I don't like to do that."

"Calvin, you are the boss now. You are not paid for running a popularity contest."

The two were angry and showing it.

"No, I am not trying to be popular, but if my people think I don't trust them, they will not respect me, and I will lose my leadership foothold."

"Daddy checked behind all of you at times."

"That was different, Kate. He was the founder, and older. We all respected him, and besides, Bobby Joe, who I admit is obnoxious, is one of the best in the business. We are lucky to have him working for us. I'm sorry. I will not go out and inspect behind him."

Purposely controlling the extreme anger she felt, Kate looked at Calvin, and in an even tone of voice said, "You misunderstood me. I am not asking you to look at Nettie Lou's furnace—I am telling you to go."

"And if I don't?"

"I will give you two weeks' pay and good references."

Calvin looked at her. *She is serious. She would fire me.*

Realizing that he needed this job, he got up, and when he reached the door, he turned and said, "For the record, I think this is a dumb move." He then slammed the door behind him.

Kate said nothing, but thought, *If this had been my dad, you would have been out of the door without another word* .

Calvin fumed all of the way to Nettie Lou's. *This is ridiculous. When my vacation comes up in two weeks, I am going to Atlanta and look for a job. I'm not having some woman who doesn't know what she is talking about order me around.*

It was only when he began to check out the furnace that he cooled down. *Oh my gosh,* he thought to himself when he noticed two loose wires. Obviously, they had been cut. After fixing them and reconnecting the furnace, he saw that it worked fine. There were no problems.

Before entering Kate's office, the usually affable Calvin attached a white handkerchief to a stick and waved it in the air.

Kate saw that and laughed. "Come on in," she said. They both had obviously cooled down. "What did you find?"

"A scary scene, the pilot light was off and two wires were loose and that is why the heat was not working. They were glued in place so that most people looking for an obvious problem would not have noticed. I reconnected everything and turned on the pilot light. The furnice works fine. It was freezing in that house. It is a cheap place, and I doubt that it is well insulated. I hope Nettie Lou or one of her girls don't come down with pneumonia as a result of this."

"So what Bobby Joe probably had in mind was to take that furnace out and replace it with one that he had rebuilt. He was going to do that at a lower price than we could have matched." Kate concluded.

"Yeah. My guess is that he took an older furnace we changed out. He could have taken her furnace after he hauled it off for her, turned around and installed it for someone else, and charged a lot more money because it is only three years old. This kind of scam is not as uncommon as you might think. It especially happens with people who can't afford something new. Somebody like Bobby Joe comes along and offers them a rebuilt furnace at rock-bottom price."

"And I would bet that many people trust him because he works for us. Dad was always so careful about keeping everything above board."

"You got it."

Without saying a word, Kate picked up the phone and called the receptionist in the construction section.

"Has Bobby Joe come back?"

"He just came in."

"Tell him I want to see him now," Kate said in a rather harsh voice.

Calvin had never seen Kate act with such authority, and he was not sure what was expected of him. "Do you want me to go or stay?"

"I want you here. We are in this together." Kate added the last to sort of atone for the angry order earlier in the day. After all, Calvin was a very valuable employee, and she knew he was very much needed to make the business run smoothly.

Bobby Joe walked in—though it would be more honest to say he swaggered in—sat down and said, "What's up, boss?" Kate hated the way he used the term "boss." She knew that he wasn't saying it out of respect. Bobby Joe was a nice-looking man in a beer-guzzling, cheap sort of way. He personified the "good old boy" concept. Some women pretty much fell at his feet, and his manner showed that he was used to running the show. He had maintained a decent demeanor at work when Fred was alive because he knew he would be fired in a minute if he pulled anything.

After deciding to approach both problems that Nettie Lou had separately, Kate, in a very innocent voice, stated, "Nettie Lou was in here earlier today, and I was sort of surprised that her furnace was giving her trouble. Dad just put one in a few years ago. What happened?"

Kate noticed that Bobby Joe looked a little uncomfortable, but he quickly regained his self-assurance.

Having no idea that Calvin had been out to check his work, Bobby Joe gave a very plausible explanation of what had happened to the furnace. The only problem was that it was not true.

At that moment, Kate did not reveal that Calvin had checked Bobby Joe's work. Instead she simply said, "Nettie Lou also complained about your coming on to her.

Bobby Joe started laughing. "Aw, come on Kate. Some women actually find me attractive. I'll bet she liked it. Don't you, Calvin?" He reached over and slapped Calvin's knee.

Calvin just looked at him. Kate would have liked to have hit him, but she kept her composure.

Bobby Joe kept talking. "Listen, I'll bet that woman hadn't had anything in a long time. She was probably mad because I didn't push it any farther. Oh, she pretended to be mad, but she was pleased."

Willing herself to be calm, Kate then confronted him again about the furnace.

"Bobby Joe, Calvin checked the furnace after you left."

Bobby Joe was clearly uncomfortable, but thought he could get out of this. "Look," he started to call her Babe, but thought better of that idea. "Okay, I'll admit that I cut the wires to make it look as though the furnace had gone bad, but listen—I need some money. We don't all have daddies to drop a business in our laps."

"And then you were going to sell her furnace to another person."

Getting agitated, Bobby leaned forward and spoke in a threatening tone of voice, "You listen to me. I have always done exactly what Fred wanted, but he is gone. I'm a good worker; the best. I know that people call here and ask for me. Let's just pretend this didn't happen. What I do is my business."

Remaining very calm, but speaking with a voice of authority, Kate looked at Bobby Joe. "I will give you two weeks' pay. I want you out immediately. Calvin, please walk with him to his desk while he gets his things." She then handed him his check.

Bobby Joe was speechless. "You can't do this."

As if she had not heard him, Kate continued, "If anyone calls for a reference I will tell them exactly what you did."

By this time, Bobby was leaning forward with his hands resting on Kate's desk. Trying to sound tough and look threatening, he came back at Kate, "I'll take you to court and sue—say that you made this up. Nobody will want to work for you!"

Nonplused, Kate opened her desk drawer, did something, and suddenly they all heard Bobby Joe's voice. She had taped everything he had said.

He stood up straight and shouted, "I'll get you for this." He then turned around and stormed out of the office.

Within fifteen minutes, all of the employees knew what had happened. One worker turned to another and said, "Fred might be dead, but his spirit is alive and well in Kate. She has proven this place is going to be run her way."

Bobby Joe soon learned that he had crossed the wrong person. He could not find a job, and within two weeks had left that part of Georgia for good.

A few days later Annice approached Kate. "You did a good thing when you fired Bobby Joe. These people now know they are accountable to you. Fred would have been proud."

"Thanks Annice." Kate thought, *It sort of makes it a little easier to live with the past.*

Chapter 50

Karen smiled as she watched the students get on the bus. It was a sunny and cool October morning. They could not have asked for better weather. For four years, she and Smitty had taken the students on a college tour. They sponsored two tours a year: one in the fall, and the other in the spring. Many of the kids who went were from Mill Town. They still had a tendency to graduate and marry immediately after graduation, but often found it hard to find a job with only a high school diploma. Smitty and Karen worked hard to stress the need for higher education to all of the students at the school.

Once the bus left the parking lot, Smitty sat back and relaxed. As they drove along, he became lost in his thoughts. The last four years had been wonderful. With his mind free from the stress of the Saxtons' deaths, he had been able to put himself into his teaching with his usual work ethic. It was within the educational realm that Smitty had realized he had found his calling. He loved everything about education and leading people to the possibility of a better life. Smitty had completed his doctorate in education, and two years ago had become principal of Upton High School when Mr. Dearson retired. His marriage to Karen was stronger than ever.

Life was good, but there was a stirring in his soul, and Smitty knew that the time for change was approaching. He wondered what the next step would be, and hoped he would be equal to the task. It was a chance remark by a student later that day that helped Smitty to start formulating a plan that would not only change his life, but would also change the face of Upton and the lives of many of the people in this part of Georgia.

Chapter 51

"Happy birthday to you, happy birthday to you..." The setting was a ballroom in Dallas. Jen was there to attend a gala for literacy, one of her pet charities. Word had gotten out that today was her birthday, and the decision was made to end the dinner with a delicious cake from one of the finest bakeries in the city. Jen was surprised. She had forgotten that today she turned thirty-eight. As she watched the pomp and circumstance of the celebration, her mind went back to a simpler time when she would have been surrounded by her parents and three best friends. The memory made her smile.

When she could make an exit, Jen went out on one of the balconies that overlooked the city. The view was spectacular. As she sat and relaxed, thoughts of her childhood came flooding back, and she realized more and more that the past no longer seemed so sad. Oh, the hurt over the loss of her parents would always be present, and Kate's anger still remained a mystery. Her friendship with Karen and Smitty was as close as ever. She and Tom had not spoken since seeing each other at the police station that night seven years ago. Jen's reminiscing brought joy and sadness to her. She reached up to wipe a tear from her face when one of the socialites, Cossie the Third, as she was known, appeared. Noticing the tear, Cossie replied, "Oh dear, thirty-eight is not so bad. I realize that it is close to forty, but you will be okay."

Jen just said, "You're right." She smiled to herself, *if she only knew that I was thinking I was still young. Of course in Cossie's mind, going from a size four to a size six would be cause of national concern.* The thought almost made Jen laugh out loud.

After Cossie left, Jen's thoughts drifted back to a conversation that had taken place six years ago, just after Tony announced that he was marrying.

"Tony, when did you know that you were over Susan's death?"

"My thinking began to change. As I got to know you, I knew I would be capable of loving again. That was a major issue. After that, more and more thoughts of Susan became pleasant memories, and I was able to make our relationship a part of my past. When that happened, I was open to meeting people and living."

When Jen returned to her hotel room, she knew that it was time for her to face life. For seven years she had traveled and worked hard for causes in which she believed, and while this had helped, it was not who she was. Roots, friends, and family were too important. She knew what she had to do before anything else could happen.

Chapter 52

J en got up early the next morning and left Dallas about eight forty-five. During the drive, she felt a little nervous, but she was excited as well. This was her first trip to Juarez, Texas, the place where her father had been born. Though somewhat anxious, she knew that this trip, for some reason, was a must. As Jen drove into town, she heard the church bells ringing. The Methodist church was just in front of her. It was a small, white, wooden building with a steeple. It could have been in any storybook. Jen parked the car and slipped into the back pew. The congregation was just standing to sing "Joyful, Joyful We Adore Thee." She knew the song well, and joined in with a gusto she had not known since her parents' deaths. The sermon seemed made to order. It was about forgiveness and moving on. The young minister was eloquent in his delivery, and held Jen's rapt attention. After services, some of the congregation came over to speak with the visitor. She never told them of her connection to the town. This would have caused unwanted attention. Jen was about to leave when a couple invited her to their home for lunch. They introduced themselves as the Connors.

"This is a small town, and everything closes on Sunday. You won't find a place to eat. And besides, we are the official lunch hosts for visitors," said Mrs. Connor.

Jen joined the couple in their home. It was a beautiful old place, and very comforting to her. As they ate, Mr. and Mrs. Connor asked her about herself. Jen was feeling very relaxed with the older couple, and she began to tell her story. As the tale unfolded, she noticed that her hosts had become quiet and were looking at each other in a surprised manner.

"Is something wrong?" Jen asked.

"My goodness no," Mrs. Connor said in her vibrant, outgoing way. "Honey, do you realize that you are in your grandfather's home? This is your family ranch."

Jen just looked at the two. "I had no idea. I have never been here."

"Well, this just can't be coincidence. Would you like to see the rest of the house?" asked the hostess.

"If it would not be any bother."

Jen got the grand tour of the ranch and the house. About three o'clock they all sat down again, and Mrs. Connor put out some finger sandwiches and coffee. The three visited. Mr. Connor had grown up on this ranch, and his father had also managed it. When Jen's grandfather died, they had moved into the big house so that it would be kept up. Jen noticed that the couple became quiet.

"Is something wrong?"

"No," Mrs. Connor said. "I do want to ask you, though, are you thinking about moving here or selling the ranch?"

Jen had thought the place beautiful and had said so, and now she realized that her compliments, and no doubt her presence, had given this lovely couple some fears. She quickly answered.

"Oh, no. I am a city girl. It is beautiful here, but not for me!" she said convincingly. "And besides, Mr. and Mrs. Connor, no one knows any better than I how important home and roots are. I would never take that from someone. My trip here was important in my own pilgrimage back to normal. That's all."

The couple looked relieved. "Your aunt Rachel has said the same. We were just concerned that maybe you felt differently."

"Oh, no. I'm a dyed-in-the-wool Southerner. I don't know a thing about ranches and don't care to. That is Aunt Rachel's department."

They visited for about thirty more minutes before Jen got up to leave. "Thank you for bringing some of my past to me." She hugged the Connors and left.

As she drove through town, Jen noticed a small park with a large, porch-type swing attached to a tree. She could not pass it up. While sitting there thinking about this town and what it had meant to her family, an old man walked up. He was nice looking, with thick, white hair, piercing blue eyes, and the most pleasant and gentle demeanor Jen had ever seen.

"Do you mind if I join you?"

"Oh, please do."

The old man sat down. He never introduced himself, but asked Jen some questions about herself. Without hesitation she began telling him about her family, the murders, and the loss of her friends. And then she surprised herself as she said, "Now it is time for me to go home and make a place for myself, but I don't know what to do."

The old man looked very thoughtfully at Jen before he answered, "What was important to you before your tragedy?"

Unhesitatingly, Jen answered, "Family, friends, God, church, roots, my teaching job. I loved being a part of something bigger, but things have changed so. I don't know where I belong."

"Are these things still important to you?"

"Yes. For a while I was very angry with God for letting all of this happen, but I made peace with Him about two years ago. But Kate, my best friend, will not have anything to do with me; I don't know why. And Tom, whose father committed the murders, never speaks with me. However, he did write to me a beautiful letter after his dad's arrest."

The old man looked at Jen and said, "After hardship, many people become lost because it is difficult to accept the changes that come about with misfortune. Certainly you are not the same, but one thing has not changed—that there is purpose for your life. It may be different than what you had envisioned, but never associate different with bad. We all have choices—to live or to run. You have a chance at happiness; don't throw it away."

The stranger stood. "I must go now. I wish you well." He took Jen's hands and held them for a minute. His touch was electric. As the old man started to leave, something caught Jen's attention for a moment and she looked away. When she turned back, he was gone. A peace settled over Jen, and she instinctively knew that everything would be alright.

As she was leaving Juarez, Jen saw a group of people beginning to gather at the church. She stopped and inquired about who the old man might possibly have been. No one had a clue. The identification of the stranger who had made such a profound impact on Jen would always remain a mystery.

Though she didn't have any answers as to what she would do with the rest of her life, she did know what the next course of action was. There was some fear, excitement, and dread involved, but Jen knew the steps she must take.

Chapter 53

Late on Sunday afternoon, Jen drove back to Dallas from Juarez. The next morning she caught the nine-thirty flight to Houston. When they landed, she decided to get a cab. After getting checked into the Houstonian at the Galleria, she called a taxi to go to Tom's office, which was close to where she was staying. Jen had chosen not to let him know she was coming. She didn't know if he would see her, and if he would, whether he would be embarrassed, indifferent, or something else. There were bound to be anxious moments, but Jen was positive that this visit was essential not only for her, but for Tom as well.

She looked around the building that had the name of Tom's business on it. *My, he certainly has done well*, she thought.

Jen entered Tom's suite. His secretary looked up.

"May I help you?"

"Is Mr. DePau in?" Jen inquired.

"Yes. Who should I tell him is here?" the young woman behind the desk asked.

"Just tell him Jen. He will know."

In a rather hesitant voice she said, "Tom, a Jen wants to see you."

There was a silence. Jen's heart dropped. What if he would not see her? But this fear was short-lived. The door burst open, and Tom all but ran out and hugged his old friend.

"Christy," he said to his secretary, "this is one of my best friends from childhood. She knows things about me no one should know." He said laughing.

Looking at Jen, Tom replied, "Girl, you look great. Please say you will have lunch with me."

Jen looked at her old friend and smiled. "You are the same old gregarious, self-assured person I have always known. It is so good to see you." *And you also are as good looking as ever. The gray in your hair adds distinction,* She thought.

"Why thank you, ma'am." Tom answered with a gallant bow. "And lunch?"

"By all means. In fact, I was going to ask you."

"Christy, would you please call my wife and ask her to meet us at Quincy's if possible."

The restaurant, which was within walking distance of his office, was elegant and very quiet. It was a good place for two old friends to catch up. On the way, there had been very little conversation, but once settled, they began to talk.

"I'm sorry I just dropped by this way. I was not sure you would see me."

Tom looked at Jen with utter amazement. "Jen, you don't know how much I have missed your friendship. There are things I have wanted to tell you. There will never be words to describe the utter horror that I have continued to feel that someone in my family would commit the crime my grandmother and dad did. I hope that you have always known that in no way did I condone any of that."

"I knew that. I just couldn't talk to you for a long time. After all, no matter what you felt, that was still your dad."

Tom looked out over the dining floor of the restaurant with a faraway look in his eye. "It was horrible. I had always been so proud of who I was and what my family stood for, or so I thought. When we moved here, I just wanted to pretend that I was someone else. I tried to reinvent myself. Whoever coined the phrase 'crime does not pay' certainly knew what they were saying. It destroyed my family."

Jen realized that Tom had also been victimized by the crime.

Tom then said, "But enough about me. What are you up to these days and how are you doing?"

Tom's inquiry was very sincere. Jen told him about the charity events, the traveling she had done, and about her experience in Juarez the day before: the sermon, the ranch, and the old man.

For the first time, they also spoke at length about the crime. It was something neither had planned, but the timing just seemed right. It was a healing experience.

As they were finishing, someone was approaching the table.

"Hi, sorry I am late."

Tom looked up and said, "Oh, glad you could make it."

When Jen saw her, she was shocked, but in just a few seconds she and Tom's wife embraced.

"Jen, I didn't know you were here."

"Beth Anne, I didn't know you were still Tom's wife."

The three laughed. Once lunch was over, Tom had a three o'clock meeting, so Beth Anne and Jen decided to go out to the house so that the two women could visit.

When they got home, Jen asked, "What happened? I thought that the two of you were divorced?"

"We were." Beth Anne then told the story of their getting back together.

"Right after I got my master's degree, I attended what was to be my last meeting with Tom and Bo. I just could no longer be around Tom unless absolutely necessary, and decided to break ties with the business. This was upsetting to me because it represented the end of my marriage. When I arrived home and walked in the door, the phone was ringing. My heart was broken and I could not bear to talk with anyone, so I didn't answer it. Rather, I fixed a cup of coffee and sat on the couch and had a good cry. I finally said goodbye to my marriage. After calming down, I went into the kitchen and began dinner. Within moments, there was a knock on the door.

She thought back to that night.

Beth Anne opened the door.

Tom was standing there. *"Hi. You got away so fast that I didn't have time to say anything to you after the meeting."*

"Well, you were busy with your call from London."

Tom seemed a little anxious. *"They were having an emergency in one of the offices. I tried to call you a little while ago. You probably had not gotten home. What I wanted to ask you was if I could take you to dinner tonight to celebrate your degree?"*

"Jen, it was so hard to not break down. Here was this man I still loved, but who was married to someone else, wanting to have dinner with me."

"What happened next?" Jen was fascinated by this story.

"Tom, I'm sorry, come on in and sit down. I need to talk with you."

"We sat facing each other and then I began."

"This may not be the 'in' way to act—to admit you still love someone, but the fact is that I do still love you. But you are now someone else's husband, and I must be free emotionally to move on with my life. We can deal with each other if it has anything to do with the children, but other than that, our lives cannot intermingle. It's not fair to Patty, you, or me. But thank you for the invitation."

"I stood as a sign that he was to leave."

"Beth Anne, please sit back down. I need to tell you something."

"Reluctantly, I sat."

"When dad died, the first person I thought of calling was you. In fact, if you will remember, you, the children, and I were eating when Jeff asked where Patty was. Beth, I swear that was the first time I had thought of her. I had not even called and told her I was leaving Houston or that my dad was sick, much less dead!

"I did call her later, and she offered to come, but the truth was I didn't want her there. It didn't feel right. After the funeral, I stayed on a week to help mom. I also needed time away from Houston just to think. My feelings for Patty had been waning for sometime. She was young and wanted to marry and have children, and while I had strong feelings for her, I wasn't sure she was for me. During the days of the funeral in Florida, you, the children and I were like family again and it felt good. I realized that Patty wanted something from me that I already had and wanted to get back—a family. Patty and I broke up. I told the kids several days ago when we talked, so I assumed you knew."

"Tom, this is so weird. The children and I have missed connection each time we have called each other this past week."

"Look, Beth, I know that I have messed things up with us and you don't owe me anything, but if you would just give us a chance, I will do what it takes to rebuild our family."

"Maybe this is not enough of an excuse, but when we moved here, I just wanted to be somebody else. The truth is, for some time I have wanted to give us another try, but I figured that I didn't have a chance. However, I refuse to give up without a fight."

"Tom, those are words that I have wanted to hear but never let myself think about them being said. However, you have to realize that you just can't just walk back into my life as though nothing has happened."

Tom looked shaken. "Are you saying there is no hope?"

"No. What I am saying is that I am now a different person. I have finished my master's, I'm used to running things here, and I am starting a business that I strongly believe in. The Beth Anne you left is no longer in residence. You will have to accept that."

Smiling, Tom said, "I knew you had changed the first time you met with Bo and me—never been any doubt in my mind." Looking more serious, he continued. "I understand what you are saying, and have thought about this. The truth is; I, too, am different, but I am also willing to do what it takes to make things work out."

Coming back to the present in her mind, Beth Anne continued. "We were in counseling for about a year. Six months ago we slipped off and remarried. I won't lie; there have been some adjustments, but we love each other, and will work through any problems. We know that no matter what happens, we love each other and want to be a family."

"Beth Anne, I am so happy for you. I could never imagine either one of you married to anyone else. You always seemed so well suited to each other. That crime tore so many people apart."

There was an awkward moment of silence.

Very gently, Beth Anne broke the quietness. "Jen, none of us experienced the losses you did, but we were all victimized by the heinous acts of Tom's dad and grandmother."

"I guess I had not stopped to think about it in that way, but you make sense. It must be horrible for Tom to know what his father did." She then looked embarrassed. "I'm sorry. I should not have said that."

"It's okay. You are right; he will never totally get over what happened. In these situations, everybody loses. Divorce is common, as are alienation and financial ruin. Because of all that I saw, I have started a center for victims of crime. The help extends to everyone—not just the intended victim."

For a moment Jen said nothing. Beth Anne was a little concerned that she had in some way offended her.

Jen then answered. "That is a wonderful idea. Loss because of crime is so different. It's hard for others to understand. At least I could talk about my situation. I suspect, knowing Tom, that he was hesitant to tell others."

"You got that. When we moved here, we constantly told the children not to mention the DePaus. In fact, they did not know, until recently, what really happened."

"What all are you going to have at the center?"

The two women talked for a long time about Beth Anne's new business, and though Jen had planned to go back to the hotel, have an early supper, and leave the next morning, she decided to stay. That night they all had dinner together, and the next day she took an extended tour of the center.

She flew out of Houston late that afternoon. The woman sitting next to her asked, "Where are you going?"

"I'm going home."

"You seem happy. Have you been away long?"

"Yes I have—several years, but now it's time to go back."

Jen put her head back and closed her eyes. She had enjoyed being with Beth Anne and Tom and now she had purpose. For the first time in eight years, she felt happy and hopeful.

Jen just didn't know how much things really would change with the revelations that would be made about Kate.

✑ Chapter 54 ✑

October, 1982

It had been six months since Jen had returned to Atlanta from her visit with Tom and Beth Anne. During that time, she had worked nonstop on her new project—Hope For Victims of Crime. Jen had caught the vision while touring Beth Anne's center and hearing her talk. Jen's was based on the same concept that there are many victims when a crime is committed. She was excited and working hard. Except for those obligations that had to be kept, Jen almost vanished from the social scene. However, many of the contacts she had made in the last seven years were proving to be invaluable assets as she set forth to have the best program available for victims.

One Saturday, Jen had been working since 7:00 a.m. About 1:00 p.m. she realized she was hungry and decided to go out for lunch. At the Peachtree Grill, she found a table on the patio and settled in with her newspaper. About ten minutes later, she looked up for a moment and noticed a man who seemed to be scouting out a table.

Who is that? The man, dressed in his Dockers, button-down shirt, and slightly tussled dark hair looked familiar, but she could not place him. As he moved toward the recently-vacated table close to her, Jen thought, *No, it can't be—my eyes need checking*, and returned to reading the paper. But seconds later, she heard her name being called.

"Jen?"

Looking up, she found herself looking into two beautiful, dark brown eyes.

"Richard. I didn't recognize you."

"How are you doing?" he asked with genuine interest.

"Very well, but I have missed your handling my finances."

For a moment Richard looked concerned.

"I hope nothing is wrong. I thought Carolyn would do a great job for you."

"Oh, she does, but somehow I always felt more secure with your ideas. I'm sorry, why don't you sit down and join me?" Jen realized that this might be a good time to get some answers about her financial concerns about the center. She liked Carolyn, but honestly felt that Richard's base of knowledge was stronger. He had had more experience.

"Thanks. I would like that."

"Actually, I was thinking of calling you," Jen said truthfully enough.

"Oh really? What's going on?"

She told him all about her ideas about the center, the work she had done, and her future plans for it. Jen also talked about the financial end of things.

I had planned to see if I could hire you to at least help me set up this part of my business, and, hopefully, serve on the board."

"Sure, I will be glad to. When do you want to get together?"

They set up a meeting time.

With business out of the way, Richard looked at Jen and said, "I'm so glad that you have found this interest. You seem happy."

"I am. I realized about a year ago that the traveling social scene was getting to me—that's just not who I am. I need roots, routine, and a purpose, but I didn't know what to do. However, when I visited with Tom and Beth Anne, the answer couldn't have been any clearer." She then told him about Beth Anne's center for victims.

"Speaking of business, I hear your's is doing great," Jen said.

"It is. I expected for things to go well, but I have to say, even I have been surprised at the immediate success."

"What made you leave? Just get tired of the corporate scene?"

"Well, Lea and I had talked about my going into business for myself at some point. The plan was that I would work at the firm for about five years, get some experience and make some money, and then strike out on my own. We had planned to wait to have children until that part of our lives was settled. I was twenty-eight when I had been at the firm for five years. Lea was working in public relations for a large corporation. We were happy and making good money, but something just told me that the time was not right to start my own business. For one thing, the economy was a little shaky, so I stayed at Wilson, Sterns, and Wilcox. About a year and a half later, Lea got sick with heart problems. To cut the stress, she started working part-time, and then about a year later, her health was better. We waited a couple of more years, and when Lea's problems did not return, with the doctor's blessing, we started a family. Brock was born six years ago, and then Tae was born three years ago. Two months after Tae's birth, Lea's heart problems returned, and she died three months later."

Jen was aghast. "Richard, I had no idea. I am so sorry, but no one told me about Lea, and I guess I was out of town when she died, because I didn't see it in the paper." She was very earnest in her sorrow.

"Thank you. As you know, these things are not easy, and neither is being a single parent. I had made partner at the firm, and they were very generous with me, but I know the demands that a partner needs to meet and I just couldn't with two at home completely dependent on me. That's when I decided it was now or never, so I struck out on my own. And I have to say, I love it. Being my own boss is hard work, but it also gives me the flexibility to spend time with the children."

"How have they done through all of this?"

"It's been noticeably harder on Brock, but he's a tough little guy." Richard said with a shrug and continued. "I've had him in counseling with a special child psychologist. He now seems to being doing well, but can get somewhat insecure with change. Fortunately, my sister, Susie, who is one year younger than I, and her husband, moved in down the street from us, and they have been wonderful. They have a child Brock's age and one a little older, so the kids play together, and Brock and Tae stay there a lot. Susie and I have always been close, but I don't know what I would have done without her and Joe, her husband."

"Well, you are looking good. I almost didn't recognize you." Embarrassed at how that sounded, Jen tried to undo what she had said.

Richard just laughed and waved his hand. "Don't try to explain. I was complaining about the complications of trying to meet other singles, when my sister stood me in front of the mirror and said, 'You're looking at a dork. Now is the time to change, big brother.' I was desperate enough to listen to my younger sister—hence the contact lenses, different hair, clothes—just call me Susie's creation."

They both laughed.

It was a beautiful fall afternoon, cool and crisp—a day for being outside. Jen and Richard talked effortlessly for hours. It was a lady from the next table that broke the conversation.

"Excuse me, do either of you have the time."

"Sure," Richard said, "it's four forty-five."

Then, looking at Jen, "I am so sorry, but I need to run. I promised Susie I would pick up the kids at five." Before standing, Richard looked earnestly at his newfound friend and said, "I'm no good at this single bit, and playing it cool is not my thing, but I have not enjoyed talking to anyone as much as I have you since Lea. Do you suppose we could do something together soon?"

"I can't think of anything I would like any better," Jen answered.

While Jen was driving home, it was twilight. This time of day often made her feel sad, but today was different. She knew that meeting Richard was the beginning of something wonderful.

There was a moment of sadness when she thought of how wonderful it would be if she could call her old friend Kate and tell her the good news.

"Forget that," she said to herself. "Sadly, Kate is in the past, but I will always wonder why she is so cool toward me."

Chapter 55

It was an exciting time. Smitty's doctorate was being awarded to him today, and it marked the first time in eight years that the Big Four had come together. Jen looked around Emory University's auditorium. She saw Tom and Beth Anne with their children, who were now eleven and thirteen. Up front was Karen with their three kids who were ages fifteen, thirteen, and eleven, and over to the right Jen saw Kate with Todd, who was now seventeen, and Anna Kate, who was fourteen.

"Goodness, I almost didn't recognize them."

"What?" Richard mumbled.

Jen pointed out Kate to him. "That was my best friend."

"Kate?"

"Yeah. I have not seen her children in seven years, and almost didn't know who they were. This seems so weird."

"You okay?" Richard asked, squeezing her hand.

"Yes. In fact, I'm real happy, and can't wait for you to meet the others."

Smitty had wanted to get everyone together. He was hatching a new plan and needed the Big Four's help. He also missed the group, and wanted them to try and heal the wounds of the past. Smitty and Karen and their children had spent a lot of time with Jen and Richard over the past year. They asked to give a dinner to get everyone together, to honor Smitty, and for their own surprise. After the ceremonies and pictures, they all gathered in the dining room of a posh hotel for dinner. Afterwards there were plenty of planned activities for all of the kids so that the grownups could talk. It was a fun day, and therapeutic for all, except for Kate. Jen watched her. She carefully avoided Jen as much as possible, and even with the others, she seemed stilted—almost brittle.

While the others were eating their desserts, Jen stood. "I don't believe that any of us will look back on our thirties as an easy time."

"Hear, hear," they said in unison.

"However, as I have heard it said, 'All good things have to come to an end.' I also believe that all bad things have to also end. The path of my life has certainly changed this past year. You have met Richard, and we will be married next month. It will be a small ceremony, with Smitty giving me away, and Tae and Brock will stand up for us. You are all invited." She made a point to look at Tom and Beth Anne as she said this.

They all applauded. Then Smitty stood, raising his glass. "I propose a toast to a great couple. No one deserves any happiness any more than these two. To a happy marriage."

"Hear, hear."

As Kate raised her glass and participated in the toast, the smile masked the anger she felt inside. *No one deserves happiness any more than those two. Oh, give me a break. Maybe Richard, but Jen—after what she did! I can't believe this. It's not fair.*

After Smitty laid out his plans, and as soon as she could do so, Kate made her exit.

Chapter 56

1988

It was late on a Sunday afternoon. Kate sat in the rocking chair, not wanting to move. She was still a little tired. Just three days before, Kate, her mother, Todd, and Anna Kate had returned from a two-week European vacation. It had been a fun experience—one Kate would treasure for the rest of her life. But for now, she just wanted to sit and enjoy being at home. As dark descended, she got up to move into the house. Just as she stood, Kate noticed a car pulling up in the driveway. A young woman got out. Kate could not, at first, make out who it was, but when the stranger got closer, she realized it was Bonnie Covert, Ted's girlfriend.

"What does she want?" Kate muttered to herself. A sickening feeling started forming in the pit of her stomach. She did not want to visit with this woman.

Bonnie was much younger than Ted. She was a hotshot in the DA's office in Atlanta. Kate's ex had always made sure she understood how brilliant and beautiful his live-in, as he called her, was.

With her long brown hair, wide-set eyes, and slim, tall body, Bonnie could have as easily been a model as a lawyer. Kate had only met her briefly, but as Bonnie stepped onto the porch, it was obvious that she was very direct and forthright.

"Kate. I am Bonnie Covert. We met a couple of years ago."

She held out her hand to shake Kate's.

Kate shook her hand as she answered. "Of course, Bonnie, I remember you. Please, come on in."

The two stepped into the softly lit house. It was cozy, and this sense gave Kate as much comfort as anything could at this moment.

"Please sit down." Kate motioned to a chair. "Would you like a cup of tea?"

"Thank you. That would be nice." Bonnie was glad for something to drink, as she felt stressed about the visit.

The two women sat in Kate's den with their tea. There was an awkward silence before Bonnie began to speak. "I'm sorry I just dropped by, but I had really not planned to come here. This is not easy," she said, as she looked down at her cup.

Kate could see that underneath that sophisticated, intellectual, hard-driven facade, was a sensitive woman.

Bonnie looked up. Without any delay, she began to divulge why she had driven to Upton.

"When I met Ted three years ago, the last thing on my mind was romance. I was only twenty-seven, fresh out of law school, and my sights were set on making a name for myself in the legal field. I was driven. I wanted my parents to be proud of me, and I wanted to right all of the injustices. Oh, I was a dreamer, but also a hard worker. At first, Ted seemed perfect. The fifteen year age difference worked for rather than against us. Most men my age seemed put off by my ambition—it is still in many ways a man's world, but Ted seemed to be proud of me."

Kate cleared her throat. She was not sure she wanted to hear too much about her ex-husband's relationship with the beauty sitting before her.

Realizing she was probably making Kate uncomfortable, Bonnie stopped.

"I'm sorry Kate. I know this may not be a conversation you want to have, but this part really is necessary."

Sort of curious now, Kate said, "No, go on."

"When we first started dating, he seemed like the perfect person. No pressure. Often, Ted would call the office when I was working late and say that he had made some supper, and suggest I stop by and eat when I finished work, or he would come by with a meal and we would eat at my desk. He seemed to be a light on a winding and hard path. I loved it. Though he told me several times he was in love with me, it seemed okay with him that I did not return the sentiment. The almost natural ebb and flow of our relationship made it easy for me to eventually fall in love. A year after we met, I decided to treat Ted to a special dinner at his favorite restaurant. It was then that I expressed my love for him. I expected him to be happy and excited, but the emotions I saw were stilted—he did not seem particularly moved. I was hurt, and asked what was wrong. Ted made up some excuse of just being surprised—not always expressing himself overtly—but assured me he was glad for the change in my heart.

"While I am not proud of this fact, soon after that dinner, I pretty much moved in with him. Oh, I kept my place for when my parents and your children visited, but most nights were with Ted. At first it was fun, but about four months into this arrangement, he began to gradually change. There was some withdrawing such as watching a lot of TV or staying out late for happy hour. I could not complain because I often worked late, but the difference was noticeable. When I talked with Ted, he just said that he went out because he got lonely because of my hours. What could I say?

"The biggest turnabout was his attitude toward me. Where at one time he had been proud of my ability, he now began chipping away at my self-confidence. There were never any words about how nice I looked, and little congratulations when I won a case, but there was plenty of admiration for other women and the way they did things. Also, we had been used to talking about my cases from time to time, and when I would bring something up, it seemed that Ted was always criticizing the way I handled a situation. When I complained, he said he was just playing the devil's advocate. Of course, I realize now that that was just an excuse to be critical. More and more my self-confidence began to erode, and I second-guessed myself way too often. It even began to show up in my work performance.

"Ted also did not understand my relationship with my parents. We have always been close, and I have talked with them on a weekly basis, and they were used to visiting me a couple of times a year for about a week each time. Ted thought this was excessive, and, after several months, told me I needed to grow up. I guess because he is older, I believed what he said, so I backed off from mom and dad. They were hurt, but didn't say much.

"I also had a very good friend, Sharon, with whom I went to college. She works in Atlanta, and we would try to get together for lunch or dinner at least once a week.

"My thirtieth birthday fell during the week, and since no one said anything about doing anything special, I decided to have a small dinner party. Every thing seemed fine until I had to take a call during the meal. When I returned to the table, Sharon and Ted were talking, yet Sharon was not herself for the rest of the meal and left as soon as she could.

"As we were cleaning up later, I asked Ted what was going on with Sharon.

"Taking my hands and acting very gently, he walked me over to the sofa, sat down and looked at me, and said, 'Hon, I know you like to do the right thing, and that you believe that Sharon is your best friend, but trust me; she is not! I didn't want to tell you this, but about a month ago I walked into a restaurant and saw Sharon and her secretary, whom I believe you have met. They were eating lunch, and invited me to join them. Bonnie, Sharon was saying horrible things about you. She was saying that in college you were known as a slut who would just sleep with anyone and that everyone knew you cheated your way through law school. I was shocked—didn't want to tell you because I knew it would be too painful. Tonight, she started this talk again, and this time I told her to leave and to never come back.

"I don't believe this," Bonnie said in a defiant and angry voice.

"Well, I'm certainly not lying.

"Kate, I was so angry with her that I wanted to call her and tell her what I thought, but Ted assured me that she was just a very jealous, lonely, and confused woman. He made me promise not to say anything. So I didn't."

For about two months he was so sweet that I didn't really miss Sharon."

Kate was looking at the young woman in near disbelief.

Bonnie continued, "However, after a while, the sweetness turned to anger. I will never forget. One night, I was just being silly, and accidentally knocked over a vase. I didn't break it, but did spill the water. Ted was furious. He pushed me against the wall and told me to never do anything like that again. He quickly apologized. I have never had anyone physically handle me like that, and I believed that this was a one-time experience. A month later, some little something happened, I don't even remember what it was, but Ted became angry and hit me on the arm. It became black and blue. He again apologized, but said he did not mean to hit me so hard. More and more he was hitting me in places that no one would see, screaming at me, and just being verbally abusive. I was so overwhelmed and confused, that I became more and more withdrawn. My supervisor had to talk to me on more than one occasion about my work performance. It was scary, but I didn't know what I was doing wrong to set Ted off. I was convinced that it was something about me—that I deserved this kind of treatment.

During this time, I had been doing volunteer legal work once a month at the women's center. One day, my client was a forty-year-old former teacher and now homeless. Her story got my attention. She had been an eager young teacher—even been chosen teacher of the year in her school. However, about two years into her marriage, her husband became so abusive that she did not have the confidence to continue working. The more isolated she became, the meaner he became. In fear of her life, she finally summoned the courage to leave and seek help.

As I listened to this woman's story, I realized that I was looking at me in ten years if I didn't break up with Ted.

Fortunately, Ted was out of town. Even though I had been very angry with Sharon, at that point I needed her help and support. I called, and with a little coaxing, she agreed to meet me for dinner that night."

Thinking back, Bonnie remembered the meal.

"Sharon, thank you for agreeing to meet me."

Sharon answered in a somewhat-accusing tone, "I still resent the fact that instead of telling me there was a problem, you had Ted to do it."

This statement surprised me. *"What are you talking about?"*

"The night of your birthday dinner, he told me you were very busy and tired of my calling to get together. He said you just remained my friend because you felt sorry for me."

"I never said that! One day Ted asked me why I made such an effort to always get together with you, and I told him it was because your friendship was so important. But Sharon, did you meet him about a month before my birthday for lunch?"

"One day my secretary and I were having lunch when Ted walked in. I had wanted to talk to him about having a party for your birthday, so I went over and asked him to join us, which he did. I talked about how I thought it would be fun to give you a party at the lake, but Ted said you definitely did not want one."

"Why did he say that, I wonder? I would have loved something. Is that all you talked about?"

"Yes, you can ask Stacy; she was with us the whole time."

Bonnie turned to Kate. "The light came on. I knew then that Ted had wanted to isolate me. First it had been my parents, then Sharon. I told her about the abuse—even showed her my arm. She went with me that night to his place, and I got some of my clothes and left him a note.

When Ted got home he called, and we agreed that I would come and get the rest of my things at a later date. When I went I had a police officer with me. I did not want Ted to accuse me of stealing anything. Of course he acted very polite, as he can be charming when he wants to."

Bonnie wiped tears from her eyes and continued the story. "I moved back into my apartment and started the process of trying to heal. One night I came home, turned on the light, and there sat Ted. He was drunk and looking very mean. He grabbed me and tried to force me into bed, saying that he deserved sex and I did not have the right to turn him down. The only thing that saved me was I told him if he forced me to have sex, I would charge him with rape."

Kate almost laughed out loud.

Bonnie continued. "He backed off and left, but the damage had been done. I was a wreck, and could not concentrate at work. I took a leave of absence from the DA's office and went home to my family, my roots, and my church. The pastor and his wife have been wonderful. I just lost sight of who I was and what was important to me when I lived in Atlanta. After a couple of months, I decided to move back to South Carolina. I need to be closer to family, and am starting a law practice there."

"Kate, I know you must be wondering where I am going with all of this, but I strongly suspect that this story does not completely surprise you."

"No, it doesn't," Kate whispered.

Bonnie continued, "Anyway, I have been in Atlanta this weekend, packing up. I was going to leave late this morning and drive to South Carolina. The movers left, but each time I tried to go, something happened to keep me from leaving. I finally got into my car late this afternoon to drive part of the way home when I remembered an experience I had with Ted. The more I thought about it, the more I believed I needed to come here and talk with you. I have made a promise to God to right any situation that I could from my relationship with Ted."

"What was your experience?" Kate asked curiously.

"Soon after I met Ted, we were at a party together. Your old friend, Jen, was there. She and I were talking when Ted walked up. Though they were civil to each other, it was obvious that there was no love lost between them. When we left, Ted explained that the two of you had grown up together, but said that he had ended that relationship. I was appalled, and wanted to know why he would do such a thing. He claimed that Jen had always thought she was better than anyone else and could be mean. Ted said he felt badly for lying, but was concerned about your welfare, and he believed you would be better off without that friendship.

Kate, I didn't remember that story until today. Ted actually told me that he made you believe that Jen had been making passes at him and wanted to start an affair."

Kate jerked slightly as though something had hit her. "That's exactly what he told me. I believed him!" She said with anger.

"I also thought about how he had lied to Sharon so that he could isolate me. It is so much easier to abuse someone who is totally dependent on you."

"Look Kate, I didn't come here to inquire about your relationship with your ex. However, through therapy and research I have come to realize that often a woman believes she is the only one her spouse would ever abuse—that the abuse has to do with her inadequacy, not his. I also know how valuable and powerful healthy friendships are, but they are threatening to an abuser. If what I have said speaks to you in any way, and can help, it has made my trip worthwhile."

Kate was now softly crying. "Oh Bonnie, I know this has not been easy for you, but you don't know how freeing this story was. Thank you for caring enough to come."

Bonnie spent the night, and the two women talked late into the night. It was the first time Kate had told anyone about her dark past—Ted's physical and mental abuse, and worst of all, the repeated rapes. Up until this moment, Kate thought that she was so inadequate with men that she had actually deserved the treatment.

When Bonnie left the next morning, Kate knew what she had to do. She picked up the phone to call her old friend.

Chapter 57

"**J**en."

"Kate! How are you?" Jen answered in a friendly and happy voice.

"Oh, I am fine. Listen, I know that I am the last person you expected to call, but I wanted to see if there is any possibility that we could get together today. I would love to treat you to lunch. Jen, I really need to talk to you."

Jen heard the pleading in Kate's voice. "Sure, I would love to have lunch, but could you come to my house? I can easily make something. We have some workers here, and I can't leave."

"That would be great, but why don't I pick up something so you don't have to go to any trouble?"

"Kate, it would be no bother. Just come on—say about eleven thirty?"

"Thanks, I will be there."

After they hung up, Jen got busy in the kitchen. She wondered what was up with her old friend, as this was the first time Kate had contacted her in thirteen years.

At precisely eleven thirty, the doorbell rang. Jen smiled. Unlike her, Kate was always exactly on time.

"Kate, come on in." The two hugged. "It's so good to see you."

"Oh, Jen, you don't know how good it is to be here, and thank you for being so nice. I know I don't deserve this."

"Yes you do. I don't know what happened between us, but you have always been my friend. Now come on in."

"Your house is beautiful."

"Thank you. Okay, now decide. There are three options: we can take the grand tour, sit and visit and then eat, or eat and visit, and then tour."

"Let's eat! I am starved."

"The right answer. So am I. Follow me."

Kate looked around. Richard and Jen had restored a beautiful old home.

"We are going to eat in my little sitting room. I wanted a special, cozy place to visit with my friends."

The room was small, but beautiful. A floral chintz sofa was the largest piece of furniture. It was flanked by two very comfortable, overstuffed chairs which were covered in a plaid that made up the colors in the sofa. On one wall was a large picture of Jen, Richard, Tae, and Brock. On another wall were pictures of Richard's and Jen's parents, and the children. Kate was surprised to see that there was also a picture of Richard's first wife.

Seeing Kate's shock, Jen explained, "I decided before I married Richard that I have to accept the fact that there was a wife before me and that she is the mother of their children. I think it is important for Tae and Brock to feel a connection to her. Now sit down, and I am going to get the lunch. Look in the corner and get two TV trays."

Jen wheeled in a lunch consisting of chicken salad, fruit, asparagus, and cheese straws. This was the company lunch in the Deep South.

Kate was delighted. "Oh, my favorite. You know that your salad is to die for."

Jen smiled. "I had hoped that we could eat and talk our way through the day."

"Forget the weight." Kate added.

"Yes, let's forget dieting. Good food, good friends, good for the soul," Jen said as she held up her glass of wine.

"Spoken by the ever-thin Jen," Kate teased.

As the two sat and ate their meal, Kate explained why she had called.

"I know you must be wondering why I am calling after so long."

"The question has crossed my mind," Jen said a little playfully.

Kate started her story. "As a girl I dreamed of marrying, having children, and preferably living in Upton. When I met Ted, I believed he was the key to my happiness. When he and my father agreed that he should come into the business, I thought my dreams had been answered, and that life would be perfect. At twenty what do you know? The first two years were great. I look back now and realize that sometime during the beginning of the third year, Ted began to subtly withdraw. At first I was puzzled, but that was soon forgotten when I found out I was pregnant with Todd. During those nine months, Ted wasn't excited about the birth. I talked to my mom about his changes, but we decided that he was probably just a nervous first father. That's what I wanted to believe. After Todd was born, Ted withdrew even more. He was not a hands-on dad. If I questioned him, he would say he was working hard and was tired."

Jen responded. "I remember that you worried that he and Todd were not close?"

"Unfortunately Jen, they never have been. Looking back, I think Ted was already thinking about divorce. He would not commit to anything long-term. Our house had been big enough for the two of us, but with one more, it was definitely too small. Ted flatly refused to talk about getting another place. The only reason we got our new home was because it came up for sale at a good price. I now think Ted probably realized that if we divorced, we could make money on the place. Also, we had always talked about wanting two children close together, but he did not even want to discuss having another child. My pregnancy with

Anna Kate was unplanned, but I was happy. When I told Ted, he was furious. He claimed that I conspired to get pregnant. It was awful."

"Kate, this is shocking. Publicly he seemed to be the model father. Why didn't you say something?"

"I didn't want to admit there were problems. I wanted everyone to think my life was perfect. About the time I got pregnant the second time, Ted became friends with a salesman who came into the office frequently. He was from outside of Atlanta, and a swinging single. Ted started meeting this man and his friends at happy hour in Barkston. It was a place where singles from adjoining areas met. I went a few times, but it became apparent that I didn't belong. Being a nonworking wife and mother was not 'in'. Ted was drinking more and more, and, I believe, starting to have affairs. He would come home drunk and yell at the children and me. Nothing was good enough for him. The screaming escalated to his hitting me. Of course, it was always where a person could not see the marks. He is no dummy."

"Oh, Kate, I can't believe this was happening. Why didn't you tell someone?"

"Many reasons. I was confused and embarrassed—what was I doing so wrong? I felt that I must be a horrible person to deserve such treatment. Why couldn't I have a happy marriage like other people? I would see couples having good times together and wonder what they knew that I didn't. Also, I hate to admit this, but I bought into my popularity during high school more than I ever admitted—it was sort of like I believed my life was special and I should always be the queen. At this point I was feeling inferior to everyone, but determined to make everything work out.

"Soon before I delivered Anna Kate, I was miserable. One night Ted came in drunk and demanded sex. I said 'no' emphatically, but he forced me. It was a wonder she did not come immediately. Anyway, after that, our sex life usually happened when he was drunk. He would force himself on me—it didn't matter what I wanted. The truth is that he repeatedly raped me. I began to feel worse about myself.

Soon before your wreck, Ted started telling me that you were coming on to him. After you went back to Atlanta, he said that you tried to talk him into meeting you. I was furious, but he said not to say anything— that you were just lonely. Later he told me that after you went back to Atlanta after your parents' deaths, you ran into him and tried to talk him into leaving me. Said you told him I was too weak for him and that you would show him what a real woman was like."

"What!" Jen shouted. "Kate, I didn't even particularly like the guy. I was just nice to him because of you. Also, telling him I would show him what a real woman was like! Please! You know that is not me." Jen was obviously angry.

"I know now, but he was convincing. Understand that Ted had been waging this campaign to make me feel as bad about myself as he could. He had to do that to convince me of your betrayal. When he told me, he was being very sweet, which almost never occurred, and for several months after that he was different—loving, considerate."

"But, why didn't you ask me?" Jen was bewildered.

"Because Ted made me believe that you were just lonely, so I tried to put it behind me. I couldn't, of course. That was the reason I became so cool. Of course, after a period of time, when Ted realized that I was not going to confide in you, he became more and more physically abusive."

"Wait a minute, Kate," Jen said with some anger. "After all those years of friendship, you were willing to believe that I would actually make a pass at your husband yet you didn't say anything to me?"

Kate was quiet a minute. "I understand that this sounds unbelievable, but try to see it from my point of view. I lived with the master of abuse. He would constantly degrade me, and just as I thought I couldn't stand any more, he would go for days as a wonderful, loving, and caring man. I would start to believe that maybe things would be okay, and he would turn on me.

"Jen, I can remember his last compliment. Just before we found out I was pregnant with Todd, he told me I looked terrific in a dress I had just bought. That was twenty-one years ago. Our sex life could have been called 'rape time,' and being hit was the norm. With those living conditions, I was too confused to think straight. I needed to blame someone for our problems—even if it was you. At least if it was your fault, I was not the only bad person. Can't you understand?"

Realizing that she had, at one time, been afraid that her best friends had been involved in the murder of her parents, Jen answered, "Yes, we can all be misled. Did you ever tell anyone what was happening?"

Kate looked down for a minute. "I went to your dad. Ted had pushed me, and I had fallen and hit my ribs. I was so sore I could hardly move. I told Dr. Joe that I had fallen, but he saw the bruises. He asked if Ted was abusing me and I said 'yes.'

We talked for a long time. I told him how Ted acted. He was horrified. Your dad insisted that the children and I move in with them until something could be decided—remember, my parents were in Europe at the time. Your parents were going to help me move right after they returned from Atlanta. Oh, Jen, for the first time in years, I felt safe and hopeful. Unfortunately, the plan never worked out, because they were killed before I could make a move. I was crushed at losing two people I adored and thought of as another set of parents, and also, without your dad's strength, I was stuck."

"After you had admitted the situation to dad, why didn't you turn to the rest of us?"

"I did go to Smitty and told him something of the abuse. I asked him if he would help me find a place to live in Atlanta. What I was really looking for was a place to hide out, because I knew if I left with your parents gone and mine out of the country, Ted would feel free to do anything. And while I didn't think he would take my life, I knew he could go on a rampage that would cause untold problems. Unfortunately, someone mentioned to Ted that they had seen Smitty and me talking a lot, and he started claiming that we were having an affair. We had to start meeting in Atlanta, at the Forest restaurant, to talk about the situation. I finally told Smitty to forget it. It was almost time for my folks to return, and I always felt safe with them around. Ted may be crazy, but he is not stupid. As long as daddy was in Upton, Ted wasn't going to do anything that would leave an obvious scar."

Jen didn't say anything, but she remembered the day she and Tony had seen them at the Forest after Kate had said she was going to LaGrange. It seemed like a lifetime ago.

"Oh Kate, I am so sorry. Whoever thinks that crime does not have a far-reaching effect is stupid. But I have to ask. Why did you wait so long to tell me this? Why did you continue to be cold after the divorce?"

"I was left with two children to raise alone, broken dreams, and the belief that I was a very inferior being. Ted constantly dated smart and beautiful women and made sure that I knew that. In my mind I saw these women as having perfect relationships with him. I just knew that he never abused them as he had me. This made the abuse even worse. I felt like such a failure. You, on the other hand, moved on with your life. You made it look effortless. It was easier to think that part of the problem was that you had gone after Ted. It made me seem less of a failure—gave me someone to blame.

However, yesterday his ex-girlfriend came to see me. She told me about their relationship, and I realized that he had been the same way with her. Bonnie mentioned that one of his other ex-girlfriends had confided that he had hit her, and that was the reason she had left him. It has just been within the last twenty-four hours that I have understood that I was not the only one he abused. Also, I realized I was not to blame, and that it was not my fault that Ted acted the way he has. This man is sick, and he tries to separate friends so he can have more power."

"I am so sorry this happened to you," Jen said softly.

With tears in her eyes, Kate said, "I don't know if you can ever understand what really happened to me, but could you forgive me and let's be friends again?"

"Of course I can. You always have been and always will be my best friend."

The two old friends spent the afternoon talking, and the weekly luncheon became a fun ritual and a healing experience.

Chapter 59

The Upton Celebration

Smitty sat at the head table and just looked around in awe. He noticed the four banners that read:

Thanks to the Big Four—Seven. You Did It!

Everyone in town must have signed them. He smiled as he looked around. The celebration committee had taken over the college cafeteria and turned it into a walk into the past. This was the only place large enough to host the fiftieth anniversary of the Upton Celebration—an event for which many former residents returned to attend. The theme this year was the community college. The Big Four and their spouses were the honorees.

Smitty began to take his own trip down memory lane. He looked out of the window and saw the bell tower of the school that had once stood in what was known as Mill Town. His thoughts drifted back to eighteen years before. It was a beautiful fall day; he was still the principal of the high school, and the students were taking one of their annual tours of Georgia colleges. On each trip the group visited one junior college and one four-year college.

Michael Trebar, a chaperon and former student, walked up. "Mr. Jarvis, we need a junior college in Upton."

"Why do you say that? Are you interested in going to one?"

"You bet. Like most of my family and friends, I married right out of high school and started my family. Don't get me wrong; I love them, but man, it would be great to have my own business. There is really not much future in the maintenance work at the factory."

"Your own business. What would you do?"

"Well, according to this information, Junior colleges have to have a vocational school attached. I would take air conditioning and refrigeration, and open a repair shop.

Why don't you try to get a college for Upton?" The tone of Michael's voice made it obvious that he was serious.

That night when Smitty told Karen about his conversation with Michael, her reply was, "Well, why don't you?"

This had been the beginning of a dream. Before presenting the idea to the county supervisors, Smitty took it to the Big Four. He had missed his old friends, and had felt that a good way to galvanize the splintered group would be to get the members involved in a major project. It had done the trick. Because the others did not live in Upton, only Kate had served on the committee to make the college a reality. However, the whole group's support of resources had given Smitty the courage to go forward with his vision, and within two years, Upton Junior College, now known as Upton Community College, had opened its doors.

As its president, it was Smitty's responsibility to see that they offered the best academic and vocational programs. This was where the group had come in. Tom and Beth Anne had been the main contributors to the technological school both monetarily and equipment-wise. Tom kept the school outfitted with the latest in computer technology. He also helped them to set forth a yearly technology plan. Tom and Beth Anne had also set up a scholarship in honor of Tom's mother for a deserving student who had a financial need, and who was also in good academic standing.

Jen and Richard had built two dorms and a library in memory of Jen's mother. They had also set up a scholarship for medical students in memory of Dr. Joe.

Kate had set up a scholarship for women returning to get an education. She also offered a paid internship each year for a second-year woman in the business field. Kate was one of the business department's most sought-after and frequent lecturers.

The contributions of the Big Seven had made Upton Community College one of the best in the south. Its reputation was being recognized in national publications.

As Smitty looked over the crowd, he saw Michael, who was one of the first graduates of the vocational school and owner of a successful business. Scanning the audience, he saw other graduates who now had better jobs than many would have dreamed possible.

His thoughts then went back to two poor but starry-eyed college students at the University of Georgia dreaming of returning to Upton and making a difference. He looked at Karen, who now had her PhD and a counseling practice, and thought, *We did it! Not without problems, but we are living our dream!*

⁓

Tom and Beth Anne were walking around campus. They had agreed to meet with the young reporter. One of the major Atlanta papers was covering this event for the Sunday magazine.

"Mr. and Mrs. DePau, I am Cynthia Gertland. Thank you for agreeing to see me."

Tom and Beth Anne shook hands with the young woman.

Tom laughed. "Oh please, call us by our first names. Also, we are glad to meet with you."

The three enjoyed the interview. As the talk was coming to an end, Cynthia turned to Tom.

"Tom, how have you lived with the stigma that your father and grandmother did such a horrible thing?"

Beth Anne put her hand over his as he talked.

"For a long time my father's actions made me feel worse that I can ever describe. Finally, the realization came that I was no more responsible for what he had done than anyone else, and there was nothing I could do to change things. With these thoughts in mind, I set out with my wonderful wife to give the best to my family, my God and others. This is where my concentration is—not on something over which I had no power."

～

Kate walked into an office that adjoined the cafeteria for an interview.

"Mrs. Stroud, my name is Cynthia Gertland. Thank you for agreeing to see me."

"It's nice to see you Cynthia. And please, call me Kate."

"The story of the Big Four is fascinating. You have all 'made it', so to speak, but certainly not without trials. In fact, I believe that your book, *Making It In Spite of Circumstances*, is due out soon."

"That is correct."

"You have been a leader in this town not only in your work, but also in your helping to build centers and groups for abused people and people in need; your training of individuals, both men and women, who need work experience; and, of course, your business success is legendary. The good you have done seems endless. What helped you to take charge of your own life and move from being a divorced, and, by your own account, very miserable single parent to a seemingly happy, successful businesswoman and parent? Was there one defining moment when things started to click?"

"Well, I believe that there is a defining moment every time we dare to move forward, but there is some advice that has always served me."

"What was that?"

"Being a stay-at-home mom was something I liked, and I believe, if given the chance, it is the most rewarding career. My life changed and did not allow for this. For a long time, I kept trying to find something or someone to rescue me. Finally, through some good counseling from a former Sunday school teacher, I realized I had one of two choices: keep living in the past and staying in my rut, or take the faith I had always proclaimed and reach out into the unknown. I knew the latter would make me a better role model for my children, so, with fear and trembling, I went forward.

It's funny. Once I got past the hurdle of moving into my own home and committing myself to helping to build up the business, my life became very fulfilling."

"Did you close the door on ever marrying again?"

"No. In fact, there is a man in my life, and we are thinking about that very question."

"How would you sum up your life?"

"Wonderful! I have not walked the way I would have chosen, but I am very happy. My children are outstanding people—I am so proud of them. I am also profoundly grateful that I decided to do what it took to move forward."

"Kate, I know you have some things to do before the dinner gets started, but thank you for your time."

"Thank you. It was fun."

⮑

Upon entering the cafeteria, Jen just stopped and looked around. Everything was beautiful. Few people were there yet, as she and Richard had come early. As she scanned the room, Jen almost expected to see her parents. That deep and very familiar pain of loss struck her heart, and for a moment, she was immobile. Sensing what was happening, Richard put his arm around her for comfort. Within seconds the pain lifted, and the couple moved through the room, speaking to those who were there.

"Mrs. Nottingham."

Jen turned to face a young woman.

"I am Cynthia Gertland from the Atlanta Press."

"Oh, hi Cynthia."

"Is this a convenient time for your interview?"

The two women retired to the same office where Kate had been earlier

"Mrs. Nottingham—"

Jen interrupted. "Please, call me Jen. The other is too formal, and makes me feel way too old."

Cynthia smiled. "Okay. Jen, how do you do it? I have heard you speak, and seen the works that you have done through the years, yet there seems to be no trace of hostility or bitterness. How?"

Jen just looked down at her hands for a moment. She knew that what she had to say could sound preachy, or like a lot of clichés, yet she had to answer truthfully.

"Though I denied it, I was very bitter. When I watched a tape of a talk show I had done in Colorado, I was appalled. The bitterness and anger, though perhaps not obvious to many people, were so real to me. Hearing myself, I knew I had to turn things around or the crime would completely destroy me. I knew my parents would never want such a thing."

"What did you do?"

"I changed the way I looked at things. It was almost by accident. Several weeks after the taping of the Colorado show, I went to see a friend of mine who had a terminal illness. Because I had been out of town and had not seen her for a while, I was shocked at what I saw. She was in such a fragile state. When I left, I sincerely thanked God for my health. Thanking God was not something I had been doing much of. In fact, I had been pretty mad at him. Within that time frame, maybe two weeks later, or a month—I don't remember—I was watching the news. It was a hot summer, and they were reporting that people in Atlanta were dying of heat. I realized that individuals living in the same city as I were miserable because of the weather, and here I was sitting in an air-conditioned townhouse, cool and comfortable. It was apparent to me that even though many circumstances in my life were negative, all of them were not. I began to feel very blessed for what I had, so I thanked God for that. These two events made me aware of the things that I have but take for granted—clothes, food, a nice home, friends—the list is endless. Each day I would decide to thank God for five or ten or fifteen things. The more you do this, the harder it gets to justify your bitterness. This may seem trite, but it helped me to see life with different eyes."

"How do you feel about the murders now?"

"As sad as ever. I will always miss my parents, but by looking at what I do have and not at what I don't have, I was able to build a good life. It doesn't make what happened okay; it just means that I am not being controlled by it."

The two women talked for about twenty minutes. As they parted, Cynthia watched Jen walk away. *I will never see life through the same eyes,* the young reporter thought.

⤛

The dinner was truly wonderful. The Big Four—now the Big Seven—ate together, and their affection for each other was apparent. As the dinner came to an end, the mayor got up to speak.

"Tonight, we honor the Big Four and their spouses—the Big Seven—for all they have done for the county and the town through Upton Community College. This institution has given and will continue to give many people in this region a better life." Then, turning to the group, she continued, "You have a history of giving to this town; would you please allow us a glimpse into what gave you the strength to rise from the ashes of bad circumstances to lives of such victory."

The room fell very quiet as Jen took the microphone. "It was our faith, friends, family; and we learned to dream new dreams."

The mayor then raised her glass and said "To the Big Seven."

The audience rose, raised their glasses, and in unison repeated, "To the Big Seven!"

The End

About the Author

I was raised in the small town of Goodman, Mississippi. It was there that I witnessed and experienced the strong bonds and ties that are formed among people who live in close proximity.

Holmes Community College is located in Goodman. This school, of which I am very proud, had a profound affect on me. I grew up hearing stories of many of the students who, often at great sacrifice, attended Holmes. However, it was there that with hard work they began an educational path that led to a better life.

Murder in a Small Town is not only a mystery, but it captures the profound ability that lies within all of us to move forward even in the most extreme conditions.

9 781425 968328